LOVE, LIFE, AND THE LIST

Love, Life, and the List

KASIE WEST

SCHOLASTIC INC.

ISBN 978-1-338-28128-6

12 11 10 9 8 7 6 5 4 3 2 1 18 19 20 21 22 23

Printed in the U.S.A. 40

First Scholastic printing, January 2018

Typography by Torborg Davern

To my *Abby, who works hard, laughs hard, and dreams big.*
You are an absolute joy and I love you!

ONE

"Hot or cold?"

"Hot. I hate being cold. You know that about me." Just the thought made me shiver even though it was the middle of summer, which was probably what prompted Cooper's question. It was hot. So hot that sweat was beading on the backs of my knees. We had been standing in line for the movie on the beach for twenty minutes already, and I was looking forward to when the sun went down and the breeze picked up.

He shook his head. "I do know that, but I mean, would

you rather die from freezing to death or overheating?"

"Morbid." I pursed my lips. "But you're right, that's a different question. I've heard that dying from being cold is blissful."

"Who did you hear this from? Are ghosts of people who froze to death visiting you?"

"Yes. Every day. Speaking of, would you rather be cursed with seeing ghosts or zombies?"

"Cursed? *Cursed?*" He gripped one of my shoulders and shook it. "Neither of those is a curse in my opinion. Totally amazing. I'll take them both."

"That's not how the rules work. You have to pick one."

"Ghosts. Hopefully they can tell me about my future."

"Ghosts don't know the future," I said as we shifted forward in the line, inching closer to the ticket table. Sand slid between my foot and flip-flop and I shook it free.

"Says who?"

"Says everybody, Cooper. If anything, ghosts know the past."

"Well, yours may not, Abby, but my ghosts are future-telling ghosts. It will be awesome."

The girl standing in line in front of us turned around and smiled at Cooper. She probably thought he was adorably charming. Because he was. She was around our age.

Her hair was pulled up into a purposefully messy bun and I wondered how people made that look purposeful and not just messy.

"Hey," he said to her. "How are you?"

"Better now," she said with a giggle, then turned back around.

I shook my head. "Don't mind me. You know, the girl standing next to the boy you're flirting with."

I was sure by my tone she knew I was joking, but Cooper still put his hand over my mouth and said, "The best friend of the guy standing here. Just friends. Said guy is totally available."

I freed my mouth and laughed, even though the "just friends" part was not by choice. I had, in fact, professed my love to Cooper Wells exactly one year ago that very month. It had been more than obvious by his reaction that the feelings were not reciprocated. So I had to play it off like some joke. Some joke he had been more than willing to go along with. And I let him, because I didn't want to lose him as a friend. He was the best friend in the world.

A voice sounded from behind us. "Which begs the question, would you rather hang out with your best friends one more night *or* pack all night for the trip your parents are dragging you on for the entire summer?"

I whirled around, a smile taking over my face. "Don't

use the word *begs*, Rachel. My eighty-year-old grandpa uses that word," I said.

Rachel stood there with her hands on her hips and her dark eyes sparkling. "That's where I picked it up. And he's only sixty-eight."

I bumped her hip with mine, then gave her a hug. "How did you know we were playing *would you rather*?"

"Aren't we always?"

"I thought you weren't going to make it tonight," I said.

There were four of us in our tight-knit group of friends: Cooper, Rachel, Justin, and me. Justin had left last week and would be gone for the summer on a mission to South America with his church. Rachel was leaving tomorrow for a tour around Europe with her parents. So for the rest of the summer it would be just Cooper and me.

"Me too. Now, back to my begged question," Rachel said. "Packing or best friends?"

"That's a tough one, Rach," Cooper said. "Probably packing."

She shoved his arm. "Funny."

We finally reached the front of the line. Cooper stepped up to the covered table that served as the ticket booth every Friday night throughout the summer. A guy standing behind a cashbox said, "Are you Cooper?"

"Yeeees," Cooper said warily.

"That girl paid for yours." The guy nodded to Messy Bun, who had been standing in front of us and was now walking toward the entrance. She must've heard me say Cooper's name at some point.

"What about ours?" I called after to her, linking arms with Rachel.

The girl threw us a smile over her shoulder, then waved.

"You punk," I said to Cooper. "Where are the people willing to buy my Friday-night entertainment?" I dug into my beach bag, past the towels and sweater, until I found my wallet. I handed the cashier my money and collected a ticket. Rachel did the same.

"You have to work on your charm," Cooper said.

"I am the most charming person here." I slung my beach bag back onto my shoulder and it rocked back and forth like a pendulum. "Charm oozes from my pores."

"Gross," he said. "If that's the case, you're doing it wrong."

"Come get your oozing charm, boys!" I yelled to the line behind us.

"Move your ooze along," someone called back.

Rachel dragged me away from the line, probably embarrassed. Cooper headed left, toward the food stand just past the barriers.

"We're getting expensive food tonight?" I asked.

"Seems I have some extra money. I can afford a ten-dollar popcorn now."

"I hate you. I'm eating all your popcorn," I said.

He laughed. "You do ooze charm, Abby Turner. Loads of it."

I blew him a kiss. "We're going to stake a claim on our spot. You get food."

"I'm on it."

I had already committed to walking away with Rachel when I saw that the girl who'd bought Cooper's ticket was now in line at the food truck. I almost changed my mind and sent Rachel to our spot without me so I could join him. But then I didn't. I didn't need to witness *all* his flirting. I already saw enough of it.

"So you're never going to guess what my parents decided," Rachel said as I pulled a couple of towels out of my bag and we spread them out on our spot next to the right-side barriers.

"That you don't have to go with them and you get to stay with me all summer instead?" I guessed.

"I wish."

"You know how spoiled you sound that you're complaining about traveling Europe for nine weeks?"

"With my parents. My parents. It's not like a youth hostel backpacking trip with friends. We're going to have to visit ancestors' graves and random plots of land that they think my great-great-grandfather's brother once peed on or something."

"Wait, your ancestors are from Europe?"

"Some of them. You don't think there are any black people in Europe? Come on, Abby."

"It's not that I don't think . . . you're right, I'm dumb. So, anyway, what did your parents decide?"

"That it's a technology-free trip."

"What does that mean?" I sat down on the towel and slipped off my flip-flops. "No Google Maps?"

"No cell phones."

My eyes went wide. "You can't take your *phone*?"

"A detox, they called it."

"That's torture."

"I agree!" She plopped down next to me. "You're not allowed to do anything fun this summer, because I won't be able to hear about it."

"Don't worry. You'll come home and everything will be exactly the same," I said. Exactly. The. Same.

"It better be."

I dug my toes in the sand and watched Cooper walk toward us holding a popcorn and a bottle of water. His blond hair was slightly wavy tonight and was reflecting the last bit of sunlight like a halo. His blue eyes, lit by his smile, met mine and I couldn't help the smile that spread across my face.

"How was the concessions truck?" I asked.

"Concessions? And you made fun of *Rachel* for sounding eighty?"

"Blah blah blah, whatever."

He sat down on the yellow-and-white-striped towel on my right side and handed me the bottle of water.

"What's this garbage? I want caffeine."

"Just yesterday you told me you were giving up soda. You said it quite dramatically, in fact. And then you said, *keep me honest, Cooper.*"

"What?" Rachel asked from my left side. "You had forty-four ounces of Mountain Dew at my house last night."

"Shhhhh." I pressed my finger against her lips. "We're not talking about that."

Cooper scoffed and Rachel pushed my hand away.

"Who do you all think I am? Wonder Woman? Geez." I uncapped the water and took a drink.

"Her name is Iris," Cooper said, nodding back toward the food truck and the girl who'd bought his ticket.

"Oh no," Rachel said.

I gave a faux sympathetic hum. "The kiss of death—an unshortenable name. Little did she know telling you her name would be the end for her."

"It can't be shortened at all. *I.* I'm supposed to call her I?" Cooper asked.

"You could get over your lazy tendencies and just call her by her full name."

"It's not about being lazy. It's about my relationship goals. I want to be able to call my girl by a shortened version of her name."

I huffed. "I know you think that makes you seem sexy or whatever, but really it doesn't."

He took a handful of popcorn and shrugged. "Regardless."

I thought for a minute. "What about Ris?" I wasn't sure why I was trying to help him with this new girl aside from the fact that it made me feel like I had been successful in smashing down my feelings. The feelings nobody knew about but me . . . and my mom . . . and maybe Cooper, though I was pretty sure I'd convinced him I was joking last summer.

"Ris is cute," Rachel agreed, taking her own handful of popcorn from Cooper's bucket.

"Huh," he said. "That might work. Good thing I got her number."

"She should've bought *me* a movie ticket. I just saved her chances." I watched the sun sit atop the edge of the ocean before it dipped below it.

"What about you two?" Cooper asked. "What are your relationship goals?"

"My immediate goal," Rachel said, "is an Italian boy

with long wavy hair and an accent so thick I won't know what he's talking about, but he'll be an exceptional kisser, so it won't matter."

I laughed. "Is this before or after you and your parents find the plot of land your great-uncle peed on?"

"Definitely before . . . and then after as well. What about you, Abby?" Rachel asked. "Relationship goals?"

I flopped onto my stomach and began drawing in the sand with my pointer finger. "An artist for sure. Someone who can paint or draw or something."

"But then what if he's better than you? Why would you want someone who has your same skill set?" Rachel asked.

"Yeah," Cooper agreed. "It would turn into a competition."

"Just because you turn everything into a competition, Coop, doesn't mean everyone does."

"See, my name is perfect. It can be shortened with epic results."

"I don't know that it qualifies as epic, but it's adorable," I said.

"Actually, that reminds me," Rachel said. "Someone was asking about one of your pieces the other day. He remembered seeing it in the art room before school let out and hasn't been able to get it out of his head."

"Who was asking?"

"I didn't know him. He stopped me in Starbucks. I guess he knew we were friends."

"Cool," Cooper said.

I bit my lip and smiled. I wanted to yell, *see, Cooper, I have something going for me. I'm not so laughable a catch. I'm an artist.*

"So as far as relationship goals go," Rachel said. "Would appreciating *your* art be just as good as being an artist? Because if so, you need to ask mystery boy out."

"Yes! You should," Cooper said.

"Appreciating art would be a close second to being an artist. Good thing you have so much detailed information about who he is, Rachel."

"Minor setback."

The movie started on the large screen in front of us, music blasting out of the speakers.

Rachel leaned close to my ear. "I need to go to the bathroom. I'll be right back." She scurried off.

Cooper moved onto his stomach, positioning himself alongside me so our shoulders were touching. He started drawing stick figures in the sand next to my art. "Just you and me this summer, kid," he said.

My heart gave a jump at those words. We're over him, I reminded my heart. He's one of your best friends, after all. We could handle a summer alone with Cooper Wells. "Yep." I reached over and added wheels onto the bottom of one of his stick men. "You racing at the dunes this week?" Cooper raced his quad in an amateur local league put together by some serious quad lovers.

"Wednesday. I expect you there with a big sign that says, 'Cooper is number one.'"

"But what if you come in second? Then that will be awkward."

He bumped his shoulder into mine.

"I will be there. Am I ever not there?"

"Well, you usually come with Rachel and Justin, so I wasn't sure."

"I used to come without them all the time." I'd met Cooper first, eighth grade. We'd been friends ever since. Rachel and Justin joined us freshman year.

"That's true. And I've decided you're my good-luck charm, so you have to keep coming for all of eternity now."

"I will." For all of eternity I'd be Cooper's fangirl. That pathetic thought almost made me march out of there that second and gain back some of my dignity. But then he smiled at me.

TWO

In the summer, I usually slept in as long as possible. But the next morning a strip of light from the window crept into my room through a partially open blind and wouldn't go away. I stood up, crossed my room, and shut the blind completely. I snuggled back under my covers, pulling them up around my ears. It didn't stop me from hearing my phone buzz on the nightstand next to me. I thought about ignoring it, but when it buzzed again, I couldn't help my curiosity. A text from Rachel lit my screen.

This will be the last text I send you for 9 weeks.

That text was followed by: What will you do without me?

Probably get more sleep.

True. Me too. What happens if I like being without a phone? No. That can't happen. Even if I like it, I would never let my parents know. They'd enjoy that too much.

I smiled and rubbed my eyes. **I'll miss you! Don't like any hot Italian boys more than me.**

You too!

Pretty sure I'm not in danger of liking any hot Italian boys in the near future.

Funny. I meant the missing you part.

I know. Safe travels. Call me from a pay phone if you ever get a chance. Do you think they still have pay phones?

I don't know. We shall find out.

I stared at my phone, but there was nothing more to say, and it stayed quiet in my hand. It really was going to be a slow summer without Rachel and Justin. My finger, almost as if it had a mind of its own, swiped across the screen and pulled up a website I had saved as a favorite. Wishstar Art Institute Winter Program Application. The program of my dreams. The program that my art teacher told me would bolster my college applications and help me get into a really good art school. Plus, it was Wishstar. They had amazing instructors, and I was dying to spend part of the winter holiday with other artists. We would spend two solid weeks learning new techniques, working with all sorts of mediums, and being inspired by the speakers sharing their success stories. I wanted to meet actual professionals in the field and, along with bettering my own art, this would help me do that.

I studied the page again, like I had a million times in the last six months. I read through the requirements, which hadn't changed. Age, experience, letter of recommendation, display/sales history. I was finally old enough. They only accepted high school seniors and above. And in the fall I would be. I had heard most attendees were college students and even older, but that wouldn't stop me. I had experience—a whole portfolio of paintings I could attach. I knew who I wanted to write the letter for me. I had only one more thing to accomplish before sending off my application: display/sales. I had never had my art on display anywhere outside of school. And I had definitely never sold a painting before. But I had a plan. I smiled, excited by the thought again, and threw my covers back.

I shuffled down the hall into my bathroom, where I nearly tripped over my mom, who was lying on the floor. The cupboards were open and shampoo bottles and hairspray and window cleaner lined the floor next to her. In one hand she held a flashlight, which she was pointing under the sink, and in her other hand was a flyswatter.

"Uh. What are you doing?" I asked.

"Have you ever heard of a brown recluse?"

"The spider?"

"Yes. I was just making sure you didn't have one under your sink."

"Did you see a web under there? Or is there a sucked-dry mouse corpse?" I squatted down to get a better look and sent a bottle of conditioner toppling.

"No, I read a story about a teenage girl who got horribly disfigured by a brown recluse spider when reaching under the sink for her Herbal Essences. Then I remembered that's where you store your extra shampoo. I figured I'd better check."

"Mom." I picked up the bottles on the floor and began shoving them back under the cupboard. "Stop reading horrific internet stories and immediately applying them to our lives. If I'm going to be horribly disfigured, it better be in my own original way."

She sat up and gave me a stern look. "Abigail. Don't joke about that." Her dark hair stuck up in crazy waves around her face, like she'd rolled straight out of bed and into my bathroom.

I clicked off her flashlight and brought it to my mouth like a microphone. "Can I have my bathroom now? I need to use it."

She sighed and stood. "I have to check the other bathrooms anyway."

I locked the door after her and turned on the shower. My eyes went to the cupboard. I opened the door and peered in, then shut it quickly. I rolled my eyes. There were no spiders in the bathroom.

After a quick shower, I pulled on my standard summer wardrobe of cut-off shorts and a tank top. I arranged my blond waves up into a ponytail and went to the kitchen. The oatmeal was on the top shelf in the pantry, so I stood on my tiptoes and fished two packets out of their box, poured them into a plastic bowl, and added water. By the time the oatmeal was done heating and the timer went off, my grandpa was awake. His feet made a scuffing noise on the tile because he didn't pick them up very high when he walked.

"What's this?" he asked, coming into the kitchen. "The princess doesn't need her beauty sleep today?"

"Funny, Grandpa."

"Your grandma used to think I was funny. No woman has found me as funny since. It's a tragedy."

"Her death or that no one has found you funny since?"

"Oh, a wise guy, huh?"

My grandma had died from cancer three months

before I was born, so it was literally a lifetime ago. Not knowing her made it so *I* couldn't really miss her. But I knew my grandpa did, even when he joked about it. Grandpa had moved in with us after she died.

"Do you want some oatmeal?" I asked Grandpa, holding out my bowl, which I hadn't eaten from yet.

"No, I want something with lots of sugar in it."

"I'm sure this has plenty of sugar. It's two cinnamon-and-spice packs."

"But it's masquerading as healthy, and I can't forgive it for that." He got himself a bowl and a box of cereal from the pantry.

"Grandpa, how did you live to eighty when you eat so bad?"

"I am not eighty. Why do you always insist on adding years to my life? It's like you're trying to get rid of me."

I retrieved a spoon from the drawer and sat at the table. I pulled my bare feet up under me and took a big bite, then immediately regretted it, because my tongue was on fire. I sucked air into my mouth.

"That's instant karma right there," Grandpa said.

"You're mean," I mumbled through my mouthful.

My mom joined us. "Our house is spider free."

"Did you spend the morning killing spiders?" Grandpa asked.

"No, hunting spiders," I said. "Internet spiders."

She put her hunting gear on the counter.

Grandpa sighed. "You need to stop reading stories on the internet."

She ignored his statement. "What are we eating?" She peered into my bowl and then my grandpa's.

"Oatmeal," I said.

She raised her eyebrows at Grandpa. "That isn't oatmeal."

"I didn't say it was. Your daughter is eating oatmeal. I have Cocoa Krispies."

"Dad."

"What?"

"That's too much sugar for a prediabetic."

"Well, when you feel like going to the store to stock up our shelves with acceptable items, let me know."

The smile fell from her face. My mom hated going to the store. She hated going anywhere outside of her comfort zone. Especially when my dad was gone, like now, deployed to the Middle East until the end of August. Eleven more weeks. We could handle eleven more weeks. My mom was always a lot better when he was around. It hadn't always been like that. She used to have a tight community of military wives at each place we moved (five different cities between my first year of school and my seventh), who seemed to help her transition better. But four years ago she decided she wanted me to have more stability, so when we moved to the central coast of California, we bought a house away from military housing, and she declared it our permanent home. I was so happy. For the first time, I had friends I knew I wouldn't have to leave. But my mom seemed to struggle. More every day.

"Right. The store." Mom disappeared into the pantry and I shot my grandpa a look.

"What?" he asked.

"Mean," I whispered. Then I called out to her, "When does Dad get to video chat with us again?" We'd just talked to him last week, so I probably shouldn't have asked. It would only make her more upset. But when my mom started obsessing over internet stories and rarely going out, I always thought of my dad and how I wished he wouldn't leave so much. I knew if he had a choice he wouldn't, but it was easy to blame the person not here.

"Probably in a few weeks," she said, coming out with a box of shredded wheat. She set it on the table, then took a clean bowl out of the cupboard and rinsed it thoroughly under steaming-hot water. "What's on the agenda today?"

"Not much," I said. "I'm scheduled to work at the museum. Mr. Wallace has me cleaning the storage room. You should see it. It's a nightmare. Almost like a bunch of creative people are in charge of it."

"Is Mr. Wallace going to let you display your paintings in the July showcase?"

I bit my lip to contain my smile. I'd finally gotten all my pieces organized, copied, and put into a portfolio that I was going to show him. "I don't know, but I'm going to find out."

Mom kissed the top of my head. "How could he say no? You are so talented."

"Did you include my favorite piece?" Grandpa asked. "The flower fields?"

"I did."

"Then you're golden," Grandpa said.

My phone buzzed from where I'd left it on the table. It was a text from Cooper: Did I leave my green and white board shorts at your house?

I headed for my room to check.

Sure enough, Cooper's board shorts, along with one of his T-shirts, were thrown over a chair in the corner of my room. He must've left them after we went swimming at the beach last week. I picked up his shirt and absentmindedly held it to my nose. It smelled just like his beach scent—cherry ChapStick and sunblock.

Yes, they're here, but I'm on my way to the museum so you'll have to get them later.

Are you going to ask Mr. Wallace about the show?

Yep!

Good luck!

The once-a-year showcase Mr. Wallace hosted to raise money for the museum was the perfect opportunity not only to display my paintings but, hopefully, to sell one too. Problem: there was an age requirement of eighteen. But I had my art, my persuasive speech, and the fact that he liked me on my side. This was happening.

THREE

The problem with the storage room at the art museum was that Mr. Wallace was a hoarder and he didn't even know it. He saved everything. Every piece of signage, every program, every single decoration from all his past exhibits and shows. The room was bursting at the seams. I'd worked at the museum for about a year (a job I'd applied for because of my love of art), and I'd never had to clean it. By the looks of it, none of the other employees had cleaned it either. Not that they would. As the newest employee, I did the grunt work around here. The docents conducted tours, Tina mainly did ticket sales, and Ralph, the security guard, never traded his badge for a mop. So the storage room was probably the result of years of neglect.

The second the museum closed for the day, I moved a box of papers out into the hall and started sorting through it.

I'd made three piles so far: one was "definitely throw away," one was "maybe," and the third was "keep."

Mr. Wallace came by and saw me, and I wished he'd leave, because otherwise my "definitely throw away" pile was about to shrink.

"What's this?" he asked. Mr. Wallace looked nothing like what I'd picture an art curator to look like. Not that it was something I'd pictured on a regular basis. But if I had, the curator in my mind had an eye for fashion and style. Mr. Wallace looked like a used-car salesman, with a cheap, slightly too-large suit and slicked-back gray hair. But he was nice and seemed to have an eye for art, if not the kind he wore on his body.

"Just piles," I told him as he stood over me. "I'm organizing."

"Why are there three?"

I picked up a few pieces of the "definitely" pile. "Look, these posters have dates on them. You won't use a decoration for any event this year that has a date from five years ago, right? So this is in the 'definitely get rid of' pile. That one is the 'maybe.'" I pointed to the middle stack. "And this is the 'keep.'"

He toed the definitely pile. "I never planned on using this thing again, but I saved it so I could remember the idea. It was a good theme."

I pulled out my phone. "Then we can take a picture of it and save it that way." I snapped a picture. "You can have a file on your phone or computer of decoration ideas."

He nodded. "That's a good idea, Abby. I knew I kept you around for some reason."

"Funny. You better watch it or I'm going to turn your name in to that hoarders show, then you'll be in trouble."

"You wouldn't."

I smiled and he left. It had just been Mr. Wallace, Ralph, Tina, and me on the clock tonight. Tina had taken off right when we closed, so I had the wide hallway all to myself.

Now that I'd basically been given permission to take pictures and throw away, my discard pile grew bigger by the second.

A text came in on my phone in between shots: Where are you?

It was Cooper. **I told you. At the museum.**

Still?!

Just getting started. Where are you?

Waiting for little sister outside of music lessons.

I actually know Amelia's name. And fourteen isn't so little anymore.

I know. Our girl is growing up. Have you asked him?

I'm going to in a little bit. If I clean some more, he'll be happier.

You shouldn't have to bribe someone to put your art in the show. Your art speaks for itself. It's brilliant.

A bribe never hurt anyone.

Ask him!

Ask him. Ask him, I told myself as I transferred the discard pile into two big trash bags. As I took those trash bags out to the Dumpster in back. I was going to ask him. I stopped by my car on the way back inside and grabbed my large portfolio. It was mostly pictures of my work, because the canvases themselves were too big to lug around. But I did bring a few of the original smaller pieces. My grandpa's favorite piece was the first, and looking at it made me happy.

Mr. Wallace was in his office writing something in a notebook. His office was almost as bad as the storage room—piles of papers on his desk, easels in need of repair leaned in a messy pile against one wall, a trash can overflowing in the corner. He looked up when I stopped in the doorway.

"You heading home?"

"I am, but first I wanted to ask you about the show at the end of July."

His gaze went to the large folder I held.

"I brought some samples to show you." I set my portfolio on his desk.

"Abby, there is limited space, and I have applications from all over." He opened a drawer and pulled out a stack of papers, as if I wouldn't believe him.

"I'd like to throw my hat in the ring too."

"Eighteen is the age requirement." He pointed at a random spot on one of the applications.

Now for my well-rehearsed speech. "Sir, I believe that art doesn't have an age limit. Michelangelo sculpted *Madonna of the Stairs* at sixteen. Picasso was granted entrance into a prestigious art school at fourteen. At the age of fifteen Salvador Dalí had his first public art exhibit. I'm not saying I'm anywhere near as talented as they are, I'm merely pointing out that age shouldn't be an indicator of ability."

"You've been doing your homework, I see."

I slid my portfolio closer to him. "I'm just asking for a chance."

He sighed and reached for my portfolio. I sunk into the chair opposite him in relief. I'd accomplished the hard part. My art spoke for itself. He began slowly flipping through the folder. I'd blown up most of the pictures to at least ten by twenty. He studied each one closely. After what felt like forever, he closed the cover and looked up at me.

I gave him my winning smile.

"Abby, you will be perfect for the show when you meet the age requirement. Is that next summer?"

"Wait . . . what?"

"You'll be the right age next summer." He patted the closed folder. "Bring me some more samples then."

The smile slid off my face. "Yes. But why? I've seen the art you've had in here for amateur exhibits. Mine is just as good. Are you really going to hold me back because I'm not eighteen yet?"

"It's not just about your age."

"Then what?"

"We have limited space and I need every sale I can get to keep this place going. This is my one and only fundraiser for the year. We're a museum, not a gallery, so I don't get to do this just anytime I feel like it."

I moved to the edge of the hard chair. "But what if I sell a few of my allowed paintings? That would help you, right?"

He pushed my portfolio back toward me. "You won't."

"Why not?"

"Because you're not ready. Your paintings aren't good enough yet."

The air went out of my lungs so fast it felt like someone had punched me in the gut.

When I didn't say anything, he went on. "I have every reason to believe that they will be. But you're not quite there."

"What do you mean? What are my paintings missing?"

He stared at my closed book. "Experience . . . heart."

"Heart?"

"They're technically good, but they look like you copied a picture. I want to *feel* something when I look at your paintings. They're missing a layer, and that's understandable. You're young. You haven't experienced enough in life to add that depth to a painting. But you will. You are exactly where you should be in your progression as an artist. Just keep moving forward. You'll get there."

I nodded numbly. After years of art teachers, my parents, my grandpa telling me I had talent far beyond my years, this was hard to hear. I stood and tucked the book under my arm.

"I'm sorry," he said as I walked away.

I went through the back to avoid Ralph. I didn't want

him to ask me about the huge folder I held. I didn't want to have to explain to him what I was doing with it.

The museum had a courtyard, and right now, outside, a recycling exhibit was on display. The artist had taken trash and turned it into art. I passed a tree made of shaped iron for branches and green tinted bottles for leaves, then I wound around two old bicycles that were fused together. They seemed to defy gravity by balancing on a single wheel. The last piece I flew by before reaching the side gate was the rusty hood of a Volkswagen Beetle. On the domed section was carved a lopsided heart. I slid to a halt.

These were all pieces in a traveling exhibit that we only had for two weeks. Next week we'd pack it up in wooden crates with shredded paper and ship it up the coast, to Pismo or Santa Cruz or some other artsy beach community like ours. I'd spent some time out here admiring the pieces. I loved art. All different kinds. But now, this rusty old hood with its uninspiring heart seemed ridiculous. Mr. Wallace considered this art, but not my paintings? Was this really that much better than what I had shown him? Maybe I had no idea what art was after all. And maybe I had nothing to offer anyone.

FOUR

"Has anyone seen my angled brush?" I called down the hall. I was lucky. I knew that. My parents, fully supporting my art, had turned one of the spare bedrooms into a studio for me in our house. It had easels and canvases and a hutch full of paints and brushes and the best lighting in the house.

My mom came to the door holding my brush. "It was in your washing jar by the sink."

"Thank you." I hadn't told anyone what Mr. Wallace had said to me Saturday night. I had expertly avoided the questions with answers like: *he's considering me.* Leaving off the second part of that sentence: *for next year.* I was pretending he hadn't said it. I was going to ignore it. I didn't need his show. There were others I could apply to. I couldn't think of any at the moment, but I'd research it.

"What are you painting? Something amazing . . ." She stared at the poster board that I'd set up on the easel. "Or something not so amazing."

"I think it's a pretty awesome poster."

"Do you have to make Cooper a new poster for every single race? What's wrong with recycling?"

"That's the beauty of this, Mom. It *is* the old poster. I just add another layer every time."

"It is a pretty cool poster," she admitted. "But the paint is what I was talking about. So much paint."

I had painted over the bottom half of the orange backdrop from before, and it was now various shades of blue, melding together to create the effect of movement. Then I had painted encouraging words over the top.

I snatched the angled brush out of her hand. "A painter has to paint, Mom."

She went to the window and opened it. "I thought we talked about airflow when you're painting. You need better ventilation in here. The fumes aren't good for your lungs."

"I don't smell anything."

"That's because you've desensitized yourself to them."

"Mom, painters have been painting for centuries without good ventilation."

"And they probably all got lung cancer."

It was useless to argue with her sometimes. "Okay, I'll open windows. But then what if I get hypothermia?"

She smacked my back playfully, then looked at her watch. "I thought the race started at two."

"It does. Wait. What time is it?"

"One forty-five."

"What? Crap." I added the final black words under what I'd already written and yanked the board off the easel. "I can take the car, right? You don't have big plans for this afternoon?"

She gave me a little shove instead of responding to my sarcasm. "Text me right when you get there. And when you're leaving."

"How about I text you if there's an emergency."

She leveled a stare at me.

"Fine, I'll text you."

"Thank you."

"I'll clean up when I get home," I called over my shoulder as I rushed for the door.

"Sunscreen!" she yelled after me.

I wheeled back around, made a pit stop in the kitchen at our drawer of sunscreen, grabbed one of the twenty bottles there, and left.

I carefully placed the poster flat in the trunk, hoping that the heat from the day would help it dry on the way over, then climbed into the car.

I was still wearing my painting shirt, a long-sleeved plaid button-down covered in old splatters of every color, over a tank top and shorts. I wiped my hands on the shirt and started the car. Hopefully Cooper's race wasn't the first one.

I cheered wildly from my spot toward the finish line. I had arrived just as he started, so I hadn't had time to find his parents or sister, but I was sure they were there somewhere. I held my sign up nice and high. Cooper wore a bright-green helmet, and he took the dunes at breakneck speed. I always worried about him when he raced, but he always told me that he was born on the dunes so I had no need to worry. To which I would always reply, *gross, and no you weren't.* But I knew what he meant—he'd been riding since he was little. And it showed. He won nearly every race, and this one was no different.

After he crossed the finish line in first place, he stood up and pumped his fist in the air. I wove my way through the watching crowd, mostly made up of tourists, to his trailer, where he'd load up the quad. Cooper and his family were already there when I arrived.

Cooper's helmet was tucked under his arm, and when

he saw me, his smile widened. "Abby! Over here!"

I nodded and finished the walk to him. "Hi!"

"Hello, Abby," his mom said. His dad nodded at me. His sister, Amelia, hugged me. I'd never met a family that looked more similar to one another than Cooper's. They were all tall and lean and blond.

"Hi, everyone. Great race, Coop."

Amelia looked at my sign. Cooper was studying my sign now too. He read it out loud: "'Cooper is number one.' Yes, I am."

I pointed to the part he was ignoring. The smaller words inside a pair of parentheses. "Or number two."

He shoved my arm. "But I wasn't."

"I like to come prepared."

"You also like to come covered in paint, I see."

I looked at my outfit to make sure I had, in fact, taken off my paint shirt and left it in the car. "Do I have paint on my face?"

"Yes, you do." He ran a finger down my right temple, then my left cheek, sending tingles down my arms. I shook them out.

"Cutting it close today?" he asked.

"I made it," I said, wiping at my face. "I saw your whole race and brought a sign."

His dad patted his back. "You did so good today, son." Cooper's parents hadn't always been so supportive of his racing, but when they realized how much he loved it, they started coming to more events.

"Thanks, Dad."

"Should we get your quad loaded up on the trailer?"

"Sure." He gave me a nod and patted the seat. "Come on, Abby, you want to go for a ride?"

"Nope, I refuse to get on that death trap."

His sister laughed. "I've ridden it."

"You must trust your brother more than I do."

In a loud whisper behind his hand, Cooper said, "Abby is a huge wimp."

"I will ignore that comment and take you out for a bacon burger to celebrate your win," I said.

"My parents are taking me out to celebrate this time, but come with us. That's okay, right, Mom?" he asked.

His mom smiled, but I couldn't tell if it was real. "Yes, of course."

It wasn't that I thought Cooper's parents hated me. In fact, much like him, they liked me as a friend. I knew they were happy we weren't a couple, though. They wanted something different for Cooper—better. Not the girl with the hand-painted signs, weird mom, and always-gone dad. Cooper had never said that's how his parents felt, but I could see it in the way they reacted to stories about my life, about my art, about my mom.

"Okay," I said, not sure if I should accept the invitation,

but wanting to celebrate with him.

"We'll be at Cheesecake Factory at five," his mom said. "That will give us all plenty of time to go home and clean up."

She meant that would give *me* plenty of time. But she was right. I didn't need to show up at a restaurant with paint face. "Yes, okay . . . I'll see you all there then." I walked away, but Cooper caught up with me.

"What?" he asked.

"What?"

"You have your sad face on. What happened?"

"Nothing. I'll see you in a little bit."

"Fine. Don't tell me." He jogged back toward his family.

"Don't be a baby," I called after him.

"But being a baby is my favorite."

I knew I'd have to tell him what Mr. Wallace had really said eventually, but right after he won a race didn't seem like the right time. Maybe after dinner.

FIVE

Or maybe I'd never tell Cooper about Mr. Wallace. The denial thing was working out okay too.

I had put on my nicest sundress, pulled my bleached-by-the-sun hair into a loose braid, and put on makeup, even though I rarely wore more than a swipe of mascara in the summer. It was too hot for more than that.

Cooper's mom kissed my cheek when I arrived at the table, and his sister patted the empty chair in between her and Cooper.

"I love it when you dress up for my parents," Cooper whispered when I sat down.

"Shut up," I mumbled back.

Cooper wore shorts and a faded blue T-shirt that made his eyes look even bluer. His skin was bronzed to a perfect tan from all his time outside. His blond hair, still slightly damp from his recent shower, curled up on the ends. Yes, he was still as adorable as ever. I scolded myself for noticing, then opened my menu and looked over the options.

I was so busy trying to distract myself from Cooper's cuteness by burying myself in my menu that I didn't notice someone was standing over me until I heard a "Hey, Abby."

I looked up and saw a guy I recognized from school—Elliot Garcia. "Hi. I didn't know you worked here."

"Just for the summer," he said.

"Awesome."

"Hi," Cooper said to Elliot. "Why don't I know you?"

I punched his shoulder. "You don't know everyone in the world."

"You know what I mean," he said. I did. Cooper and I knew the same people, and they knew us. It was Cooper, Abby, Justin, and Rachel. Or Rachel, Cooper, Justin, and Abby. Whatever the order, usually people didn't know one of us without knowing the others. But we did have separate classes, so occasionally, like with Elliot, I knew people they didn't and vice versa.

"I know of you," Elliot said. "You're Cooper Wells.

We've just never met before."

"Now we have," Cooper said.

I analyzed the two of them as they spoke. Elliot was cute, but in the nearly exact opposite way as Cooper. Where Cooper's eyes were blue, Elliot's were brown. Cooper's hair blond, Elliot's curls were nearly black. Cooper was tall and muscular, Elliot was lean and an average height. The differences were so noticeable seeing them side by side like this.

"I think we're ready to order," Mr. Wells said, pulling my attention back to the moment.

Elliot straightened up. "Oh, your waiter will be right here. I'm just a host. I'll grab you some waters." He smiled at me. "I'll be right back."

As he walked away, Cooper said, "You should take Abby out."

I gasped.

Elliot turned back. "What?"

"Nothing. Ignore him," I said. Cooper fancied himself a matchmaker at times. He was not good at it.

Once Elliot left the table I shot Cooper my meanest look.

"Sorry," he said. "But that guy has a crush on you. It was obvious. I was trying to help him out."

"You can never just let me do my own flirting, can you?"

"Were you going to flirt? Because it was looking pretty questionable."

I wasn't going to flirt. I had no interest in Elliot or any other guy right now. I had just gotten horrible news about my art and my heart still picked up speed when Cooper smiled at me. I was not in the proper emotional place to be dating.

I ignored Cooper's super-sarcastic question by asking a question of my own. "Have you heard from Justin?"

He pulled out his phone and showed me a picture of a halfway-finished stone wall. "Did he send you this text?"

"No. Why is he not sending me texts?" I read the words he had sent with the picture. Working on a schoolhouse for the local children. I could picture Justin there, speaking Spanish, the language he spoke all the time at home, and playing with the kids.

I pulled out my own phone and sent a text to Justin. Where are my update pics, punk?

"Ah. I'm sure that will inspire immediate obedience," Cooper said, reading over my shoulder.

"I'll be equally happy with obedience or guilt."

Cooper chuckled.

Elliot came back with our waters, followed by the waiter, who took our orders.

"How is your art going?" Mr. Wells asked from across the table as soon as the waiter left.

"It's good."

"Will you paint something for *me*?" Cooper's sister asked.

"Of course," I said at the same time his mom said, "No, that's not polite to ask, Amelia."

"Why not?" Amelia asked.

"Because Abby doesn't have time for that."

"It's true, Amelia," Cooper said, reaching behind me to tug on his sister's hair. "Abby wants to paint five brand-new pieces for an art show she's going to be a part of in six weeks."

"No, I don't," I said.

"Yes, that's what you said to me. You said none of the pieces you already had were good enough."

"They aren't," I said. "Can we not talk about this right now?"

"I completely disagree. They're amazing. But whatever, you're stubborn, so you'll paint new ones."

"I won't," I said.

"So are you going to use some you already painted? Which ones?"

"No."

Now he was confused. I could tell. "You can't both paint and not paint," he said.

"There is no show."

"He canceled it?"

"For me. There is no show for me."

"I thought he was considering. He'll say yes."

"He said no."

"Oh." His smile immediately slid off his face.

"Yeah. But whatever, it's not a big deal. I'll find another show." I could feel my cheeks go hot and I wanted to move on as fast as possible. I pulled my water glass close and took a long drink.

His parents looked at each other and then back at me. One of them was about to ask a follow-up question to clarify what I meant. Or say something like, *but it is a big deal*, or *but your work should be in the show.* His dad even cleared his throat, getting ready for whatever was coming next. I knew if he said one more word about it I'd break down in tears before the sentence was through. The tears were already threatening, clinging to the backs of my eyes, causing them to sting.

That's when Cooper said, "You're right, it's not a big deal." He squeezed my knee once, under the table, then dropped his hand. "Tell me I wasn't awesome today out there on the dunes?"

His sister took the bait first, probably realizing as much as Cooper did that I needed a subject change. "You caught air on that back jump."

His parents were a little slower to let go, his mom meeting my eyes and holding them before turning her attention to Cooper. "Yes, we are here to celebrate your amazing race. Let's celebrate."

By the time the waiter came back with our food, everyone had moved way past my failure and was well into celebrating Cooper's success. I was grateful Cooper knew that was exactly what I needed.

"Abby's going to bring me home," Cooper said at the end of dinner, when the bill was paid and we'd all stood to leave.

"I am?" I asked. I really just wanted to go home and crawl into bed. I'd managed to push the thoughts of Mr. Wallace and the art show to the back of my mind (or at least the middle of it) for the last couple of days, but admitting the truth out loud had brought them flying back. What he'd said, and what, through all my anger and denial, I knew I believed.

"Yes, you are."

"Be back by curfew," his dad said, then took his wife by one hand and his daughter by the other and headed out of the restaurant.

"Cooper, I'm tired. Can we just talk tomorrow?" I asked when they were halfway to the door.

"Nope. You have to talk now. I can tell it's bothering you. Come on." He led the way toward the exit.

"Of course it's bothering me, but I'm fine. I'll get over

it. Let's get cheesecake instead." I stopped at the lit glass case and surveyed all the beautifully displayed cake.

Cooper stopped beside me. "It looks like they don't have white chocolate raspberry."

"Maybe I want to try a new one."

"You never try something different. Once you find the best, that's all you ever want."

"So true, Cooper, so true."

He gave me a sideways glance, like he thought I was talking about something other than cheesecake. I was.

He shook his head with a breathy laugh, grabbed hold of my hand, and led me outside. His hand was warm and slightly callused, and I always thought it fit perfectly in mine. My car was parked in front of the restaurant, but he walked past it and toward the pier. He must've realized I was going to follow him without force, because he let go of my hand, much to my disappointment.

After a block and a half he said, "I got something for you."

"You did? What?" Without my permission, my heartbeat sped up.

He pulled a white napkin out of his pocket and handed it to me. There was a phone number written on it. I swallowed my disappointment.

"I already have your number," I said.

"Ha-ha. That is Elliot's number. You're welcome."

"You still think you're some sort of matchmaker?"

"I'm an excellent matchmaker."

"Elliot gave me his number six months ago, but thanks anyway." I knew Elliot had been interested back then. I'd kind of blown him off, exchanging a few texts but nothing more. I shoved the napkin back into Cooper's pocket, then walked ahead of him. The planks on the pier were warped and I had to slow down once I got there so I didn't trip.

Cooper caught up. "Did you ever call him?"

"We texted a little. I'm not interested, Cooper."

"Did you ever tell me about this?"

"I'm sure I did."

"Huh," he said.

When we reached the end of the pier, I leaned against the wood railing and looked out into the water. At first glance, the ocean appeared black at night, but between the skyline and the shoreline there were so many variations of color and movement that it always made me itch for a paintbrush.

"Talk to me, Abigail. I hate it when you get inside your head. What happened? You said Mr. Wallace was considering you. What did he *really* say?"

"That I have no heart."

"He said you were an android?"

I draped my arms on top of the railing and laid my

forehead on them with a moan. The smell of salt and fish and seaweed overtook me.

Cooper rubbed my back. "He said you have no heart? What does that even mean?"

"He said I have no depth. That my paintings are basically one-dimensional. They don't make him feel anything."

"Oh. So *he's* an android. Got it."

I buried my head deeper in my arms.

"But seriously, he obviously doesn't know what he's talking about."

But doesn't he? I wanted to say. *You feel the same way. You're missing that piece when you look at me too. The piece that makes you feel something.*

I turned my head sideways and looked at Cooper. "I have an agoraphobic mom and a war-zone dad." And I couldn't forget the unrequited-love thing I had going on. "How much deeper can a person get?"

"Not much." Cooper chuckled, a sound that made my heart thump hard in my chest.

I groaned again and reburied my head. Several waves crashed against the supports below before he spoke.

"Your mom isn't agoraphobic."

"I know. But it seems as though she's studying really hard to become one. She's getting worse."

"Worse how?"

"She used to at least go out. Leave the house. I can't remember the last time she did that. She needs friends. That always seemed to help her before we moved here."

"I can probably get my mom to ask her out to lunch."

I didn't need to say anything, just stared at him until he realized that was a ridiculous suggestion.

"You're right," he said. "They aren't a good match."

"It's fine. She'll be fine when my dad gets home in August."

"Your dad gets home in August?"

I smiled at that thought. It was right around the corner. "Yes, I can't wait. But he'll miss the show. I mean, he would have missed the show. Now it doesn't matter."

"Maybe you misunderstood Mr. Wallace."

"Nope. He was straightforward. Very. He actually used all the words I told you. No emotion, no depth, no heart. All of them."

"That's harsh."

It *was* harsh. Being an artist defined me. It was the one thing I felt I was good at. The one thing I thought people, and Cooper, admired me for. And now I didn't even have that. The tears I'd managed to control at the restaurant threatened to spill down my face.

"It's just one person's opinion, Abby."

"He has a doctorate in art. He is a museum curator. And he is the only person close that can show my art.

I needed this experience." The lump in my throat was growing by the second, and I kept having to swallow it down.

"What about another museum? Or gallery?"

"I've been looking. It's a long shot. Hundreds of people apply for shows. I thought I had an in with Mr. Wallace. But if he doesn't like my art, you really think some stranger is going to take a chance on me?"

"Don't let him get in your head."

"He's already there." With those words the tears escaped, much to my frustration. I swiped at them angrily.

Cooper pulled me into a hug. "Don't cry. I hate it when you cry. It makes me want to beat people up."

"I'll be fine."

"I know you will be. And you'll figure out a way to prove him wrong." Cooper's hand went up and down my back and I melted further against him.

As comforting as Cooper's words were, I wasn't sure I would figure out a way to prove Mr. Wallace wrong. I wasn't great at changing people's feelings.

SIX

I stared at the blank canvas. Experience. Depth. Cooper was right. I needed to prove Mr. Wallace wrong. I'd get in that art show, get accepted to the program, and prove to Mr. Wallace, to Cooper, to everyone that I was a real artist. I'd paint something new. Something different. He wasn't making final decisions on the applications until two weeks before the show. I'd show him that I was more than what he'd seen.

I had about four weeks to paint five paintings better than I'd ever painted before. The time wasn't what was causing a growing panic in my chest, though. I had time.

Depending on the size, how detailed it was, how many continuous hours I could devote to the piece, I spent anywhere from a day to several days on a painting. Since it was summer, I had nothing but time. The tightness filling up my chest was due to the fact that I had no idea what I was going to paint. I had no idea what would be new or different or better.

I flipped through my scrapbook of inspirational photos and prints, which normally gave me ideas. But nothing was coming to me. And wasn't the point to do something different than I normally did?

I shoved the scrapbook back in the hutch and dropped my paintbrush into the jar. I turned to leave the room and let out a scream when I saw my mom standing in the doorway behind me.

"You scared me," I said.

"You didn't paint anything."

"I know."

"Cooper told me what Mr. Wallace said."

"What? That traitor. When did he tell you that?"

"He texted me this morning."

"I will kill him."

"What I want to know is, why *you* didn't tell me."

"I don't know. The more times I say it out loud, the more I believe it. I wasn't even going to tell Cooper. He forced it out of me."

She shook her head. "That boy doesn't have to force anything out of you."

"I know. I told him without much effort. I have no willpower when it comes to him. Keep that to yourself."

She smiled. My mom knew about my history with Cooper. She was the one I cried to last summer after that fateful late-night walk on the beach where I told him how I felt and he laughed it off.

I brushed by her and out to the living room, where Grandpa was sleeping in the recliner. I sat on the couch, thinking my mom wouldn't try to talk to me in here with Grandpa napping. I should've known better.

She sat next to me. "I think your paintings are beautiful."

Grandpa snorted awake. "I wasn't sleeping," he said.

"It's okay, Gramps, when a man gets to be your age, he can't help it."

"Would you punish your daughter for me?" he said.

My mom laughed. "We're talking about Mr. Wallace."

"No depth, huh?" Grandpa said.

"You told him?" I threw my hands in the air.

"I'm not allowed to know?" Grandpa asked, indignant. "Since when am I not allowed to know?"

"Since I have no heart," I said.

Mom patted my shoulder. "You have a heart, baby. It's your art Mr. Wallace is referring to."

"So you agree with him?"

"I never said that. You know your father and I love what you do."

"Wait, did you tell Dad? He doesn't need to worry about this right now."

"He likes to be kept up to date too."

I sighed. "I need to start waking up earlier."

My mom gestured to the paintings hung around the living room. They were like windows that let in no light, but made the room seem endless. Each one was a different scene of the outside world. I'd painted busy places like Times Square and the Strip in Vegas, but also serene places, like countryside villas in France and green-covered bluffs in Ireland. Not that I'd ever been to any of those places, but I'd seen a lot of pictures. I'd painted these one by one since our move here, thinking they could inspire my mom to see more of the world, but I wasn't really sure they helped. Maybe they actually made her feel like she didn't need to go anywhere, since she had the whole world in her living room.

"Just look how talented you are," she said.

The paintings looked nearly real. But wasn't that Mr. Wallace's point? They weren't unique. They weren't my own. They were based off pictures. But what did I feel when I looked at them? I just thought they looked like nice places to visit. I couldn't feel the wind on my face or taste the air. Is that what was supposed to happen when looking at really good art?

Maybe Mr. Wallace was right. But maybe there was something I could do about it. “I need experience.”

“You’ve been painting for as long as I can remember,” Mom said.

“No, I mean experiences. What experiences will help me find depth—find my heart?” I needed to find inspiration from life, not from pictures. And not just inspiration, but emotion too.

“I think you have a perfect heart,” Mom said.

I rolled my eyes. “You’re my mom, you have to say that. I’m being serious. I need to do something. Lots of somethings, apparently. But what?”

“What kind of qualities are you looking to develop?” Grandpa asked.

I thought about that as I tapped my finger over and over again on the arm of the couch. My gaze drifted to my grandpa, one of my favorite people in the world. What were my favorite qualities about him?

“Courage. Like you,” I decided.

“Me?” Grandpa asked.

“Yes, you say what you’re feeling no matter what the people around you think. You know how to stand your ground. How did you learn that?”

"A really mean drill sergeant in boot camp."

"So I should join the army? Follow in yours and Dad's footsteps?"

He nodded. "Sure, when you're eighteen, you should. It made me a man."

"You want me to join the army and become a man?"

He let out a growl. "Stop pretending to take me so literally."

"You're not joining the army, Abby," Mom said. "Grandpa was saying that he gained courage by standing up to someone even when it was hard."

"Right. I have no idea how to do that."

"You'll figure it out," Grandpa said.

"What else?" Mom asked. "What other traits do you admire?"

"I like how you know something about everything, Mom."

She laughed. "I'm pretty sure you hate that."

"Well, I'm not a fan of the brown recluse stories."

"She means she's not a fan of your paranoid reading," Grandpa said.

I swatted my hand through the air in his direction. "That's not what I said."

My mom patted my leg. "Well, whatever the case, reading is right. I'd say that books can give you a new perspective on things. I know you already read, so may I suggest reading something out of your comfort zone? Like a classic."

"Hold on." I jumped up. "Let me go get paper. I need to write these down." I went to the junk drawer in the kitchen and found a pen, then plucked a piece of paper from the printer on the counter. I grabbed a magazine off the coffee table and sat back down, positioning the paper on top of the magazine. At the top of the page I wrote *The Heart List* and underlined it two times. "Okay, so, stand up to someone and read a really old book."

Mom rolled her eyes but didn't protest. "What other traits are important to you?"

"Dad is always somewhere new and doing something different. I think that made him who he is. The kind of person who is flexible and adventurous."

"So try something new?" my grandpa said.

"And he doesn't mean drugs," Mom added.

"Because that was the first thing I thought of."

"Try more than one new thing. Make it five. Try five things you've never done before," Grandpa said.

"Five? What do you think I am? A newly minted person? Five is a lot. Are there five things I haven't tried?"

My mom rolled her eyes. "Please. There are a hundred things you haven't done."

"Okay, fine. You're right." I wrote it down. Three things were on my list. That wasn't enough. If I had to drastically change the way I saw the world, which would hopefully change the way I painted, I needed more experiences. I thought of my friends and things I admired in them. "Rachel is kind to everyone. I think everyone likes her. What experience could I possibly have that will grant me that quality?"

"What about learning a stranger's story?" Mom said.

"What do you mean? Just walk up to a random person and ask what their deal is?"

"No, care enough about something you see someone do to *want* to know more about that person. To let what you hear change you in some way."

"So, learn a story." I added that to my list. "What else?" My pen was poised, eager to soak up their wisdom, which I was sure was going to transform me into the best painter in the universe by the time the deadline for the showcase came around.

"You tell us," Grandpa said.

"My friend Justin is on a service mission in South America right now. I bet that experience will give him more depth than anything I could dream up."

Grandpa grunted. "You don't have to go to South America to do service. There's plenty here."

"Like what?"

"I have complete faith that you'll find something," Mom said.

I added *service* to my list, with Justin's name next to it. Then I added names next to the other items on the list they had inspired. I had Grandpa, Mom, Dad, Rachel, Justin . . . "Cooper," I said aloud.

"What about him?"

"I don't have a Cooper-inspired experience."

"What do you like best about Cooper?" Mom asked.

I closed my eyes for a moment. What *didn't* I like about him? Every laugh and story we shared raced through my mind. I stopped myself from saying *everything.* "He's fearless. Nothing scares him. Maybe I need to overcome some of my fears."

"How?" Grandpa asked.

"By facing one."

"I don't like the sound of that one," Mom said.

"Nothing dangerous."

"It's a good one," Grandpa said as I wrote it down.

"How about, quit a bad habit," my grandpa said. "That's always character-building."

"I don't drink or smoke, Gramps."

"Are those the only bad habits in the world? What about that horrible sarcasm of yours? That would be a good one to nip in the bud."

"Nobody says *nip in the bud.* And I'll quit being sarcastic once you do."

He curled his lip. "Or you can pick another thing."

"That's what I thought." I added *quit a bad habit* to my list.

"If you're looking for character-building, you should add *fall in love* to your list," my mom said.

As I wrote it down, Grandpa asked, "Didn't she already do that one?"

I gasped. "Did you *tell* him?"

Mom narrowed her eyes at Grandpa and I rolled mine. "So I guess I can check that one off."

"Fall in love with someone who loves you back," she said.

"Ouch. Now you're just being mean."

She patted my leg. "It will change you."

"Okay, so I'm going to add *have my heart broken* to the list, because I can already check that one off."

"Are you looking for things you can already cross off?" Mom asked.

"No." But I wrote it anyway and put a tidy check next to it with a smile.

My mom let out a breathy laugh. "How about, see life come into the world."

"Uh . . . you're getting weird now. You want me to case hospitals? And by the way, gross."

"That sentence can be interpreted in many ways, and I definitely didn't mean follow pregnant women."

"Okay, I'll write it, but I don't know how that can be interpreted in more ways than the obvious one."

"How about," my grandpa said, with a dramatic pause, "see a life go *out* of the world."

"And that is the end of my list. When you people start talking about death, I'm done."

"It changes you, child."

"I don't want to see that. Even if it does make me a deeper person."

"Understandable."

Besides, I felt like I could already put a check mark next to that one too. I hadn't exactly seen my grandma die, but I felt like I saw the heartache it had caused often enough. I wrote it down, but didn't add the checkmark. Maybe there was another way to interpret that one as well. I hoped this worked. Because if it didn't, maybe I really wasn't an artist. And if I wasn't an artist, what was I?

SEVEN

I read, then reread, the list I'd made the day before. I hoped that the best traits of the people in my life cobbled together into this list would turn me into a Frankenstein's-monster version of the lot of them. The nonfreakish version. There were eleven things on the list. Well, technically ten if I didn't count the one I'd already checked off. How to become deep in ten steps . . . or less? I hoped it would be less.

Maybe this was why the art institute winter program asked for sales history, because they knew how hard it was to make it past the gatekeepers of galleries. That could narrow down their list of applicants dramatically.

I fished a pushpin out of the container on my desk and found a spare bit of wall space between a quote about love and a picture of a dandelion, all its seeds but one floating away on the wind. I'd pinned all sorts of inspiration on my wall—art, quotes, poems, scenery—over the years. Muses for my painting. It was all things I'd seen while flipping through magazines or scrolling through my phone—some I added to my scrapbook, some to my walls. I laughed a little as I turned a circle, taking in everything now. They were all things that had made me feel something, I realized. It's why I'd pinned them there. Oh, the irony that *my* paintings weren't doing the same thing for someone else.

I snapped a picture of the list with my phone and out of habit was about to send a group text to Rachel, Justin, and Cooper, when I remembered Rachel wouldn't get it and Justin was in the middle of being philanthropic. He didn't need to see my attempt at depth right now. Instead, I emailed the picture to myself, then sat down at my laptop to compose a letter to my dad.

Hey pops,

Attached you will find a list of activities that will make me so full of heart you might not recognize me when you get home. And since you're always gone so long that I forget who you are, we'll be in the same boat this time. You're welcome. Also, I figured out what I want you to bring me home this time. I want a small rock shaped like a heart. You should scour the desert to find it. It's the only way I will know you truly love me and think about me every day. Plus it will represent my heart growing three sizes. Is that how many sizes the Grinch's grew? I forget. Remember when we used to watch that every Christmas and you said that you almost named me Cindy Lou Who? I'm still eternally grateful you didn't (even though I now know that's not a true story). Love, your appropriately named daughter.

I picked up the little vial of sand I kept on my desk that Dad had brought me home after I requested it during his last tour. He always brought me home something. Sometimes it was something I asked for, sometimes it was something he said reminded him of me, like painted beads or glass art.

I turned the bottle sideways, letting the sand move along the vial as I tipped it back and forth.

There was a knock on my door, followed by Cooper's voice: "Are you presentable?"

I set the small bottle down, hit Send on my email, and shut the laptop. "Presentable? Do you mean decent?"

"Same thing."

"Well, one of those things I am and one I'm not, so I

don't think they *are* the same thing."

He let out his overly dramatic sigh, which I could hear even through the closed door. "Do you have clothes on, Abby?"

"Yes."

He opened the door and flung himself into my room, landing on his stomach on my bed, then rolling onto his side. "Hi."

His eyes narrowed in on the list I'd pinned to my wall. "What's that?"

"My ten-step guide to a deeper life."

"It only takes ten steps? Maybe I should do it then."

"You totally should. These can be our summer activities."

He scooted off the bed and came to stand next to me, looking over the list. He smelled good. Like vanilla and oranges. That was his usual scent. But sometimes he smelled like sweat and fabric softener and sometimes he smelled like toothpaste and face wash or cherry ChapStick and sunblock. Or chocolate. Or . . . *stop*, I told myself. Not helpful at all.

"I'm not going to watch a baby being born," he said.

Right, the list. I turned my attention back to it. "That's what I said. But my mom said there were other ways to interpret life coming into the world or something like that."

"I can only think of one way to watch life come into the world."

"Same. But whatever. We don't have to do all of them. I sense depth will occur after five."

He laughed. "Good, because I also don't want to have to kill anyone."

I smiled. "I don't think that's what Grandpa was suggesting with that one."

"I have your number six."

"You do?" I glanced at the list to remember what number six was. *Face a fear.* Of course he'd pick that one.

"Why is my name next it?" he asked.

"Because certain ones were inspired by certain people." I pointed at his. "You, my fearless friend, inspired that one. And you don't get to pick my fear. I'm picking my own for that."

"Come on. You'll give yourself an easy one."

"And you'll give me an impossible one."

"Everything is possible."

I stared at him expectantly.

"What?" he asked.

"Are you going to finish that thought? Everything is possible . . ."

"That's all I was going to say. Is there supposed to be more?"

"There's always more with that start. Everything is

possible through hard work or through perseverance or through never giving up or through God."

"Huh. Okay . . . everything is possible when you're with me."

I rolled my eyes. "I liked my options better."

"Well, right now, my option fits, because you're going to face your fear—with me."

"What have I gotten myself into?"

He laughed evilly as we left the room.

He held out a red helmet for me.

"No. Absolutely not. I told you I was just going to watch. This is *your* thing." Over his shoulder I could see the other quads and dune buggies zooming through the dunes. The sun beat down on the sand and made everything in the distance appear wavy, adding to the nausea I already felt at the thought of being out there with them.

"A fear is not going to be something that's *your* thing. Then it wouldn't be your fear."

"I'm not scared of this. I just think it's stupid. And dangerous."

"You are terrified of this. I can see it in your eyes. Don't try to pretend this isn't one of your fears. And if it's not your fear, you can put one check mark in the *trying something new* box."

I huffed and took the helmet from him. "Fine. It is my

fear." I'd seen too many crashes while he was racing, and I did not want that to be me.

He smiled big and started walking to where his quad was waiting by the trailer.

One of his buddies passed, obviously just finishing his run, and said, "Be careful out there. It was really windy last night."

"Thanks," Cooper said and when we were out of hearing distance added, "for nothing."

"We can't go now," I said, walking faster to try to catch up with him. "I know what wind means on the dunes. I've been out here with you enough. It means there's hundred-foot drops carved into the sand. It means we hit them at the top of a hill out of nowhere and we go plummeting."

"Don't listen to him. We'll be fine. I was born on the dunes, remember?" he threw over his shoulder.

"And now you're going to die on them, and I'll be able to check off the last item on the list."

He stopped suddenly, me nearly running into him, and turned around. He put his helmet on the sand between his feet, then stood and placed his forearms on my shoulders, looking me in the eyes. "I know you can do this. I know we'll be safe. But if you don't want to, you don't have to."

And that was it. I was toast. Was it possible he knew

what this proximity and those eyes and that voice did to me? Even if he didn't, I knew my weakness, that tiny voice inside my head that was saying, look at him, he wants you to do this, maybe this will make him fall for you.

But being aware of my weakness and resisting it were two totally different things. Ugh. I'd thought I was more over him than this.

I nodded. "I'll try."

"Yeah?" he said, his sparkling smile back.

I took a fistful of the front of his T-shirt. "Yes. But after this you will buy me a milk shake."

"Only if you don't barf," he said, taking a step out of my hold, swiping up his helmet, and finishing the walk to his quad.

"Wait, what?"

He took the helmet I still held and popped it onto my head.

"Ow." My voice was muffled inside the only thing now protecting me from a cracked skull.

He lifted up the visor. "What?"

"Nothing. Let's get this over with." My stomach was already in knots, and I realized that maybe he was right. Maybe I wouldn't want a milk shake after this, because I was certainly going to barf.

He hopped on the quad and powered it to life. Then

he turned and patted the seat behind him. I lowered my visor and climbed on. He took my arms and wrapped them around his waist. "Hold on tight, okay?"

I nodded. He hadn't needed to tell me that. Then he put his own helmet on and we were off.

I should've gone on my own. If he taught me how to use the quad, it would've been better. I would've gone slow and taken it easy and life would've been better. But I wasn't on my own. I was behind Cooper, the guy who was in frequent dune races. The guy who was *born* on the dunes. And he wasn't taking it easy. Acid crept up my throat. The landscape ahead was terrifying. The sand was pocked with bowls carved into its otherwise smooth surface. Some of those bowls were shallow and harmless. But the ones Cooper liked to take on were thirty-foot drops that we had to race down the side of, into the hole. Those were the kind that needed momentum to come out of, so he took them at speeds that had me gripping him even tighter. I might've enjoyed this setup if I wasn't so terrified.

"I hate you. I hate you. I hate you," I said as he revved the engine to make us go even faster. He couldn't hear me, but those words echoing through my helmet made me feel better.

On the bright side, this wasn't a feeling I purposefully had very often. I couldn't remember the last time

I'd felt this amount of sheer panic. Or this amount of hatred toward Cooper. So maybe this would help me paint emotion.

Cooper skidded to a stop at the top of a hill. Our two right tires were on the edge of a sandy cliff. One more pump of the gas and we would've been flying down the eighty-foot drop. Had I not been here, he probably would've taken that drop, happy and hoping not to somersault down it.

He turned on the quad to talk to me. "Are you having fun yet?" he yelled.

I shook my head back and forth, unable to open my mouth for fear I'd be sick.

"Really? I thought for sure you'd like it once you tried it."

I shook my head again.

"Okay, I guess we head in then."

I nodded.

And he was back at it just as fast as before. When we arrived at his trailer, I stumbled off the quad and tripped to the ground on wobbly legs.

He took off his helmet and sat down in the sand next to me. "So . . . you *are* actually a wimp. I had been kidding when I called you that in front of Amelia. But now I know."

I threw a handful of sand at him, then shakily took

off my helmet. "I might've liked it better had *I* driven."

"You want to drive?" He swung his keys in front of my face.

I held up my hands. "No."

"So, what do you think?" He pointed out at the stretch of sand we'd just made our mark on. "Is this list of yours going to accomplish anything?"

I thought about the fear that gripped my chest out there, that clawed at my insides in a way I'd never felt before. And now it was gone. I'd faced that feeling and overcome it. A surge of pride expanded my insides. "Yeah . . . maybe."

I looked back up at him. A teasing smile lit his eyes. He needed to feel the same thing I'd just felt—that mocking smile would be wiped off his face real fast. I had told my grandpa and mom that Cooper was fearless. And that seemed to be the case. But I was probably wrong. Everyone was afraid of something. "You're next. What are you afraid of?"

He held his helmet in the air. "I fear nothing, Abby."

"No, really. You said you wanted to do the list with me. What fear are you going to face?"

He tossed the keys to his quad once, then caught them. "Huh. I really can't come up with anything. I'll think about it."

I handed him back the helmet. "So will I."

EIGHT

"My legs are sore," I said. "Why are my legs sore? We were on that quad for thirty minutes." I held the milk shake Cooper had bought me as a reward as we walked down Main Street toward his car.

"You were gripping the seat with your thighs like your life depended on it. Of course they're sore."

"My life *did* depend on it." I hit my right thigh three times with a closed fist. "Ouch. That seriously hurts."

"Then stop doing that. And stop walking like that."

"Like what?"

"Like you just spent hours on a horse."

"That's what I'm trying to tell you. I can't help it." I hit my thigh again.

He stepped in front of me, presented his back, and squatted. "Jump on."

"I will. Because maybe carrying me a hundred yards will make *your* legs sore." I jumped onto his back and rested my chin on his shoulder. This wasn't exactly helping my sore legs, or the feelings I was crushing down.

Main Street was mostly tourist shops—kites, beach trinkets, surf gear—but Cooper still looked in each window we passed, like he might actually buy any of those things.

I caught sight of a sign on a post and said, "Wait. Stop."

"Why?"

"There." I pointed to the sign. "Read that."

He walked closer. The sign was taped up to the silver light post, and Cooper read aloud the words on it: "Come audition for the community theater summer musical, *The Music Man*." Cooper hitched me up farther on his back and started to walk away. "Nope. Pass."

I pulled on his shoulders, like I really was riding a horse now and he would back up with my command. When he didn't, I kicked free of his grip and hopped off his back. "Cooper. The tryouts are in three days." I pointed at the date on the sign. "That is exactly when I need to complete another experience by. This is fate. Neither of us has ever tried out for a play before. It's perfect."

"Fate?"

"Yes. Fate. Destiny. We happen to be walking by a sign. We happen to be working on a list. This is happening." I took a picture of the info with my phone.

He threw his head back and groaned. "I miss Justin. He wouldn't make me do crap like this."

"Yes. We should let Justin know what he's missing out on." I texted Justin the pic I'd just taken with the words Cooper begged me to try out with him.

"You are such a punk," Cooper said.

"Are you scared?" I asked. "Is this your fear?"

"No. I just don't understand the point. We won't make it. We are both horrible singers."

"Hey. Speak for yourself."

"You think we'll make it?"

"No. But it's not about making it. It's about the experience. That's the point, Coop." I hooked my arm in his elbow. "This will be so much fun."

"That's one word for it."

My phone buzzed with a text. Justin had written back: Um . . . I don't want to know.

"See, he thinks it's crazy too."

"I will see you at my house Monday morning at ten

a.m. That's not tomorrow or the next day but the day after that."

"I know what day Monday is."

"Just checking. It's summer. I know how days blend together."

"What about tomorrow?" he asked.

"Tryouts aren't tomorrow."

"I know. But I'll probably see you tomorrow."

"I have to work in the morning. After that?"

"Sure. First day back since Mr. Wallace told you you're an android?"

"Yep."

"Good luck."

I collapsed into my desk chair after work. It had been a weird day. Mr. Wallace posted me at the ticket desk. I never worked the ticket desk. Even though cleaning and directing visitors seemed like a worse job, it put me right in the middle of inspiring art. Today I got to stare at the lobby and the street for four hours. There was nothing inspiring about that. I sensed Mr. Wallace was trying to avoid me.

I signed into my computer and pulled up my email. The time difference between Dad and me usually meant that he wrote me when I was sleeping. Sure enough, I had an email waiting.

To my daughter, whose mother named her and didn't ask for my vote,

Your heart does not need to grow three sizes. One, maybe, but definitely not three. May I suggest you take the following items off your list for the proper amount of heart growth: face a fear (that sounds dangerous and I don't support it), fall in love (you're not allowed to do that until you're thirty), have your heart broken (this seems counterproductive, seeing as you're trying to grow it), learn a stranger's story (don't talk to strangers), see a life go out of the world (I've seen enough of that for our whole family). That should do it. That leaves six on your list. You're welcome. As for the impossible request you have tasked me with, we shall see if rocks exist in the shape of hearts. Thanks for keeping me updated. How is your mother?

Love, that guy you won't recognize when he gets home.

My dad was the best email writer. And considering that's how we communicated a lot of the time, it was a good quality to have. I typed him a reply.

To the most overprotective dad in the world,

Thanks for your input, but you don't get a vote on the list. In fact, I've already done one you vetoed. I faced a fear yesterday. I rode on a quad for the first time. It was not something I will do again for a while, but it was definitely an

experience. And I can guarantee that heart-shaped rocks exist. We'll see if you are dedicated enough to find one. Mom is doing okay. Not as good as when you're here, but nothing to worry about. Stay safe.
Love you, [insert the name you would've voted for here]

I pushed Send, then looked up at the list on my wall and grabbed a pen from the desk drawer. I put a small checkmark next to "face a fear." Could I also count the quad ride as trying something new? No, one experience could only equal one checkmark, I decided. No combining. I really wanted this to work. New experiences would give me new images and emotions to draw from for my art. I usually painted what I knew, what I'd seen in my life or in pictures. I didn't rely on emotion or pushing myself to feel or see or try new things.

I surveyed the rest of the list. Aside from the tryouts in a couple of days, I wasn't sure what I'd do for the rest.

There was one, however, that was simple. One I could start now that would take me at least a couple of days to complete—read a classic.

"Mom," I announced when I arrived in the kitchen. "I'm going to the library."

She looked up from a book she was reading titled *True Crime*. Not good reading material for my already overly worried mom.

"Any input on which classic I should pick?" I asked.

Grandpa called from the other room "I've read a lot of classics. Do you want my input?"

"Nobody is talking to you, old man. Keep watching your *Matlock*."

I heard an exasperated grunt. "I don't watch *Matlock*."

My mom gave me her disappointed look, the one that said I had taken my joking with her dad one step too far.

"I'm sorry for calling you old man," I yelled.

"And what about the *Matlock* thing?"

"There's no shame in watching a show about an old-man lawyer who always manages to save the day. There's something to be said about characters you can relate to." My grandpa had been a lawyer before he retired, and he hated being compared to TV lawyers.

He said something I couldn't understand, probably mumbling some silent curse.

"There are too many classics for me to limit your choice." She pointed to the living room. "And you burned any bridge you had there. Looks like you're on your own."

"Do we have a library card? We need a library card. Do you need to fill out a form for me since I'm a minor and all? They probably don't trust me with their books." My attempt to get her away from that book and out of the house was beyond transparent, but I didn't care.

Mom's brow immediately went down, and I could tell she was trying to reason through that, hope for some other solution than her needing to go to the library with me. "I don't think they need me there. Kids have library cards, right? I don't need to go."

"There's not very many people in the library, Mom."

"You don't know that."

"Plus, it's only five minutes away," I said.

"By car."

"Yes, by car."

"I'd rather walk."

"I know. But that's a long walk." One I knew she couldn't make. "It's fine, Mom. It's just been a while since you pushed yourself a little." I usually didn't say things like this to my mom. I usually let her off the hook easier. I didn't want to upset her or make her more anxious about life. But maybe clinging to Cooper on the back of that quad the day before made me realize that pushing yourself to do hard things was actually pretty liberating. There was a sense of accomplishment about it, after the fact.

She sighed. "I'll call the library and see if they need me there for you to get a card."

Blasted phones, I thought, always ruining my best-laid plans with their usefulness.

I pulled out my useful phone and sent Cooper a text:

I'm going to the library to pick out a classic. You want to come?

Can't. Family BBQ at my dad's work. Call me with an emergency in about an hour.

What kind of emergency?

The best friend kind. I don't know. You'll think of something.

I'm sure your parents will love me even more for that. I'm not faking an emergency. I'll be reading Crime and Punishment. I had looked up a list of classics, and that one sounded the most interesting to me.

What crime are you planning to commit?

That's the title of a book.

Cool. Get me that one too. It sounds awesome.

We can't read the same classic. We need to read different ones and then tell each other about them. It will be double the depth.

Okay. I call dibs on Crime and Punishment.

You are a brat.

This is true. I have to go now.

Okay. Have fun.

He added: Call me in one hour.

No.

I put my phone in my pocket and looked up just in time to see my mom come back into the kitchen.

"Good news," she said. "You can sign for your own library card."

"Oh. Okay."

"Don't look so disappointed, hon. I'll walk to the park with you after dinner tomorrow. How about that?"

"Promise?"

She hesitated a moment, then nodded resolutely. "Yes."

"I'm holding you to that."

"I heard it too," Grandpa said from the other room.

"I'm being ganged up on now?" she asked.

"Not ganged up on, Mom. Supported. You have lots of support."

She smiled and hugged me, then handed me a bottle of antibacterial hand gel.

"What is this?"

"Do you know how many people touch those books?"

I handed her back the gel. "You should read some stories on this stuff. It's creating superbugs."

"Really?"

I shouldn't have said that. Now she'd spend the next two days on the computer reading about superbugs. I snatched the bottle back. "You're right. I'll bring this." I lifted the car keys from a hook by the door and left before she decided I couldn't leave the house after all.

NINE

There were lots of books considered classics. A whole section of them. Some I'd never even heard of before, like *Ulysses* or *Middlemarch*. Some I had, like *The Scarlet Letter* and *The Sun Also Rises*. A lot of them were on the list I had looked up, but a lot of them weren't.

I'd already found *Crime and Punishment* and was reaching for *Frankenstein*, thinking it reminded me of the mash-up of qualities that had inspired my list, when someone else reached for it at the same time. "Sorry," we both said, then laughed.

The girl smiled and gestured for me to take it.

I recognized her immediately. She had curly red hair and bright-green eyes. "Oh, you're the . . ."

"Zit commercial girl?" she finished for me when I stopped myself in time.

"Yes."

She gestured to her beautifully clear skin. "Keeps them gone for weeks."

"Do you really use that zit cream?"

"No."

I smiled. "You go to my school too, right?"

"Pacific High? Yes."

"I'm Abby, by the way."

"Oh, sorry. I'm Lacey." She nodded toward the book I'd reached for. "Are you getting a jump start on the honors English summer reading list? Do you have Engle?"

"No, I'm not taking honors English. I'm just looking for an interesting classic to read."

"Why?"

"For fun, I guess." I didn't want to explain the heart list to her. "You can take that one. I'll find a different one."

"What kind of stories do you like to read? Maybe I can help you pick one."

"Have you read a lot of classics?" I asked.

"I've done a lot of theater, so I've read almost all of Shakespeare. Other than that, not really. I'm not sure why I offered like I was some expert."

"If you say anything with enough confidence, it's true, right?"

"I can get behind that." She pulled a book down. "There's always the summaries on the backs. Those are sort of helpful." She began reading the back of the book she held in an English accent.

"Is the writer of that one British?" I asked.

"I just assume all the writers of classic literature are British." She shrugged. "But more importantly, I do a killer British accent."

"You really do."

"Wow, that sounded vain. I promise I'm not vain." She bit her lip. "Is that the kind of promise vain people make?"

I let out a single laugh and held out my hand for the book. "I have to get that book now."

She handed it to me.

"*A Tale of Two Cities*, by Dickens," I read off the cover.

"Aha!" She patted the book. "See. It *was* a safe bet."

My phone buzzed in my pocket. Saaaavvvveeee me! It was a text from Cooper.

I tucked the two books I now had (one for me, one for Cooper) under my arm and typed back. **Just tell your parents you want to leave their party.**

Can't. They'll be disappointed. You've seen their disappointed faces.

You need to go into the army. I hear it makes you a man.

Lacey slid *Frankenstein* off the shelf and waved at me with it. "It was nice to meet you. I hope you enjoy *A Tale of Two Cities*."

"Thanks." I pointed to her book. "You too."

She walked away, and I dialed Cooper's number. He answered. "Hello."

"I ran out of gas."

"Abby, why would you do a thing like that? Don't you pay attention to your gas gauge? It's that little one right above the steering wheel."

"Watch it or I'll hang up right now."

He laughed. "Of course I'll come save you, even though I'm right in the middle of my dad's really cool work party. You should see it, they have live singers and everything."

"Sounds amazing."

"What's this group called again, Dad?"

A deep voice said something I couldn't understand.

"The Patriotic Quartet. There's four of them and they walk around the party only singing patriotic songs."

"I would've never guessed that by their name," I said, heading for the checkout. A few people shot me looks on my way, and I guessed I was being too loud for the library.

"I know."

"And it's not even the Fourth of July," I said, quieter this time.

"Barely two weeks. Imagine how booked they are for that day."

"Would you rather have to listen to only quartets for the rest of your life or screeching cats?"

"That's a hard one. But quartets, I think. Unless they can only sing patriotic songs. Then the cats."

"I'm getting our books now. Are you going to come rescue me and my empty gas tank or not?"

"Abby ran out of gas," Cooper's muffled voice said. He was obviously relaying the message to his dad. "I have her on the phone and can ask her exactly where she is. Otherwise we have the Find Your Friend app on each other's phones."

His dad must've asked what that was, because he said, "It's like a GPS thing that lets me track her phone. What? Yes, it's safe. You don't let strangers track you, just your friends." Back to me he said, "My dad doesn't know what Find Your Friend is."

"I figured."

"I'll be right there."

"My hero," I said dryly.

"See you in a bit."

"I'll be back at my house. No need to use the app."

"Copy."

I hung up and handed my books to the librarian.

"These are due in two weeks," she said with a smile.

"Thanks."

She used a wand to scan the barcode on the covers. "These are character-building books. They'll make you think."

"That's what I'm hoping for."

I hoped they built character fast, because it felt like the clock was ticking.

TEN

The next day Cooper and I sat in my room reading our books.

"Was work any better today?" Cooper was lying on the floor. He'd rested *Crime and Punishment* on his chest and had his hands grasped behind his head. He looked so at ease in my room that it seemed like he should be a permanent fixture there.

From up on my bed, I responded, "Nope. Ticket counter again. Tina got the floor. Tina doesn't even *like* the floor."

"Stupid Tina."

"I know!" I sighed and turned the page of my book.

Cooper was silent for several long moments, then asked, "Would you rather have to read only that book for the rest of your life or only be able to watch one movie for the rest of your life?"

"That's hard. I love movies, but I can't imagine never being able to pick up another book either."

"I know."

"I don't think I can give up movies. I'm visual," I said.

"I don't think I can either." He held up his book. "You want to switch?"

"Switch? I'm on chapter six." We'd started reading the day before, after he'd "rescued" me. And I was actually enjoying Charles Dickens. The language was hard to get into at first, but I felt like I was starting to understand. It was an interesting story that brought to life some of the things we'd studied in world history about the French Revolution.

"Let's summarize what we've read so far and then switch for the next hour. Double the depth, right?"

I laughed. "Okay." I Frisbeed the book to him. "Oh. I forgot to tell you I ran into Lacey Barnes at the library yesterday."

"Zit cream girl?"

"Yes."

"I've never talked to her before. Does she really use

that zit cream? Does it help?" He ran his hand over the side of his face, where he must've had a blemish. I couldn't see one. Cooper had nice skin but, like me, broke out on occasion.

"She doesn't use it. She has perfect skin."

"Figures," he said. "What's she like?"

"Really nice, actually. And not vain at all."

"What does that mean?"

"You don't know what vain means?"

"I know what vain means, but why did you bring it up?"

"Nothing. Inside joke."

"You already have an inside joke with Lacey Barnes?"

I almost said I had been kidding but then realized "Yes, I do."

"There you go oozing your charm again, Abby."

I threw a pillow at him and he laughed, then tossed me his book. It landed next to me on the bed. He picked up the book I'd thrown him and reclined back.

"Wait. Summary." We each summarized what we had read so far and then began reading from the books we now held. I wasn't sure how much time had passed when my mom knocked on the frame of my open door.

"Have the classics swallowed you both whole or would you like to eat dinner?"

Cooper set his book aside and immediately stood.

"Mrs. Turner, if you are offering food, I will eat it. It's the least I can do."

She beamed at him.

I joined Cooper and we followed my mom down the hall. "I can see why you wanted to switch books, by the way. *Crime and Punishment* is disturbing."

"I know. I sensed nightmares. I'm not as tough as you," he said.

"Didn't you just call me a wimp the other day?"

"A wimp about some things. Not others."

"Wow. Thanks."

He chuckled. "No problem."

Mom had made chicken and rice, and four plates sat on the table, where my grandpa waited.

"Cooper," Grandpa said. "Again."

Cooper smiled. "You sick of me, Grandpa Dave?"

"Always," Grandpa said.

Mom swatted the air near Grandpa. "He's kidding."

"He's not," I whispered at the same time my grandpa mouthed, *I'm not.*

Cooper let out a single laugh. "It's kind of creepy how you two are the same person," he said, looking between Grandpa and me.

"Except he's a hundred years older."

"How's the list coming?" Mom asked, loading up a plate and handing it to me.

"Cooper made me ride on a quad in the dunes. I'm not sure how much depth that gave me, but it was an experience."

I was about to talk about how terrifying it was but pressed my lips together. Mom had stopped scooping rice midscoop, frozen.

I changed my tone. "It was fun. Cooper is a professional, so it wasn't really scary at all."

Cooper laughed, taking the plate full of food in front of me and sliding it in front of him. "Right. You should've seen her."

I grabbed hold of his knee under the table and dug my fingers around it.

He shot me a look but then noticed my mom. "She did great," he said with hardly a pause. "We took it slow."

Grandpa sighed as if he knew what we were doing.

Finally my mom snapped out of her daze. "That's great, hon. That's definitely a new experience. Next time, will you run risky activities by me first?"

"Yes. Sorry."

"I kind of sprang it on her. She wasn't sure what we were doing. Sorry, Mrs. Turner."

Mom smiled at Cooper. "It's okay. I know you're careful."

If she had seen how *careful* he was, she would never trust him with me again.

Grandpa retrieved the plate my mom was extending and then said, "Didn't you promise Abby a walk to the park after dinner today, Susan?" This was his way to push my mom, because I certainly hadn't, with our downplayed ride. I shot him a look but then smiled at Mom. Because it was true. She had promised. "We can all go," Grandpa said.

Mom's lips formed a tight line. She finished filling the last plate, then sat down. "Yes, I did promise. That sounds good."

I wasn't sure what it was about having Cooper with us that made my mom more relaxed. Maybe it was his general happy nature, or maybe she sensed that he feared nothing, so she didn't need to either. Whatever it was, when he was there, our success rate at getting my mom out the door was almost as high as when my dad was around.

Grandpa and I walked arm in arm, trailing Mom and Cooper. Cooper was doing most of the talking, like I generally did when I walked with my mom. But she was looking up more, laughing more, not hesitating as much. I couldn't hear what they were talking about, but I'd ask him later so I could pick up a few pointers.

"How was your quad ride really?" Grandpa asked me.

"Terrifying," I said. "Too fast."

"That's what I thought." He patted my arm. "And did it give you newfound depth?"

"It actually gave me an idea for one of my paintings."

"That's great. So does that mean you're going to be racing on the dunes alongside Cooper next week?"

"Not on your life."

"How are you going to retaliate?"

"You mean what fear am I going to make him face?"

"Yes."

"No idea."

We arrived at the park, and my mom sat on a bench. I chose a swing close by, Cooper taking the one right next to me. Grandpa stood behind me and gave me a push.

"You're surprisingly strong for your age," I said.

"I'm strong for any age."

I pushed myself higher with a pump of my legs.

"Which classics did you end up picking?" Grandpa asked.

"It was the best of times, it was the worst of times," I yelled out from the top of my swing.

"*A Tale of Two Cities*," Grandpa said. "Good choice. About two vastly different realities existing at the same time. And what about you?" Grandpa turned to Cooper, who was twisting in his swing, the chain getting tighter and tighter.

"*Crime and Punishment*."

"Ah. About a man getting away with murder . . . or does he? Our internal judge can be the worst punishment of all."

"Don't tell us the end, Grandpa!"

He laughed. "I haven't."

I glanced over at Mom as my swing slowed to a stop. She was intently taking in our surroundings. "What's next on the list?" she asked when she noticed me looking.

Cooper lifted his feet and began spinning violent circles as the chain unraveled.

"Dizzy," he said when he planted his feet again.

"What's next on our list, Cooper?" I asked.

He groaned. "We're trying out for a musical tomorrow."

Grandpa raised his eyebrows and said, "Really?" as if he thought it was a horrible idea.

I grunted. "It's a new experience!"

A buzzing noise sounded from Cooper's pocket and he pulled out his phone. A smile played on his lips.

When he looked up I nodded at his phone, asking him who it was.

He just shook his head and started spinning the swing again.

As we headed back to the house, my mom arm in arm with Grandpa this time, I leaned over to Cooper and whispered, "Who were you texting with?"

"Remember that girl I met at the outdoor movie a couple of weeks ago?"

"I?"

He smiled. "No. Ris."

"Oh, right. Ris. Yes, I remember her." I had hoped *he* hadn't. That she was quickly forgotten. Apparently not.

"It was just her. We've texted a few times."

"Oh. Cool."

"I think you'd like her."

I was sure I wouldn't. "Yeah. Bring her to one of our outings sometime and I'll see."

"I will."

When we got to my house, he went straight to his car.

"Your book is inside," I said.

"I'll get it tomorrow."

He drove away and I watched him go, trying to ignore the sinking feeling in my chest.

ELEVEN

That night I pulled out a painting I had done over a year ago. It was Cooper on a quad, flying over the sand dunes. It was good, realistic, but that was it. I studied the painting, remembered the fear that had coursed through me when I was in the same position, and set out to alter what I'd created. I tried to mask its portrait feel and make it more dramatic. More shadows, more sand flying, more expression. I didn't refer to a real picture while working out the details on his face. I didn't care so much if it was true to life. Just that it was real.

I stood back and glanced up at the wall clock. Three

hours had passed. It hadn't felt that long. My hands were covered in paint—black and deep blue streaked along all my knuckles. I used a clean corner of my paint shirt to wipe a blob I could feel under my eye, and then I assessed what I had done.

It was different. There was emotion on Cooper's face that didn't exist in the picture this was based off, along with steeper dune angles and misty sand flying and much more shadow. I wasn't sure if all this made it better or just different. I wasn't sure if *I* was better. The doubt that had lodged in my chest with Mr. Wallace's summary of my work had built a sturdy nest there that wasn't going to be easily disassembled. I dropped my paintbrushes in the jar and went to clean up.

"I can't believe you talked me into doing this," Cooper said. We were sitting in the red velvety seats of an auditorium with a hundred other people. They all held some sort of paper, and I stretched up to try and see what it was.

"What do they have?" I whispered. "We don't have anything."

Cooper looked around too, as if my mention of it made him realize that people were, in fact, holding papers. He was taller than me, so he had a better view. "Sheet music?" he said, as if not sure his guess was right. "It looks like sheet music."

"Were we supposed to bring our own sheet music to try out with?"

"Obviously," he said. "I guess that means we should leave." He moved to stand, and I grabbed hold of his arm, pulling back down.

"We are not leaving."

The click-clack of heels echoing through the room drew my attention to the stage in front of us, where Lacey now stood. I gave a small hum of surprise.

"What?" Cooper asked.

"Lacey Barnes is here. And apparently in charge."

"And that surprises you?"

"I guess not. She *is* the star of a commercial."

"And almost every single one of our school plays."

"I guess I should watch more school plays."

Lacey cleared her throat and spoke. "Welcome, everyone. We're so excited to have you. I'm Lacey Barnes, assistant director of *The Music Man* this year. Thank you all for coming out. We'll be starting soon. Our pianist today will be Mac Lawrence." She gestured to the piano on the floor in front of the stage, and a man stood up and waved. Everyone clapped and I joined in.

"Myself and Jana Kehler, the director, will be sitting at that long table back there. So make sure you project." She smiled, then held her arms out to the sides. "If I could get the guys to come up the stairs and gather behind the curtain, stage left, and the ladies stage right, we can get started."

Everyone stood and filed up a set of stairs on either side of the stage.

"I'm thinking of a proper punishment for you after this," Cooper said.

"You'll be fine. You love the spotlight."

"Not this kind," he said right before we separated and joined our respective groups on opposite sides. Lacey saw me and walked quickly over.

"I thought that was you," she said. "I didn't know you liked theater. Be honest, was it my amazing British monologue at the library?"

"Yes, so inspiring."

"That's what I thought." She smirked.

"Speaking of that amazing monologue, why aren't you starring in this thing?" I asked.

"My acting coach suggested trying all the different aspects of theater as a form of growth. That's exactly how she said it too."

"I figured."

She laughed. "Here's to growth."

"So," I said before she expected too much from my audition, "this isn't my thing and I didn't know I needed to bring music."

Girls were trying to walk around Lacey and me to get

backstage, so she pulled me to the nearest corner. "That's okay. People who don't bring their own music get to sing 'Happy Birthday.'"

"Nice."

"Did I see Cooper Wells too? Did you guys come together?"

"Yes."

She wiggled her eyebrows.

"Oh, no. Not together like that. We're just friends."

We both looked across the stage to where Cooper stood staring at us, like he found it weird to see us talking.

"You don't keep someone who looks like that in the friend zone for too long," Lacey said.

"Yes, I do, I mean, no, I don't want . . . didn't want to. He . . . it's complicated. Please don't repeat that," I added, realizing I'd just revealed more to her than I ever had to Rachel.

"I have no idea what you just said, so I will gladly not repeat it."

"Thank you."

She gestured over her shoulder. "I better go. Someone has to run this thing."

"Okay."

"Break a leg," she said and was off.

The next hour went by like someone had pushed a fast-forward button. Lacey would call people out one by one to sing. She and the director would take notes, and then the next person would be up.

Cooper went out before me. I thought he would be nervous, but he smiled at the judging table. "I didn't bring music," he said. "But I can sing some Metallica if you want. Or a little MJ."

I held in my laugh.

"Happy Birthday is fine," Lacey said.

He nodded, and the piano gave a frilly intro. Then Cooper sang. A few of the girls standing near me giggled.

One behind me said, "He's nice to look at, but not good on the ears."

I didn't think his voice was all that horrible. It wasn't like the other guys we'd heard who were polished and perfect, but he could carry a tune. When he got to the part where he had to insert a name, he sang Lacey. I peeked around the corner to see her smile at that.

When the piano played its last note, Cooper bowed and left the stage.

Finally, it was my turn. I'd been the one to suggest this, and now my palms were sweating, my heart racing.

A spotlight I hadn't noticed before shone right in my eyes. I tried to look at Lacey and the director, but I couldn't see them through the bright haze. I held up my hand to block some of the light.

Lacey gave me the thumbs-up.

"I need to sing Happy Birthday too."

Without another word, the piano began its opening notes. I dropped my hand and let the light take over my vision. I always thought I was a better singer than Cooper, but there on the big stage in the middle of the even bigger theater, my voice was swallowed whole. I tried to sing louder, but I was already forcing my voice, so it cracked. I was so happy when I sang the last "you" and I rushed offstage.

"Good job," the girl who'd been mocking Cooper said.

"Really?" I asked.

"You were kind of quiet, but you have a nice voice."

"Thanks." A surprising feeling of happiness coursed through me. I peered across the stage to the other side to see if I could get a glimpse of Cooper. He was standing there beaming, and the happiness in my chest expanded even further.

When all the singing was done, we were handed reading parts we had to perform. It felt like we'd been there all day, listening to people with varying degrees of talent read, when finally Lacey dismissed us. She handed out a paper that explained the callback process, and everyone filed toward the doors.

I hooked my arm in Cooper's and we headed to the exit.

"That was torture," he said.

"It wasn't that bad." It was something new. Something I'd never tried before, and it had pushed me outside my comfort zone to feel nerves I hadn't felt in a while.

"You have a good singing voice," he said to me.

"Thanks."

"I don't think I realized that before."

"Abby!" Lacey ran down the aisle toward us. Cooper and I turned to face her. "Hey," she said, when she stopped in front of us. "I wanted to tell you about a small barbecue I'm having at my house for the Fourth. You should come. Both of you."

I'd actually heard about Lacey's parties. There was nothing small about them. She lived in a huge house and threw even bigger parties. We'd never been invited, though. Cooper looked at me. We always watched the fireworks on the pier for the Fourth of July, and I wondered what he thought about this change of itinerary.

"Um," I said, hesitating. Cooper didn't say a word, obviously leaving this decision up to me.

"There will be people and food and fireworks. It'll be fun," she added.

Maybe I could count it as something from my list. The one about strangers or trying something new. I had to think of five of those, after all. "Okay."

"Really?" Cooper said under his breath, and I elbowed him.

Lacey took the paper I held about callback information and wrote her name and number on it. "Text me and I'll give you my address and stuff."

"Okay."

Cooper held his tongue until we'd waved good-bye and were outside. "Are you and Lacey friends now?"

"No, I hardly know her." We hadn't had a new friend join our group since it originally formed. We all got along too well and were too comfortable with one another to try and force an expansion.

"So no pier this year?" he asked.

"Rachel and Justin aren't here, so it will already be different. We don't have to stay at her party long if you don't want to."

He shrugged. "Maybe we should. Maybe I'll bring a date."

I tried to keep my voice casual when I said, "You might want to ask Lacey first."

"If she's just going around inviting random people, I'm sure she'd be fine with it."

"Random people?"

"No offense."

I laughed. "Well, too late, offense already taken."

"You know what I meant." He paused for a moment. "I wonder if she got a lifetime supply of zit cream from that commercial."

I pushed him. "You're a dork."

With late afternoon light shining through the windows of my art room later that day, I started a perspective piece—the view from the stage. Again, I tried to go just from my memory and how I had felt. It had been so hot up there on stage. And bright. The light shining in my eyes basically blinded me. I squeezed a large amount of yellow and white onto my palette. I mixed a bit of each color and blotted it onto the middle of the canvas, making a quarter-size spotlight. I squeezed out some red and cream, some black and brown for the chairs and people and stage that would surround that spotlight, and got to work.

The window in the room had grown dark, and now only my lamp lit the painting. I moved to the switch and turned on more overhead lights to assess my progress. It was wrong. There was something wrong with it. Too many chairs. Too many eyes from too many people looking forward. That's not how I had felt on the stage. I had seen hardly any chairs and almost no eyes. I swiped a clean brush through more yellow and white. I pulled out the light from the spotlight wider and wider. I streaked it across the chairs. The not-dry red mixed with the white and yellow and made orange swirls on the outside. The side of me that had obviously always loved my paintings to reflect reality almost painted more yellow over it, but I stopped myself. It was interesting movement. The spotlight in the center now made it almost impossible to see the surrounding chairs or people watching or edge of the stage. It took over the painting.

My eyes were tired. They had been straining too long. I resisted the urge to rub them with my paint-covered hands. I wasn't quite done with the painting, but it was time to call it a night. I stepped back but then stopped when I noticed a face in the few that remained just outside the spotlight. I leaned closer and squinted. It was my mother. I'd painted my mother into my painting without even realizing it. My mother—the least likely person to be in that auditorium today.

TWELVE

"What about her?" I asked Grandpa as we pushed a cart through the produce section.

Grandpa was squeezing nectarines and placing only a select few into the clear bag he held. "That woman? You want to know her story?"

"Why not?"

"I'm just wondering why all the people you are pointing out are women in their sixties." He tied the top of the bag in a knot and added it to the cart.

Grandpa always tried to set me up, and I always tried to set him up. And we both never actually agreed to the setup. It was our thing. "No reason," I hummed.

He pushed the cart forward. "That's what I thought. Your list isn't a matchmaking opportunity for me. It's a growth opportunity for you."

"I don't see why it can't be one and the same."

Grandpa bonked me on the head with a red pepper and added it to the cart. "Let's not mess up the dynamics of our already precariously balanced home."

"Precariously balanced? We have a perfectly balanced home."

"Exactly."

"No." I huffed. "That's not what I meant. I meant that we are lovely people and can add another lovely person to our mix."

Grandpa stopped the cart near a bin of apples and turned toward me. "Now that you're thirteen, we need to have a serious conversation."

I knew he was throwing an age joke at me to counterbalance the ones I always threw at him, so I chose not to react. "You want to have a serious conversation in the middle of the produce section?"

"What better place?"

"I don't know, maybe a more private aisle. Like the cleaning products. That aisle is always empty. Nobody buys their cleaning products at a grocery store."

Grandpa didn't give a sarcastic rebuttal, only folded

and unfolded the grocery list he had brought. That's when I realized this wasn't a joke. He *really* wanted to have a serious conversation with me in the middle of the produce section. I looked around. There were only a few people picking through a vegetable bin. I lowered my voice. "What is it?"

"Your mother was supposed to go to the store today. It was her turn."

Oh. I'd thought he was going to talk about meeting someone, but this was about my mom. "I know."

"She hasn't left the house for more than a walk to the park in weeks."

"I know. I think she needs to find a friend or two. It always used to help." I hadn't thought of it before recently, because she seemed fine. But now that she was headed in the wrong direction, I knew she needed something.

He pressed his lips together, then said, "She needs to see a professional."

"What?"

"If she won't leave the house, we'll bring one to her. I've been trying to get your father on board with this idea for a couple of years now, but he isn't having it. You know your dad, alpha male."

"My dad isn't like that," I said, feeling a little defensive.

Grandpa shook his head. "Your dad is a great guy. I've always liked him. But he doesn't want to admit she needs help."

"Is it really that big of a deal that she doesn't leave the house? In the house she is lovely and happy." Everyone had their weird idiosyncrasies. Just because hers was different from everyone else's didn't mean we were hanging by a thread.

"I think it's something she needs to work on."

"But if Dad doesn't . . ."

"You don't think she needs to work on it?"

The image of my mom's face in my theater painting flashed through my mind as an uneasy feeling settled in my stomach. Maybe deep down I did know that, even wanted it. I shook away the image. "Sometimes I do, but most of the time I'm just happy she's my mom."

"Maybe if you talked to your dad about how little she goes out."

"I don't like to worry him. He already feels so guilty when he's gone. He gets home so soon. Can't we just wait and see how she does when he's home?" She really was so much better when he was home. It was like he pushed some sort of reset button on her.

"Like I said, precariously balanced," Grandpa said under his breath and set the cart in motion again, heading toward the dairy row.

"Don't be mad at me, Grandpa."

He flashed me a smile. "I could never be mad at you, hon. I'll work on your dad. You just be their daughter."

"You just need to relax, Gramps. Everything will be fine." It had to be. She was fine. We were all fine.

"Did you ever make callbacks for that play you tried out for the other day?" Grandpa asked.

I shook my head. "No. We were horrible at acting. Pretty much everyone there, even the little children, was better than Cooper and me."

"That's probably not true, but it's good you know your weaknesses."

"Yes, I have many."

"What about him?" Grandpa asked.

We had turned down the soup and canned-vegetable aisle, and my grandpa was pointing to a guy studying soup cans at the end. At first I thought he was asking if he was one of my weaknesses, so I was confused.

"Maybe you should learn *his* story," he said.

"I thought my list wasn't a matchmaking opportunity but a growth opportunity."

"I thought one of the items on your list was to fall in love."

I choked on my own spit when I sucked in a quick breath. "Shh," I hissed between coughs. He had said that so loud. The guy looked over, probably because of my coughing fit, not because of my grandpa's loud declaration, but it was impossible to know. We took a few steps closer and I realized I knew him. Relief poured through me.

"Hey, Abby," Elliot said. "I don't see you for a month and then we see each other twice in two weeks."

"I know, what are the odds?"

Elliot looked at my grandpa and I said, "Oh, Grandpa, this is Elliot Garcia, Elliot, Grandpa."

"My name is Dave," Grandpa said, extending a hand.

"Right. I always forget you have a name," I said.

"My granddaughter is sarcastic."

I smiled. "Don't get all self-righteous. I learned it from you."

Elliot laughed. "Nice to meet you."

"Isn't it too hot for soup?" I asked, nodding to the cans in front of him.

"My mom's out of town and my dad cooks like . . ." He paused for a moment before he finished with, "Someone who doesn't know how to cook. I was going for a really cool comparison there but couldn't think of anything."

"A monkey in an apron?" I said.

"An angry porcupine?" Grandpa suggested.

"A porcupine?" I asked. "The comparison has to have opposable thumbs so that it might actually have the ability to cook. Like a monkey."

"An *angry* porcupine. I thought it could use its quills like skewers."

"Oh. Right. I see what you were going for now."

Elliot smiled. "I know who to come searching for when I need similes now."

Speaking of weird idiosyncrasies, my grandpa and I had just proven my mom wasn't the only one who had them. "Well, we'll see you around then," I said, taking hold of the cart and steering it around Elliot, feeling the need to escape any more embarrassment.

"Abby," he called after me.

"Yeah?"

"Are you going to Lacey's Fourth of July party?"

"Yes, actually."

"Cool. I'll see you there."

Maybe Cooper was right. Lacey was just inviting whatever random people she ran into.

"Well, there you go," Grandpa said after we were out of hearing range (thank goodness). "You can all but check the *fall in love* item off your list."

"Funny," I said. "And no."

"We don't like him? He seemed great. And he found you amusing too, which is a good sign."

"You just like him because he found *you* amusing."

"That didn't hurt." Grandpa took control of the cart

from me and pushed it toward the registers. "We better get going."

I hooked my arm in his elbow, my mind wandering back to our produce-section talk. "You're not *too* worried about Mom, are you?"

"She'll be fine."

"Are you sure?"

"As sure as the sunrise."

I furrowed my brow. "Is that an old-person saying?"

He grunted. "That is the saying of a person who has lived a lot longer than you."

"Exactly." A thought came to me. "You are a genius!"

"That's what I've been trying to tell you."

"No, you just gave me the best idea for my list. I can do it first thing tomorrow." And I'd force Cooper to join me.

THIRTEEN

It was an unearthly hour and my body screamed at me along with my alarm the next morning. Who set their alarm in the summer anyway? I thought about hitting snooze and forgetting my plans. But I knew I couldn't. I was already behind in completing my experiences if I wanted to finish my list before Mr. Wallace picked the final artists. And since I hadn't found a stranger to accost the day before, I needed to do something else from the list to stay on track.

It was four in the morning, still dark outside. Cooper would probably kill me if he knew what I had planned.

Or not come. That's why I wasn't going to text him. It would be easier for him to refuse a text. I would just show up at his house. I left a note for my mom on the counter and quietly lifted the keys off the hook by the front door.

Nobody in Cooper's house was awake either. The porch light was still on and all the windows still dark. I decided it was best to let myself in through his window like I sometimes did. I hoped he hadn't taken to locking it. He had a window facing the front of the one-story house. A fact his parents really should've been more concerned about, knowing Cooper. However, they apparently still hadn't even noticed there was no screen. That had been taken off two years ago, when he set up a middle-of-the-night game of parking-lot bowling with Justin and a couple of other guys from school. I shone my phone light on the window and slid it open. Unlocked. I took a breath of relief before I became irritated. Any criminal could just waltz up here and have instant access to his house.

I hefted myself inside. It had been a while since I'd done this, and my knee scraped along the casing, scuffing my skin. I sucked in some air, and one foot found the carpet. My other leg, while swinging in, found a baseball trophy on his nightstand and knocked it to the ground. I cringed, but Cooper didn't stir.

I turned on his nightstand lamp and sat on the bed next to his shirtless body. When had he started sleeping without a shirt? I really should've just texted him. I shook his shoulder. "Hey, wake up."

He grunted and turned onto his side, away from me.

"Cooper," I whispered, running a finger along his back.

"I'll clean my room later," he said.

I shook his shoulder harder. "Wake up. It's me. Abby."

"Abby?" he asked, rubbing his eyes and squinting against the light.

"Yes. I thought of a way to check another item off the list."

He sat up, his eyes finally coming into focus. He glanced at the window over my shoulder. "You're right, waking up before the sun is a huge fear of mine. Go ahead and check it off."

"Nope. This doesn't count for that."

He lay back down and pulled the blankets over his head. "Then let me sleep."

"Seriously, Cooper. Wake up. I didn't account for this taking fifteen minutes. We have a time constraint here, and if we miss the window, I'm going to be back again tomorrow at four thirty."

"It's four thirty?" he asked in exasperation.

"We are going to see life come into the world."

"Someone is having a baby right now? Who?"

"Of course not." I pulled off his covers. "Get up. Put a shirt on. Brush your teeth and meet me outside."

I quickly averted my gaze as he climbed out of bed, boxer shorts and all, and pulled on the pair of jeans that were in a crumpled heap on the floor beside his dresser.

"I hate you so much right now," he said.

I smiled and headed for the still-open window. "I'm okay with that."

"This better be good," he said when he came out through the front door and joined me outside five minutes later.

"It will be." I tugged on his arm, pulling him to my car.

"Like, life-changing good. I don't even wake up this early for school."

As I drove I explained. "So, we have seen about a thousand sunsets."

"Yes. We live by the beach. Ocean sunsets are pretty much unavoidable."

"You act like we should try to avoid them. They are gorgeous."

"No, I just mean, if we're at the beach when the sun is setting, that's it. It's the ocean and the sun. It cannot be missed."

"Yes. But when have you ever watched the sun rise?"

I grabbed hold of his bicep and gave it an excited shake to try and sell my pitch.

He was silent for a minute before he said, “Never. I value my sleep.”

“Exactly. Me too. But besides that, there’s nothing spectacular about it, because of all the houses and buildings and stuff in the way.”

“True.”

“So we are going up the mountain. We are going to see it rise in splendor. We are going to see life come into the world.”

“Ah, look at you being all metaphorical and stuff.”

I smiled.

“I still hate you.”

I laughed.

I had researched this well. The perfect spot to watch the sun rise that was less than an hour away from our houses. Did I not tell my mom and grandpa because it felt a little like a romantic gesture? Maybe. I could imagine the look my mom would give me and the joke my grandfather would make, and had decided I just didn’t feel like dealing with either. Besides, it wasn’t romantic. It was on my list. I’d committed to doing my list. This was another event to bring me depth. That was the mantra I kept mentally repeating that made this all seem perfectly normal, at least.

When we arrived, I pulled a blanket out of my trunk.

"Why didn't you bring two blankets? You are a notorious blanket hog," Cooper said.

"What? I am not."

"Do I need to go down the list of times you've hogged the blanket? Most of them involve movie nights."

I pointed to a bag in the trunk. "Stop whining. I brought you doughnuts."

"You brought doughnuts?" He snatched up the bag and opened it. "And chocolate milk too? Okay, I don't hate you anymore."

"That's what I thought."

There was a picnic bench, and Cooper sat down immediately and started to pull out a doughnut.

"Wait! Don't touch. We're not there yet."

"Not where yet?"

We were at the bottom of a trail. I pointed to the top.

"What? You're going to make me hike?"

"That is not a hike. That is a five-minute walk."

"Hiking is when you have to walk uphill for any length of time. Therefore that is a hike."

"That is not the definition of a hike."

"Then what is the definition?" he asked, reluctantly standing.

"I'm not sure. But not that."

The sky was lightening and I knew we didn't have a

lot of time. I put the blanket over my arm and led the way. Cooper grabbed the bag full of sugar and followed behind.

The top had a gorgeous view—a valley of green-blanketed scenery. It was hard to believe I'd never been up here before. With the ocean five minutes away from my house, complete with its own set of hills and cliffs and hiking trails, it wasn't often I went seeking nature in the opposite direction. From here, I couldn't see the ocean, even though I knew it was somewhere behind us.

I settled against a tree, facing east, and Cooper sat down next to me.

"Can I eat these yet?"

"Yes. Eat." It was really cold, and the air smelled of pine and dirt. I draped the blanket over my shoulders and watched the sky.

"You want one?" he asked with his mouth full of doughnut.

"In a minute." I checked my phone. We had more time than I thought. Sunrise was at five forty-three today, and it was just after five thirty.

Cooper held up the half gallon of chocolate milk. "Is this to share?"

"Um . . . yes!"

"Okay, okay, just gauging how much to drink."

I nudged him with my shoulder and he smiled. If he

stopped smiling so much, my life would be a whole lot less complicated. He passed me the carton and I took a drink.

"Chocolate milk makes everything better," I said.

"I agree." He leaned back against the tree, then tugged on a corner of the blanket. "Hey, blanket hog. You gonna share?"

I lifted the half of the blanket closest to him and he wrapped it around his shoulder, which pulled me up against him.

"You're warm," he said, inching even closer.

"I've heard the coldest time of day is right before sunrise—that moment in time when the earth has been without light the longest. And then the sun rises and slowly warms up the world again."

Cooper reached around my waist and tickled me. "That sounded like a Discovery Channel narration. It would be accompanied by a slow camera pan across a scene like this right before sunrise. Take out your phone. Let's do that."

"No. This is a no-technology moment."

His hand that had reached around my back to tickle me was still there, now resting on my hip.

I closed my eyes for a second and concentrated on pushing feelings down. I'd gotten so good at it this last year it was almost second nature.

"I'm going to take Ris out tomorrow night. Where should I take her?"

My eyes flew open. "Who?"

"Um. You know, that girl I've been texting." He took his arm back, resting it on his knee.

"Right. Ris. Yes, I knew that. I thought you were going to take her to Lacey's party."

"I am. But I mean like a real date."

"Aren't *we* going to the movie on the beach tomorrow night?"

"Oh, sorry, I forgot about that. We'll go next time for sure."

"For sure." I wasn't disappointed, I told myself. This helped even more with that feeling-smashing thing.

"So where should I take her?"

"I don't know," I said. "I don't know her."

"I know, but where do girls like to go on dates?"

"You're the one who takes girls out, not me."

He huffed. "But you are a girl."

"I am? Thank goodness I have you to tell me these things."

He squeezed my knee. "Be serious. Help me."

I thought back to dates I'd had over the years. They were all pretty basic—movies, dinner, beach. "I don't know. I don't go out much."

"Well, think about it for a minute. Your perfect date.

Where would you like a guy to take you?"

A perfect date was different from one that had actually happened. A perfect date required imagination. "My grandpa said there's this amazing underground garden somewhere close. I think that would be cool." For me, at least. Things like that gave me inspiration to paint.

"Good idea. I've heard about that too. I'm surprised you haven't been to it."

"I know. Me too. We're always busy doing other things." I turned back toward the view in front of us. "Oh! Shhh. Look. Here it comes." I gestured toward the mountain in the distance with my head.

"We have to be quiet while it rises?" he whispered.

"Shhh." For some reason I did want to watch it in silence. He seemed to sense I was serious, because he didn't say another word, and we both sat, taking it in. The rays came first, stretching across a section of the mountain, making it look like it had caught fire. And then slowly, one millimeter at a time, the sun showed itself. It looked smaller than I thought it would, but the higher it rose, the brighter the sky became. For the first time since we'd arrived I heard birds chirping above us. I had never watched the world come alive like this before. It was gorgeous how something could go from dreary, cold, and gray to full of light in such a short amount of time. I breathed in the air, which was still cold, despite how warm the sky looked.

Beside me, I could feel Cooper draw his breaths too. And with each of those breaths, my body leaned in until my cheek rested on his shoulder.

"How much longer are we staying?" Cooper asked when the sun was well above the mountain.

"I thought we'd stay for a week."

"Only if we get more doughnuts." He set the bag with my doughnut inside on the ground in front of me. "This doesn't mean you're a morning person now, does it?"

"No way. But I'm glad we did this."

"Me too." He looked at me, our faces so close together I could see the flecks of gray in his blue eyes.

"Let's go," Cooper said, jostling me as he stood up.

"Yes. Let's go. . . ."

FOURTEEN

"Here's those dried crickets." Grandpa held the small, clear bag up in my doorway. "You left them in with the other groceries."

"Oh. Right. I'm trying to forget I thought they were a good idea."

"Crickets are always a good idea." He set them on the end of my bed, then left.

It had been three days since the early-morning sunrise outing. Since then, I had visited a soup kitchen and helped serve dinner, for the service experience on my list. It was both fulfilling and depressing. I didn't like to imagine children without food, but it was hard to deny it when they stood in that line waiting for a ladle full of the chicken-noodle soup I had served. I wished I had thought to do something like that on my own, without a list forcing me to. I signed a volunteer form when I left and let the director know she could call me when they were shorthanded.

I'd gone to the shelter without Cooper. In fact, I hadn't seen Cooper since watching the sunrise. I tried not to think about why. Had he taken Ris out? Was he spending every spare minute with her since then?

Hey, if you're still doing the list with me, you need to find a service experience. I did mine yesterday.

Done and done. I'm doing service right now. My dad volunteered me to paint some guy's house. Paint. A house. Painting is your thing.

Oh. So it wasn't Ris that was keeping him busy. He actually had a real excuse. That shouldn't have made me so relieved. **Not that kind of painting.**

I'm on day three here.

I texted back: **So can we add painting to your skill set now?**

Of course. I'm awesome, but that's beside the point. The point is that I'm tired and sore and want to be done.

You're not done yet?!

I think we'll finish up today.

Nice.

First some crazy whack job got me up at four thirty, and then my dad's been waking me up at six. Not cool. When this is over I will soak in an ice bath and sleep for a week, followed by my best friend giving me a massage.

Justin's home?

Funny.

I would not be giving Cooper a massage. That would send me into major relapse. It was hard enough *looking* at his body. I didn't need to feel it as well.

Four thirty in the morning. You owe me.

That's why I brought you doughnuts. I owe you nothing.

He sent me back the pile of poop emoji and I laughed.

I pocketed my phone and made my way back to my art room. I'd set up a canvas yesterday before work, and it still sat on its easel, only a coat of white primer to show for my time. I had been avoiding it. My initial thought was to paint the sunrise. I had pulled out all my warm colors—reds and oranges and yellows—and they still sat on the dresser waiting for me. But as I looked at them, it seemed like such a literal interpretation. I remembered how cold that morning had been. How it smelled like pine and made my nose numb. How the birds hadn't come alive until the sun was sitting on the mountain. I remembered the feeling of life being awakened a little bit at a time. Awakened.

I took out more tubes of paint—gray and black and silver. At the bottom of the canvas, I started with cool colors. I drew rusty dried leaves and black bare trees and silver sleeping birds. As I moved up the canvas I added more colors and more life until I reached the tops, where the birds burst out from the green mountain, their flight mimicking the rays of the sun, the sky behind them bright and yellow.

"Wow."

"I thought I taught you not to sneak up on me when I'm painting. That could've sent my brush across the canvas." I'd managed not to jump. Barely. Cooper was normally a quiet observer until he saw me back away from the canvas.

"Sorry. I should know that, seeing as how I'm an expert painter now."

"True. I should just let you finish this for me," I teased.

"No way. That's amazing. I love it."

"You love everything I paint."

"It's true. But this one is . . . different. Are those birds dead?" He was referring to the ones on the bottom.

"That's a little dark for you."

"They're not dead. They're sleeping. Do they look dead?"

"They look cool. This is supposed to be the sunrise, isn't it?"

"That was my inspiration."

I set my palette on the hutch to my right, the one whose drawers were full of art supplies, and turned to Cooper. "I thought you were going straight to bed for a w—" I stopped. "Whoa. You have paint all over you."

"I know! That's why I had to come by here first. It was important for me to show you that we're twins now."

I smiled and stepped forward. "I don't think I've ever managed to get this much paint on me. Did you bathe in it?" I pinched a section of his shirt between my fingers and pulled it away from his body. "Coral? You painted the house coral?"

"It's not coral. I think the official name is soft peach."

I bit my lip and dropped his shirt. I now had some soft peach paint on my thumb and pointer finger. I wiped it on his cheek and he scrunched his nose.

"The house actually didn't turn out half bad."

"Huh. Well, I'm surprised my mom let you in looking like that."

"Your mom loves me."

This was true.

"Besides, she's used to letting people covered in paint walk around this house." His finger brushed along my collarbone, tracing a line of paint I had there. Tingles shot down my arms and I took a step back.

"How do you get paint on your neck anyway?" he asked.

"The same way you did."

"Have I left any clothes over here lately?"

"I think your board shorts are still here."

He turned and headed for my room. I shook out my still-tingling arms and followed after him.

"Why?" I asked.

"Because I'm going to shower here and then you're going to work a knot out of my neck."

"No, I'm not."

He went to the corner of my room, where his clothes were still draped over my chair. He picked up the shorts, snapped my leg with them, then headed for the door.

"What about the shirt?" I asked.

He waved his hand through the air. "It's dirty."

"But you need a shirt." I went to my closet and flipped through my stacks until I found the biggest one I owned, then tossed it to him.

He held it up. "You want me to wear a hot-pink breast cancer run shirt?"

"Yes."

He shrugged. "Okay."

"Oh, and before you shower. I got something." I snatched the crickets off the end of my bed and held them up for Cooper to see while I pointed at the list. "Try something new."

"What is it?"

"Dried crickets."

"Crickets? Are you being serious?"

I tore open the bag and poured them into my hand. There were six of them. Cooper stepped closer, took one off my extended palm, and popped it into his mouth.

"Mmm. Salty." Then he walked to the door.

I let out a huff of air. I had hoped he'd put up more of a fight than that. I'd hoped that maybe I'd found something he was afraid of. When he got to the door, he turned. "Are you going to try one?"

Without thinking too hard, I stuck one in my mouth and chewed it up quickly. He was right—it was salty and crunchy and tasted a bit like dry grass. "That wasn't too bad."

"Not at all. But that doesn't count for me."

"What? Why?"

"I've eaten dried crickets before."

I threw the rest of them at him, but they landed on my floor five feet away. "You brat. Well, it counted for me."

"Okay, but we have to try something new together too. Something we both haven't done. Something epic. Like that sunrise."

I smiled, hearing he thought our outing was epic. "Okay."

He backed out of my room, and I watched him disappear behind the bathroom door across the hall.

FIFTEEN

"You really shouldn't shower here!" I called out to him. Like I needed the person I was trying not to be in love with waltzing around my bathroom . . . showering.

I thought he hadn't heard me, but the door popped back open and he leaned out. "What?"

Gah. I was being ridiculous. He'd showered here before. "Nothing. Go shower."

I picked up the dried crickets from the carpet and deposited them in my trash. Then I added another check-mark to my list. I was still on track. Three paintings almost done and nearly half my list. I was convinced I could make the deadline now, but not completely convinced Mr. Wallace would see any growth. Different didn't necessarily mean better.

When I walked by the bathroom, Cooper was humming some tune I didn't recognize. I joined my grandpa and mom in the living room.

"Where's Cooper? Trailing more coral paint through the house?" Grandpa asked.

"Coral, right? I'm glad we agree on the color." I gestured down the hall with my head and sat down. "He's washing the coral paint down the drain."

My mom, who had been sitting on the couch reading her *True Crime* book, raised her eyebrows. "How's the list coming?"

"Pretty good. I still have a few to do. But I *am* halfway in love, according to Grandpa."

"Oh yes, I heard about Elliot," she said.

"You two are like gossipy tweens. No secrets can be shared here."

"I am a vault," my mom said in faux offense.

"And I am the safe inside the vault," my grandpa said.

I rolled my eyes.

"We don't tell anyone else," Mom said.

I almost said, of course you don't, you don't *see* anyone else. But there was some sarcasm even I resisted.

"Well, except Dad."

"You told *Dad*?"

"Of course, honey, he likes to hear these things. He said you haven't emailed him lately."

I cringed. He'd sent me a response to my last email where he'd listed off several alternative name choices I could pick from and asked what other experiences I'd done off my list that he could tell me he disapproved of. I'd read the email on my phone, meaning to respond once I was in front of my laptop, but I never had. "I know. I forgot. At this point, I'm just waiting for his weekly phone call. That's easier."

My mom sighed. "Easier does not promote communication."

"I'm going to put that on a T-shirt."

"Seriously, Abby."

"I know, Mom. I'll email him." I headed for the kitchen. "I'm going to get some ice cream. Cricket aftertaste isn't great."

By the time I had scooped myself a bowl of mint chip ice cream and gone back to the living room, Cooper was sitting on the couch, hair still dripping and hot-pink shirt too small on him. It stretched tight on his biceps and across his chest. I quickly looked away before my grandpa saw me staring.

"Did you eat a cricket too?" Mom asked him.

"Yes. It was flavored, I think." He tugged at the neck of the shirt.

"Salt and pepper," I said.

"Abby is working on number five on the list," Grandpa said.

"You know the numbers?" I asked.

"No, it was just a stab in the dark. But I mean the falling in love one."

I had just taken a big bite of ice cream and I swallowed it too quickly, causing a brain freeze. I hopped around until the pain subsided, then pointed to my grandpa first and then my mom. "Cooper, meet the vault and the safe inside the vault."

"I didn't say anything," my mom said.

"Falling in love?" Cooper asked with a teasing smile. "Did you meet someone?"

"Nope. We just saw Elliot at the store. Grandpa is overreaching."

"Elliot again?" Cooper asked. "That's twice in two weeks. Maybe it's *fate*." He emphasized the word I liked to use. "You two should come on a double date with me and Ris."

Grandpa put up his finger. "Elliot said he was going to a Fourth of July party."

"Perfect!" Cooper said. "We can all hang out together there. I'm going to call him."

"You don't have his number."

"I do. I got it on that napkin, remember?"

"Hey, Grandpa? Remember that deep-tissue massage technique you taught me?"

"Yes."

"Cooper has a really bad knot in his neck. Can you work it out for him?"

Grandpa pushed the ottoman that sat in front of him out with his foot. "Have a seat, my boy. Let's nip that knot in the bud."

"I'm going to bed." It probably wasn't even nine o'clock, but I was annoyed at everyone in the room. I finished off my ice cream and put the bowl in the sink. "Let's all try this again tomorrow."

Once in my room, I opened my laptop and typed a quick email to my dad.

From the daughter who is bad at emails, to the father who is the master of them,

Sorry! I've been busy growing my heart. It takes work. Let's see, what have I done? I tried out for a play. Not sure what it taught me. Maybe that making a fool of myself is something I excel in. I'm reading two classics simultaneously. They are both equally old and mind stretching. I thought I knew English, but apparently I don't. I watched a sunrise. How come you and Mom have never forced me to do that before?

Does this make you horrible parents? It's up for debate. I helped at a soup kitchen. The kids there are so little. It was heartbreaking, but also taught me that I have so much to be thankful for. I also heard that Mom told you about Elliot. That is nothing, so no need for twenty questions about him. I don't think I could even answer twenty questions about him. Maybe three, and they'd all have to be about how he looks. Speaking of Mom, she went on a walk with us the other day.

I paused in my writing, remembering what Grandpa and I had talked about in the grocery store. I wondered if I should put my two cents in about Mom and therapy. I shook my head. He didn't need the extra worry. Plus, I wasn't sure I agreed with my grandpa. We were fine. I typed some final thoughts into the email.

She did great. Love you tons. Talk to you soon.

Then I sent it off. I turned out the lights, crawled into bed, and listened to Cooper joke and laugh with my family in the other room. Just the sound of his voice made me happy. I sighed. I had been right, spending all this alone time with Cooper was not helping in the feelings department. Something needed to change.

My phone sat on the nightstand, and I picked it up. I wished I could call Rachel. Why hadn't I ever told her how I felt about Cooper? Probably the same reason I played off my feelings as a joke to Cooper when it was obvious he didn't like me back—I didn't want to change the friendship dynamic. Our tight-knit group lacked drama, and I didn't want to be the person to single-handedly change that.

I scrolled through my contacts until I stopped on Lacey. I took several deep breaths as I stared at her name. I wasn't one to try too hard with new people. I had my friends, and I was comfortable with them. But I could ride a quad and eat a cricket without the world ending, so why not this? I pushed the button.

She answered quickly. "Hello."

"Hi, it's Abby."

"Abby! Hi. I'm so glad you called! I didn't have your info. You were supposed to text me."

"Yeah, I was going to before the party to get your address."

"I'm so sorry you didn't make the play. It was more about your lack of experience than anything."

"Experience?" I grunted. "That sounds familiar."

"Are you mad? It's not too late. I got the feeling you didn't want a bit part in the ensemble, but I can make a case for you as trombone player number five."

"Oh, no. Don't worry about that at all. We just tried out as an experience. I really don't have time to commit to a full-on production."

"An experience?"

Oh no, had I offended her? "I'm sorry, we wasted your time by showing up when we weren't planning on following through."

She laughed. "No, no worries. What do you mean by *an experience* though?"

"Long story. I'm trying to gain new perspective to help with my painting."

"Really?"

"It sounds weird, I know."

"No, not at all. I'm just surprised because I do something similar."

"You do?" I sat up in my bed.

"Yes, me and a few of my friends from drama. We force ourselves into new situations to expand our perspectives. It helps with characterization and things, gets us out of our ruts and our normal ways of thinking."

"Yes. Exactly." A feeling of validation made me smile. Every time I talked to Lacey, she surprised me. It felt like we clicked.

"So . . ." Lacey was quiet for a moment. "If you didn't call about the play or the party, was there something else?"

"Oh. No. I was just . . ." Feeling angsty and needed

someone who wasn't Cooper to talk to and all my friends are in foreign countries. I couldn't say that. It sounded so . . . self-absorbed. It was. "How is the play going?"

"It's going well. I have to take a couple of days off this week for an audition I have in LA."

"An audition for what?"

"For a movie."

"Cool."

"I have them all the time and nothing comes out of them, so I try not to get my hopes up." A muffled voice on her end said something I couldn't understand and Lacey said, "I'll be right there."

"You have to go," I said.

"Yes, it's my little sister. She is supposed to do the dishes before my parents get home and has somehow convinced me that it's my duty to help her."

"She must be very convincing."

"She is."

"I'll see you at the party."

"I'll text you my address."

"Thanks."

We hung up. I slid back down in my bed until my head hit the pillow. Cooper's laugh rang out from the other room. *We force ourselves into new situations.* That's what Lacey had said worked for her too. It seemed to be working for me with my art. Could it also work for me in the getting-over-Cooper department? I picked up my phone again and found a different contact.

"Psst." The hall light outside my open bedroom door backlit Cooper, who now stood there. "You really went to sleep?" he asked. "It's so early."

"I told you I was."

He came in and sat on the floor next to my bed. "Your grandpa just killed my neck."

"I know. That was kind of the point. By the way, I did it. I asked Elliot out."

Cooper's teeth glowed white in my dark room. "You did?"

I had. I'd called him and asked if he wanted to go to the party with me, and he'd said yes. I was forcing myself into a new experience, hoping for something to change. I had obviously gone out with guys before. It was just that I hadn't in the last year. "I did."

"Awesome. This is going to be so fun."

I pulled a pillow against my chest and closed my eyes. How come it sounded like the opposite of that to me? "So fun."

I must not have said it with the proper amount of enthusiasm, because Cooper quietly said, "You should give him a chance, though. He seems like a really nice guy."

I nodded, my eyes still closed. "Okay, I'll give him a chance."

Even behind my closed lids I could feel the whole room light up with Cooper's smile, and my entire being glowed. "Good," he said.

"Good," I repeated, pillow tight against my chest.

He ran a hand through my hair. "Good night."

When I opened my eyes he was gone, the door closed behind him. My scalp still tingled from where his fingers had been.

"Good night," I whispered.

SIXTEEN

Do you want to meet at the party or drive over together?

I had been leaning against the handle of a mop in the museum, staring at a painting of an apple cut in half, its insides blue, happy to finally be released from the ticket counter, when the text from Elliot came in. I had kind of assumed that a date meant we were driving over together, but now that he was giving me an option, I couldn't decide what I wanted.

The party was happening five days from now. I wanted to tell him that I changed my mind. That I did the Fourth of July on the pier. I watched the fireworks light sections of the ocean bright blue or green or pink. And I watched those same colors reflected in Cooper's eyes. But that was the problem, wasn't it? I had been doing the same things day after day and year after year and expecting different results. Who had said that was the definition of insanity? Einstein? Whoever it was had seen inside my head.

My thumbs were poised ready to type something back when Mr. Wallace came down the hall. "Abby, can you take a summer preschool group through the museum Saturday at four? It was a last-minute request and all my docents are busy."

"Saturday?"

"Yes. I know you don't normally do tours, but it would really help me out."

Taking a group through the museum was like a dream job for me. Cooper had another race on Saturday. He'd texted me about it just that morning. It started at two, though. I just wouldn't be able to celebrate afterward. "Yes," I said. "I'll be here."

"Great. Thank you. Make sure there's a blazer that fits you in the closet." Mr. Wallace looked at the mop, the painting next to me, then my phone. "Is everything okay?"

"Yes." I held up my phone. "My brain hit pause while it was trying to make a decision."

He gave an agreeable grunt. "I hate it when that happens."

"Yeah. Me too."

Mr. Wallace started to walk away. "I have two weeks left, right?" I called after him.

He turned with a confused face on. "No, the tour will be this Saturday."

"Right. I know. I mean for the showcase. You're informing applicants in two weeks, right?"

"Yes. But I thought we talked about this." His face had a tired look that seemed to say, *this is why I had banished you to the ticket counter—to avoid this conversation.*

"I want a chance. I'm working on my depth."

"I can't imagine that in this short of time anything has changed enough in your technique that will affect my decision."

"I just want a chance to prove myself."

He sighed a heavy sigh, and it was probably only the super-pathetic pleading face that I'd put on that made him say, "I'll take a look."

"Thank you!"

"Don't get your hopes up, Abby. You don't meet my age requirement, and you have a lot of really strong competition." With that he finished walking away.

It was a reluctant yes, but it gave me the hope I needed to continue on my quest.

I moved to put the mop back in the bucket when I realized I still held my phone with the open text window. I sent two texts. The first was to Elliot.

Let's just meet there.

I was already changing something by going to the party in the first place. I didn't want to feel trapped, though.

The second text was to Cooper.

Hey, I won't be able to celebrate after your race on Saturday. I will be trying to convince four-year-olds that art is more interesting than snack time.

I tucked my phone away and dipped the mop into the soapy water. My phone buzzed against my thigh before I even had time to take it out again. I thought it would be Elliot, but it was Cooper.

You can't even convince me that art is more interesting than snack time. How will you ever accomplish this?

Not sure. Especially when half the art is replications of food.

But you'll still make the race, right?

For sure.

Thanks.

And I need to finish up my list and two more paintings. Help me think of something else.

I'll ponder it.

Have you finished your classic?

No.

Me neither, I texted.

Okay. I wouldn't want to be stuck in a car with me either.

My brows went down in confusion before I realized I was reading a pop-up text from Elliot.

I responded. **It's not about that. It's more about not wanting to be trapped at the party.**

We can leave anytime you want.

My phone buzzed again before I had time to answer Elliot. What does epoch of incredulity mean anyway? Cooper was asking. I vaguely remembered that line from the beginning of *A Tale of Two Cities.*

Did you start over? I gave you the summary. Did you not trust my summary?

I switched back to Elliot's text and answered. **Okay, I'll drive over with you. Do you have my address?** It's what I had originally planned anyway.

No, but if I'm going to read the book, I had to at least read that famous paragraph. I don't do things halfway, Cooper responded.

Except chemistry projects. And English papers. And cleaning your bathroom.

Fine. Things I care about.

I smiled. He cared about the list. That made me happy.

Another text from Elliot popped up. I already know where you live. But I'm not a stalker. My best friend lives on your street and I saw you pull into your driveway a while back.

Who's your best friend?

To Cooper I wrote: It's a period of skepticism. Or disbelief.

You are. Why? Cooper wrote back less than a second after I had hit send.

I am? What did that mean? I was a period of disbelief? I kind of felt like I was going through a bit of skepticism right now in regard to him, but he couldn't possibly know that. I looked at the text again. Oops. I'd crossed texts.

No, he really does. Ben Williams. Do you know him? Elliot responded to my skepticism text.

I sent you the wrong text. That was meant for someone else, I wrote to both of them.

Elliot answered first. Oh. That makes more sense. So I'll see you Tuesday then. Eight o'clock?

Sounds good.

Cooper responded a few minutes later. Who was it meant for?

Elliot.

Why were you asking Elliot who his best friend is?

Because I want to know if he's looking for one. I'm searching for a replacement.

Funny.

I thought so. Gotta run. This floor isn't going to mop itself.

You're mopping floors!? You're out of ticket purgatory??

Yes! So happy!

You're the only person I know who is happy to mop.

Shhh. Art.

BTW, good job on texting Elliot.

Yeah yeah.

When my shift was over, I made my way up the wide stairs with the glass half-wall railing and walked the halls slowly, trying to figure out which paintings and pieces to show the children I'd bring through on Saturday. We changed out the art all the time. There were very few pieces that were permanently housed here. It's what brought patrons back time and again—new artists to see. But there was a permanent one that was always a hit with the kids. Mr. Wallace had hired a paper artist to come and create a flowing, swirling design made of paper that covered an entire corner of the upstairs hallway. It was three-dimensional and mesmerizing. That was a must-see.

We'd just gotten a modern art piece on loan, and I hadn't had time to look at it until today. The kids might appreciate the bright colors and strong lines of the painting. We'd done an art workshop last summer, and I'd discovered that kids loved to paint with bright colors. Remembering those kids' paintings, I had an idea.

I ran down the stairs and searched out Mr. Wallace.

I stopped in front of him, breathless. "Could we display some of the kids' art?"

"What kids?"

"The preschool group that's coming through. Can you contact the teacher and ask her to bring by some of their drawings or paintings before Saturday, and I could hang them upstairs? I think it would be fun for them."

"You'll come in early and do that?"

"Yes, I will."

"The children would probably like that."

"Of course they would. Everyone likes to see their own art displayed." I hadn't meant to say that with a hard edge to my voice, but I did, and he noticed. I quickly finished, softer this time, with "I'd love to do that for them."

He nodded. "Good idea, Abby."

"Thank you." Perhaps it was seeing those kids at the soup kitchen that made me think of it. Or maybe it was just that forcing myself to think differently was creating new ideas in other areas of my life too. Either way, I was happy I'd come up with it.

My phone buzzed in my pocket with an incoming call as I headed for the door. I waited until I was outside before I answered it. A breeze played with my hair and brought with it the scent of the ocean.

"Hello?" Instead of walking to my car, I took the path

around the side of the building to the overlook. Two benches sat on the bluff, with a perfect view of the ocean below.

"Abby!" said a voice that sounded distant but excited.

"Hi?"

"It's Rachel! I found a pay phone! Austria has pay phones!"

I sat down on the bench. "Rachel! It is so good to hear your voice. I miss you!"

"Remember how I wondered if I'd love living without my phone?" She sighed. "I don't. Not at all. Thank goodness my parents weren't right."

I laughed. "Tell me everything."

"Aside from the phone thing, it's been pretty amazing, actually. You and your artist brain would absolutely love it. It's gorgeous, and there is so much art everywhere. Old buildings and history and culture."

"Have you been to Italy yet to find your cute Italian boy to make out with?"

"Italy was first, but it's hard to make out in front of constantly hovering parents. There were lots of really hot Italian boys though, so flirting was accomplished. We need to come back here after we graduate. The four of us."

"Four?"

"Have we shrunk since I've been gone? Or expanded?"

"Oh, right. Cooper and Justin."

"Oh no, I've been gone too long. Everything has changed."

"No. It hasn't. We're good. The four amigos."

"Did you really just say that? You've been hanging out with your grandpa too much this summer, haven't you? I can't leave you ever again."

"So true. I miss you," I said.

"You too. So, seriously, anything new happening there?"

"Nope. Just art stuff."

"Any word from Justin?"

"He sends pics occasionally. I think he sends more to Cooper."

"Send him a text from me, will you? Tell him: *This is an equal friendship circle—we all get the same things or no things. Don't be the cause of our demise.*"

"Wow, so dramatic."

"He'll think it's funny. Plus it's true."

"So if we all get the same things, does this mean you're calling Cooper next?"

She growled. "You're right. I guess I do need to call him."

"Do you want me to add something to your Justin text, like, *I miss you*? Or, *I hope your work on the schoolhouse for the disadvantaged is going well*?"

She let out a single laugh. "Yes, add: *Thank you for fulfilling the quota of good deeds required per friend group all by yourself.*"

"I will send it immediately."

"I have to go. My parents are standing by a bakery of some sort across the street and waving at me with both hands. People are starting to gather around them, as if they need help. And if I have to call Cooper now, I don't have much time."

"Okay. Tell Cooper I said hi."

"Okay . . . wait. Why? You're still talking to Cooper, right?"

"Yes, of course."

She took a relieved breath. "Okay, good. I'll try to find another time to call you soon."

"Okay, bye."

"Bye."

A loud click sounded in my ear and the line went dead. I smiled. That's what I was missing—my complete group of friends. I couldn't wait for her to get home. With Rachel gone for the last month, I had forgotten why I had never told her about my feelings for Cooper. Now I remembered, and I was glad, once again, that I hadn't. We all had the perfect dynamic, and everything would be back to perfect when they got home. I sent off Rachel's message to Justin and left.

SEVENTEEN

"My mom is going to get mad at you for bringing McDonald's into our house," I said as I held Cooper's bag in my lap the next day, the heat from the fries warming my bare legs. I tried to tug down my shorts, but it didn't help.

"I know. That woman watches entirely too many documentaries. She needs to live in blissful ignorance, like the rest of us."

"Do you think that's part of the problem? She watches too many shows and reads too many articles and books about the dangers of the world?"

"I don't know. Maybe? She seems to worry about the stuff she reads and hears more than most people."

"I know. Maybe it would make things better. If she'd just stay off the internet and away from nonfiction books." Maybe I could suggest that to my grandpa. Then we wouldn't have to take the dramatic step of a therapist. "I think she takes everything she learns, then frets about it until it turns into an irrational fear."

The car slowed, and Cooper squinted out the windshield. I followed his gaze to the right, where a big tree stood in the middle of an otherwise empty field. A man was leaning against the tree. No, not leaning. He was chained to it.

"Stop the car," I said to Cooper.

He pulled to a stop along the curb and I rolled down my window.

"Sir? Are you okay?"

The man's gaze had been on the dirt in front of him, and with my yell, he looked up.

"You weren't assaulted by chain-wielding thieves, were you?" I asked.

Cooper laughed from beside me.

"No," he yelled back. "I've done this to myself."

"On purpose?"

His smile widened. "A housing development is going

in this field, and they want to rip out this tree."

"Oh. I see. You're protecting it."

"Yes."

"Good luck!"

He lifted his hand in a wave, and Cooper drove away.

"Would you rather live in the treetops forever or in water?" Cooper asked.

"Waterworld for sure. If I can breathe underwater. Can I breathe underwater?"

"Sure. But then we need an adaptation for the treetops too. What would that adaptation be?"

"Monkey arms?"

"I can see why you'd choose mermaid, if the alternative is monkey."

I smiled and stole one of his fries.

His face went serious. "Don't eat my fries, Abby. You said you didn't want any fries, and I said, you're going to steal mine if you don't get your own, and you said, no I won't."

"Are you reenacting a conversation that happened five minutes ago?"

"Yes, because you seem to have forgotten it."

"It's my charge for holding your greasy bag."

He snatched the bag off my lap and put it on his left leg as he drove.

"You're no fun," I said.

"I am the most fun." He took a fry out of the bag and ate it.

"Speaking of, did you talk to Rachel yesterday?"

"Yes, but why is that *speaking of*? Are you trying to claim Rachel is the most fun?"

"No, *I* am the most fun. It was *speaking of* because it sounded like she was having fun."

"Yes, she sounded good. Did she tell you about the four-amigo Europe trip for next summer, after we graduate?"

"Did she call it that? The four-amigo? She made fun of me for saying that!"

He laughed. "Our end-of-summer reunion with them is going to be awesome."

When we got to my house, I made sure I put some space between myself and Cooper and his bag of poison.

"I see how you are. You'll eat it in the car but won't admit it to your mom."

"I know where my loyalties lie."

But my mom didn't say anything. She just eyed his bag once when we walked in, then asked what we were up to.

"We are going to go finish our classics so we can finally check that item off the list."

"But first I am going to fill my stomach with garbage, Mrs. Turner. And I will need to walk it off. You want to go on a walk with us in ten minutes?"

His offer surprised me. We hadn't talked about doing that. He just knew I was worried about her.

"I think I do, Cooper."

He stuck a fry in his mouth, and when my mom went back to her book, I mouthed, *thank you*.

He winked at me.

After we made it to the park and back with zero resistance from my mom, she insisted on showing Cooper my now-finished sunrise painting, like it was a priceless masterpiece. Maybe this was part of my problem. The people around me thought my paintings were much better than they were. They'd given me false confidence all these years.

Against the side wall, with soft cotton covering draped over them, were the spotlight and quad paintings. I thought about showing off those too, but I didn't. I'd save some surprises for them to see if I made it into the show.

After the sunrise painting was thoroughly analyzed, Cooper and I went to my room.

"That painting is really good, Abs."

"Thanks."

"Why do you sound like you don't believe me?"

"Because Mr. Wallace said he was willing to take a second look at my paintings, and I feel like they have to be a hundred times better than the last ones he saw. I don't know if they're there yet." I threw him his book, which he'd left on my desk when he first arrived at my house before our fast-food run, and I pulled mine out of the top drawer of my nightstand and settled onto my bed. If I could finish this book today, then I wouldn't have to worry about checking off another item for a couple of days. "I just need to finish the list."

"The magical list." Cooper made his way over to it and studied it for several minutes. "Why did you already check off 'have your heart broken'?"

My heart seemed to stop in my chest with that question. We had successfully avoided this subject for a year. Did I really want to bring it up now? I kept my gaze steady on him even though I wanted to look away. "Because I have."

Cooper's eyes shot to the ground, then met mine again. He knew. "Why did you write it on here to begin with then?" he asked softly.

"I don't know," I said. "Since I'd already accomplished it, I wrote it down. I wanted to feel like I had at least a little depth, I guess."

He nodded slowly. We were going to move past this

quickly. Continue to ignore what had happened a year ago. I could tell. I could linger. Say something. But I'd already done that once. If his feelings were different than they had been a year ago, it was his turn to put them out there.

"What about you? Can you check 'have your heart broken' off your list?" I honestly didn't know the answer to that question. I'd been a witness to pretty much all of his relationships, but I had no idea if he'd ever truly been in love with a girl before. He'd never told me he had, so I assumed he hadn't.

"No. I can't," he said. I was surprised by the relief that coursed through my body.

He jumped onto my bed next to me, back first, and opened up his book.

My phone buzzed with a new email. I pulled it up. Nobody emailed me except my dad, so I wasn't surprised to see his name in my inbox.

"Your dad?" Cooper asked, peering over the top of his book at me.

"Yeah." I read the email to myself.

To my daughter, who is better than any of my other daughters at emailing me. From her dad, who couldn't get to a computer for a few days.

Why haven't I made you watch the sunrise before? Have you

ever tried waking yourself up at five a.m.? That's your answer. I'm glad I don't have to ask twenty questions about Elliot, because I can't think of twenty questions to ask. Well, except tell me his last name so I can run a background check. What about that other boy in your life? What's his name? Your mom says he still comes around a lot. I hope he's treating you nice. We're going to be busy here for the next couple of weeks moving locations. Sorry in advance if I can't email/call as often as normal. It sounds like you're keeping yourself busy with your list. Make sure you update me, I like to hear about your adventures.

I smiled and pointed to my desk, which was closer to Cooper. "Can you hand me my laptop?"

He reached over and grabbed it, then set it on my legs. "What's the news from your dad?"

"Not much. He doesn't really tell me a lot of what's happening over there in email for security reasons. So it's mostly just him asking about me."

"Does your dad like me? I can never tell when he's home."

"My dad likes you."

"Good, because he's a little scary."

I laughed. "He's harmless."

I opened my laptop and typed a response, hoping he'd get it before they had to move their camp.

From your only daughter, who, if she found out others existed, would fight them to the death to maintain that title. Ha. Ha. Two laughs. One for the background-check idea and one for you pretending not to know Cooper's name. Thanks for those. You know I like to laugh. As for an update, I'm crawling my way through *Crime and Punishment* and nearing the end. I tried dried crickets. I don't recommend them, but they do taste decent with ice cream. Mr. Wallace is having me take a preschool group through the museum on Saturday, so that should be fun. And I decided to go on a date with Elliot No Last Name. I'm only telling you because I know Mom will. It's not a big deal. Also, be safe!!! XOXO

Before I closed my laptop, I clicked on a saved tab at the top of the screen.

"You know," Cooper said when the new page came up, "you could actually just send in an application instead of staring at that page every time you get on the computer . . . or your phone."

"I will. I'm waiting to see how the showcase plays out though. I need a sale."

Cooper jammed his finger onto my screen. "*Recommended* requirements. Last I checked the word *recommended* meant optional."

"Lots of people apply for the winter program. I want

to give myself every advantage."

"Stalling," Cooper coughed out.

"I am not."

"We should finish the list so you can show Mr. Wallace your paintings and have no more excuses."

I ignored his jab this time and said, "You're right. Let's do one of the 'try something new' items, since we have a couple of those left to do." And saying that out loud reminded me of something. "Did you ever take Iris to that underground garden? That would count for you."

"No, she didn't want to do that. We ended up at the movie on the beach."

"Hey, the beach movie is our thing."

"I know. I'm sorry. She didn't want to go to the gardens."

I swallowed down my hurt. "What kind of monster are you going out with?"

He smacked me on the shoulder once with his book, then opened it. I opened my book as well, then let my left hand fall against his right arm and rest there. When he took twice as long to turn the page of his book one-handed, rather than move his arm, I smiled, but like always, didn't let myself read into it too much.

Cooper left close to ten, and I went to Mom's room, where she was hanging clothes.

"Hey," I said. "I have a complaint to file."

"Listening," she said.

"How come when Cooper and Dad are around, you have no problem walking to the park, but when it's just us, you can't?"

She paused with a shirt halfway on its hanger and scrunched up her nose. "I go out a lot with just you."

"But more when they are here."

"I don't know. They both have a relaxed way about them. It rubs off on me, I guess."

"But I don't?"

"You do, hon."

I crossed my arms. "Apparently I'm not the only one attached to Cooper."

"He is a nice boy. I have no issues with him, aside from the fact that he likes to drag my daughter's heart around."

"I'm the one attaching my heart to his leash."

She gave me a thin-lipped smile but didn't argue.

"I'm working on it," I said.

"That's good."

I watched her add more shirts to hangers and stack them on her bed. I was constantly trying to downplay the fact that Mom didn't go anywhere to Grandpa and Cooper and Dad. Convince them that she could have a fulfilling life without venturing beyond the four walls of our house. That it wasn't a big deal. And maybe it wasn't, but I was beginning to realize that sometimes it wasn't about her. If I were being honest with myself, I knew that sometimes it was about me. I could remember only a handful of my events she'd attended in the past, and only because my dad was there.

"What?" she asked when she noticed me still standing there.

I sighed and lowered myself onto her bed. "Mom."

She turned, giving me her full attention.

I played with a hanger on the stack of clothes, nervous about what I was about to say. "If I complete this list and somehow gain a depth of emotion that makes me paint like Picasso, will you come to the gallery to see my paintings on display?"

She hesitated, and disappointment hovered around me.

I should've just dropped it, said never mind. But that painting I'd done with her just outside the spotlight, watching me audition, gave me a vision of what it could be like seeing her at the art show, so I pushed on. "Dad can't come, being gone and all. But Cooper will be there, and Grandpa. It will be like having your own bubble of protection. You'll be surrounded by familiar, relaxed people."

She pressed her lips together, and I could see the

tension on her face, but she said, "Yes, honey. I would love to see your display."

"Promise?"

"Yes."

I smiled big and jumped up to give her a hug. "Now I just have to get Mr. Wallace to let me in the show."

"He will, my brilliant daughter," she said rubbing my back. "He will."

EIGHTEEN

There's this place downtown where you can sit with your feet in water and little fish come and eat the dead skin off your toes.

And you're telling me this, why? Cooper responded.

The list. Trying something new. I needed a new painting stat, and I couldn't think of anything. It was time to force myself to think way outside the box.

My sister has a goldfish. You can stick your foot in its bowl if this sounds like fun to you.

Nope. Fish spa.

Sounds lame.

I don't hear you coming up with any ideas.

My brain is still thinking.

Well I'm going to try this anyway. With or without you. I still have three more new things to try, right?

Without me.

Are you scared of fish? Wouldn't I know this if he were? But I didn't know. Maybe I'd found his fear and I'd force him to do this with me.

No. I'm not.

Come with me, you punk.

Race today. Must mentally prepare myself to be even more awesome than I already am.

Fine.

I'll see you at my race.

"I'm going to the fish spa," I declared as I entered the living room. Grandpa and Mom were sitting on the couch. Grandpa had the television on. Mom had her laptop open. "Who's coming with me?"

"Fish spa?" Mom asked.

"Little fish eat the dead skin off your feet."

"Fish? Can't you just use a loofah?" she asked.

"It's an experience."

"Won't you catch some sort of infection?" Mom held up her foot and wiggled her bare toes.

"I don't think so."

Grandpa stood. "I'll go."

"Mom?" She was typing into the computer in a way that made me worried she was looking up the safety of fish spas.

"No, thank you. I'm writing an email to your father."

"Tell him I said hi and tell him about the fish."

She nodded without looking up. "I will."

Grandpa and I sat on the tile edge of the long, trough-like pool of shallow water. The place didn't smell like fish. It smelled like incense, and chlorine from the hot tub we had passed on our way to this room. In the water, Grandpa's feet were surrounded by fish. "You must have more dead skin because you're old," I said. My feet were unadorned.

"I am the perfect age," he said.

"The perfect age for fish."

He ruffled my hair.

The water was a little colder than room temperature, and the coolness felt like it was traveling up my legs.

"What's it feel like?" I asked.

"It tickles."

"Come here, little fish," I said, inching my left foot closer to Grandpa's right. A single fish, appearing warped from the movement of the water, worked its way over to me. My shoulders tensed as it got closer. And just as it was about to nibble, I let out a yelp and yanked my feet out of the water.

Grandpa laughed. "What's this? Scared?"

"No, it just surprised me."

"It surprised you? You watched it the entire time."

"Okay, fine, I saw it coming, but it scared me when it finally got close."

He nodded toward my still-raised legs. "Try again. You can do it."

They were just fish. Little ones, at that. I took a deep breath and slowly put my feet back in. The single fish that had braved the trip to my feet before had left, so now I had to wait once again. It was the waiting that was the most nerve-racking. The waiting and watching the impending approach. This time I kept my feet in. This time I felt the slight tickle of the fish as it made contact over and over again.

"That doesn't hurt at all," I said.

"I told you it wouldn't."

"I thought you were bending the truth."

This is when I thought Grandpa would be offended, or at least fake offense, that I had suggested he would lie to me. But he just shook his head a little and smiled.

I stared at the fish for a long time before saying, "I asked Mom to come to my art show last night . . . I mean, if I end up getting in the show."

"You did?" he asked.

"She didn't tell you?" That worried me. They talked about everything.

"Maybe it slipped her mind."

I wiggled my toes a little, but the fish stayed put. "Do you think she'll come?"

"I'll come." He smiled over at me.

"You don't think she'll come?"

"I think she'll try very hard."

More fish surrounded my feet now. "She promised. And when she promises, she always follows through."

"You're right. She does."

Grandpa and I had hit traffic on the way home from the spa and I barely made Cooper's race for the second time. I found his family and was surprised to see an addition to the little group—Iris. At least, it looked like the girl I remembered seeing once, briefly. She was cuter than I remembered. Her brown hair was pulled up into a high ponytail and she was holding a sign with Cooper's name on it. I lowered my sign to my side and finished my walk a little slower.

"Hey," I said when I reached them.

Amelia hopped up and down, then gave me a hug. "I haven't seen you in forever."

"I know. I haven't been to your house lately. Sorry."

"Have you met Iris?" Mrs. Wells asked.

"No," Iris said at the same time I said, "Yes."

"We have?" she asked.

"I was at the movie night on the beach a few weeks ago."

"Was that you?" She stuck out her hand. "Nice to meet you."

"You too." I shook her extended hand. "I'm Abby."

"Are you friends with Cooper?" she asked.

She didn't know I was friends with Cooper? He'd never mentioned me? I tilted my head, studying her expression. She looked completely serious. They really hadn't hung out *that* much. I guess I shouldn't have been surprised. "Yes, I am."

She nodded with a smile.

"Looks like they're starting," Mr. Wells said.

"Oh!" Iris turned her attention back to the course. "This is so exciting."

"Have you never watched a race on the dunes before?"

"No. This is my first time."

"Did you grow up here?"

"No, we moved here two years ago from Ohio."

"Wait, do you go to Pacific High?" I'd never seen her around school before, but I didn't know everyone. I was middle-of-the-road popularity-wise.

"No, I go to Dalton Academy," she said. Dalton was the private school right on the beach. It had marine biology classes, and surfing could replace normal PE.

"Oh, cool. Do you like it?"

"It's amazing."

The man holding the red flag lowered it, and the drivers were off.

"Which one is Cooper?" Iris asked.

I pointed. "The bright-green helmet."

She stood up on her tiptoes and let out a squeal. Cooper took a jump and landed front-tires first, his back tires airborne for a few seconds longer. Iris gasped from beside me.

"Don't worry," I said, sensing the anxiety that I knew so well. "He was born on the dunes."

She laughed. "That's what he said."

"Right . . ." Of course he would tell her that too.

This wasn't the first time a girl had shown up to watch Cooper. But seeing her there, so comfortable with his family, so excited about his race, this was the first time I felt like *I* was the outsider, the one who didn't belong here.

Cooper finished in first, like he always did, and Iris went wild, causing Mr. and Mrs. Wells to smile.

I glanced at my phone. I needed to shower and get a little more professional for the museum tour, plus I still had the drawings the preschool teacher had brought in to hang, but I had over an hour, so I could stay and at least say hi to Cooper. Maybe his presence would make things feel normal again. We all walked to the trailer where he would meet us.

"That was fun. He's good," Iris said, falling in step beside me as we walked.

"Yes, he is. Fearless."

Cooper was already at the trailer, helmet off, when we got there. The first thing he did was give Iris a hug. "I like your sign."

She let out a happy yelp.

"Did you meet Abby?" he asked.

"Yes, we met," Iris said. I waited for her to say something like, *why have you never told me about Abby before?* But she didn't. I waited for him to say something like, *she's my best friend in the world*. But he didn't.

"Are we going out to celebrate?" Mrs. Wells asked.

"I have to run, but have fun," I said.

"Where are you going?" Cooper asked me. "You don't want to celebrate?"

"I have that museum preschool group thing, remember?"

"Oh, right." He gave me a side hug.

I pushed him away a little. "Ew. You're sweaty."

He laughed. "It's hot. And this is 'winner glow.'"

"Congrats on your win. I'll see you later?"

"Yes. For sure."

I said bye to everyone else and left with only one backward glance. It wasn't a good move on my part, because all I saw was Cooper giving Iris another hug and his family all smiles.

"Are you a painter?" It was the second time the little girl had asked me that question. I had led the group and their parents through over half of the museum at a faster rate than I would've an older group. I was surprised their attention spans had lasted this long. This was the first tour I had personally led, but I'd watched what felt like a thousand. I didn't think I'd be this excited to lead one, but I was enjoying opening their eyes to art, even if they weren't quite getting it. A little boy in the back of the group head-butted his mom's leg over and over. I sensed I was seconds from losing them. But this little girl, the one in the front, with big brown eyes and pigtails, was paying attention. And apparently she knew a nonanswer when she heard one, because she didn't accept my "I like art" answer.

"Yes, I paint."

"Show us your painting here," she said.

I straightened the museum blazer I wore. "I don't have a painting here. These are famous artists on display. And once a year, we have an art show with amateur art that people can buy."

"So that's when we can see your paintings?"

"Maybe." I clapped my hands together. "But right now, I'm going to show you some really famous works of art." I was deflecting a four-year-old's question. How pathetic was I?

I led the kids down the hall and into the room where I had hung all their drawings, lower on the wall than the other paintings, so they could see easier. I'd even rearranged some spotlights to highlight them.

This focused the previously restless group.

I spoke in an official tour guide voice as I said, "Art from the Schoolhouse Preschool is on display today. This is a rare exhibit that we've never had before, so it's extra special." The kids pointed out their own drawings with loud voices. Even the parents and teacher seemed more animated than they had been until then. I noticed Mr. Wallace in the back. He gave me a thumbs-up. As the group filed out, Mr. Wallace walked with them, talking to the teacher as he went.

I began taking the drawings down one by one. The skill level of the four-year-olds was more or less the same. They could draw circles with eyes on them and sticks for legs and arms. They could draw a sun or a rough tree. But there was one drawing that was quite good, that was well above the skill level of the others. This was how I'd been with my art at a young age, ahead of the curve. This was what prompted my parents to put me in classes.

Feet scuffing along tile caught my attention, and I looked up.

Cooper's smile greeted me.

"You're here," I said both surprised and happy.

"Do you know how tempted I was to sneak up and scare you? What had your undivided attention?"

I held up the drawing I'd been looking at. It was a girl standing under a rainbow. It was obvious it was a girl; she had more than just a circle head. She had arms and legs and a body. She wore a purple dress.

"Cute," he said. "Did you draw that?"

"Funny. No. A four-year-old drew this."

"Is Mr. Wallace putting *it* in the show?" His voice was sarcastic.

"Shhh," I hissed. "Don't say stuff like that here. He's everywhere." I looked around, but the room was empty.

"Maybe I *should* say stuff like that here. Maybe it will make him think."

I sighed and pulled down the remaining drawings.

"I'm sorry, I'm sorry," he said. "What was I supposed to notice about that four-year-old's drawing?"

"Probably nothing." This child's picture may have been ahead of the curve now, but everyone would catch up with her soon enough. I stacked the papers together and looked up at him. "I thought you were out with your family."

"We just grabbed dessert this time, so we're done. And I have something for you."

"Okay."

"We were leaving the Cheesecake Factory and they had one more piece of white chocolate raspberry left. One! And I thought, it's fate. Or whatever you like to call it." He brought the white bag with colorful stripes out from behind his back.

"You're the best."

"I know. Now come on. Let's go sit on the overlook so you can share that with me."

That night I went home and set up a small canvas. I painted a fish. At first I painted it realistic, as if viewing it underwater. But I realized it didn't feel right. How I'd been feeling at the spa, how I'd felt at Cooper's race that day, didn't match up with what I'd created. I changed the painting. I made the fish warped, bent at a weird angle, its parts not aligned quite right. I made the water around it choppy, almost murky, unclear. I stepped back and studied the final product. That was how I felt.

NINETEEN

How had I never gone to a typical party before? What was I supposed to wear? Sundress? Shorts and a tank top? Something fancier? Was I supposed to put on more makeup than normal? I thought about calling Lacey to ask, but I felt stupid. I should've known this stuff. Plus, she was probably busy setting up for her party. I called Cooper instead.

Cooper picked up after three rings. "You're not bailing on this thing, are you?"

"No. Elliot is picking me up in an hour."

"Wait, what? I thought you'd drive yourself so you wouldn't be trapped there."

"I know. It was a moment of weakness. The real question is, what are you wearing?"

"You need to say that in a sexier voice for that line to work. Like this: What are you wearing, baby?" That last line he said low and raspy.

"Gross. I wasn't trying to be a pervert. I meant it for real. What are you wearing to this thing?"

"Oh."

I could almost see him look down at his outfit. Like he was just now, with the question, discovering what he was actually wearing. "Shorts and a T-shirt."

"Not helpful."

"Wear a sundress and flip-flops. Mascara. Some lip gloss."

My mouth opened and then shut again.

"I pay attention to what girls wear, Abby."

"Thank you! Now I need to go get ready."

"I'll see you in a bit. Look for us when you guys get there."

"I will." I had already planned on it. He was the conversation starter and kept the conversation going and knew when to end the conversation. He made being social so much easier.

★ ★ ★

Elliot arrived at my door right on time. He looked nice, in a collared polo and cargo shorts. His normally untamed dark curls were styled off his forehead. My grandpa answered. "Elliot, good to see you. Come in."

"He doesn't have to come in. I'm leaving. See." I stepped around my grandpa and out onto the porch.

But Grandpa didn't let go of the hand he'd been gripping in greeting. He pulled him inside. "Of course he does. He needs to meet your mother."

I groaned. "Elliot. I'm sorry this is being made into a bigger deal than it is."

"It's fine," he said with a smile.

My mom joined us in the entryway. "Hi, so great to meet you," she said, giving Elliot a hug. "Thanks for taking my daughter out."

"Yes, it is such a chore," I said.

My mom playfully hit my arm. "You know what I meant."

"Can we go now?" I didn't need to be more embarrassed.

"Come see the living room first. People love to see the living room. It has a lot of Abby's art. Her paintings are like windows to the world." She talked while leading the way, and Elliot followed.

"Mom. I will get revenge for this. You might want to

sleep with one eye open tonight."

Elliot gave all the appropriate responses—turning a full circle to take it all in, oohing and aahing at the right times. My mom beamed.

"We could just stay here tonight," I said, sitting on the couch. "I'm cool with that."

My mom put up her hands in surrender. "Okay, okay. I'm just proud. Get out of here, you two. And great to meet you, Elliot."

"You too."

He smiled at me as we walked outside.

"I'm sorry about that. She likes to brag."

"I can see why."

Not sure what to say to that, I just shrugged.

Elliot drove a Jeep with no doors. After climbing in and driving up the street, I began to question my clothing choice. The wind whipping through the cab made it so I had to hold my sundress down.

"Sorry," Elliot said, noticing my challenge. "I should've put the doors on. I was trying to be cool."

I laughed.

He reached into the back seat and produced a blanket. "Want to put this over your legs?"

"Yes, please." It helped a lot.

"You look really nice, by the way."

"Thank you." I occupied myself with the blanket

on my lap, tugging down the sides so it wrapped fully around both legs.

"You really are an amazing painter," he said after a few minutes of silence.

"I'm . . . thank you," I decided to go with. I didn't want to have to explain how professionals saw me—underdeveloped.

"Is that what you want to do after high school? Some sort of art school?"

"Yes . . . I think." That's what I'd wanted to do since I was eight. That's what I'd wanted to do until Mr. Wallace put it in my head that I might not be good enough. Now I was worried that I wouldn't make it at art school. That everyone would be better than me. That I wouldn't even get into the *winter program*, let alone art school after I graduated. "What about you?"

"Yes, me too."

"You too what?"

"I want to go to art school."

"What? You paint?" He had my full attention now.

"No. Well, I mean, I paint a little, but I sculpt more."

He was an artist. Hadn't I told Cooper less than a month ago that my relationship goals included dating an artist? "How come we haven't had any art classes together?"

"I do private lessons," he said in a mumble, as if he

didn't want to admit that.

"Oh, Mr. Private Lessons, excuse me," I teased.

"I know. It sounds so pretentious."

"I was just kidding. That's great. It's not like we have sculpting teachers at our high school. I'd love to see your stuff sometime."

"Sure. That would be great. I'd like another artist's opinion."

"Not sure my opinion amounts to much, but I do love art."

"You're the most talented artist at our school. Your opinion would mean a lot."

"You've seen my art at school?" I asked, surprised. I hadn't seen any of his art.

"I visit the art room a lot. You're good."

"Now you're just throwing flattery around haphazardly. You have to be careful with that. It can get away from you." I suddenly remembered something Rachel had said what felt like ages ago now at the movie on the beach. "Wait, did you ask my friend Rachel about my art once at Starbucks."

"She told you."

I nodded. He was mystery boy. She had said I should ask him out and here I was on a date with him. Not only did he appreciate my art but he was an artist. It was like all my relationship goals in one. Was it fate?

"You okay?" he asked.

"What? Yes." I looked to my right, away from Elliot, trying to clear my head when I saw something. "He's still there."

"What?" Elliot asked, understandably confused.

I pointed. "That man chained himself to a tree. He's been there for like four days."

"Why?" Elliot asked.

"I guess some housing development wants to tear it down. He's trying to save it." There was a big bulldozer parked to the right of the tree that hadn't been there last time. Nobody was inside of it. It sat there like a reminder or a warning of what was about to happen. "Do you think he's eaten anything? Or is he starving himself as a statement too?"

"I have no idea. I hope he's eaten something."

"I don't know that I've ever been that passionate about . . . well, *anything*," I said.

"You can't think of anything you'd chain yourself to in order to save?"

"My family, of course. My friends . . . maybe." I added that last word with a smile. "But nothing that couldn't talk."

"I guess I can't think of anything either," Elliot said. "Although . . ."

"What? You thought of something?" I asked when he didn't finish.

"If I say it, I'm going to sound pretentious twice in one night."

"Now you *have* to say it."

"There's this sculpture I did. It took me months, and I poured my soul into it. If someone told me they were going to destroy it, I might pull out a chain. Not sure if I'd follow through to the bitter end, but I'd call their bluff for sure."

He'd sculpted something he was *that* passionate about? I let my mind travel through all the paintings I had ever done. Sure, I'd be sad if someone wanted to destroy them, but . . . like Mr. Wallace had been happy to point out, apparently I'd never poured my heart into a piece.

"See. Pretentious," he said, and I realized I hadn't responded.

"No. Not at all. That's cool. Now I *really* want to see your stuff."

"Now I've set your expectations way higher than they should be." He smiled my way and then turned onto Lacey's street, which was already full of cars. I looked up and down the road until I found Cooper's car, parked on the other side. I immediately relaxed. Cooper was here, and my date was proving to be very interesting. Maybe

I'd actually enjoy this night more than a night on the pier watching fireworks. Maybe this would be my new thing. We parked the car and walked up the hedge-lined path.

"Abby!" Lacey said when she answered the door. "And Elliot. Did you come together?" She raised her eyebrows.

"Yes," Elliot said. "Thanks for having us."

She moved aside and held her arm out. "There's food and drinks in the kitchen and my dad is barbecuing out back."

Her house was full of people. "Just a small barbecue, huh?" I asked, with a smirk. I already knew she didn't do small parties.

She shrugged. "Yeah . . . it got a little bigger. Let me greet a few more people and I'll meet you out back."

Elliot and I walked through the house, which wasn't as big as I had imagined it would be from all the talk at school, but it was nicely decorated and updated. A lot of people we passed I recognized from school, but a lot I didn't. I saw Cooper across the pool, in a group of people, talking animatedly, his hands flying all around him. He must have been trying to convince his audience of whatever he was saying—that's when he'd get super animated like that.

"Do you want anything to eat?" Elliot asked, nodding

his head toward the barbecue off to our right. Smoke filled the air above it, accompanied by the smell of cooking meat.

"I'm okay for now. Do you want something?"

"I'm good. Look, there's Cooper. Should we go say hi?"

"Sure."

"Abby!" Cooper yelled in excitement when he saw me. Iris was by his side, and she waved at me. I smiled back.

"Everyone," Cooper announced loudly, "this is Abby and Elliot."

A few people said their own names. The others I already knew.

"Abby, remember that one time I pushed you into the pool at that hotel where they had the art you wanted to check out?" Cooper laughed. He'd pushed me in after we looked at their ballroom full of paintings. We'd been on our way home anyway. Then he jumped in after me, probably knowing how mad I was going to be. But we ended up splashing each other until hotel management came and kicked us out.

"Yes, and if you do that tonight, you are dead to me."

"Someone needs to be pushed in." He looked at Iris with a flirty eyebrow raise.

"No way," she said. "I agree with Abby. Death."

We smiled at each other.

Lacey joined our group by hooking her arm in mine and laying her head on my shoulder. "I didn't know you were bringing a date tonight," she said under her breath. "I was under the impression that you and Cooper . . ."

"Nope." I said just as softly back.

"By choice?"

She must have caught more of my rambling confession at the theater than she'd let on. "Nope," I said.

She was quiet for a moment and I couldn't see her eyes, but I assumed she had been studying Cooper when she said, "Well, he smiles too much and doesn't know how to dress anyway."

I held in a laugh. Those were both things I liked about him.

"And Elliot is a cutie."

We had mumbled this exchange quietly, but definitely not subtly, and when I glanced across at Cooper, he gave me a questioning stare.

I shook my head.

Then his eyes went to Lacey's arm still linked in mine, and I knew what his expression was asking—*what is that all about?*

"Do you want a burger?" Lacey asked me, louder this time. "I want a burger."

"Sure," I said.

"Come on, Elliot, let's go get food."

He followed after us. At a long table on the patio, we each filled our plates with chips and watermelon and burgers.

"Let's take this over there," Lacey said, pointing to a lounge chair under a tree that was miraculously empty.

I sat at the top end of the lounge chair, and Lacey gestured for Elliot to sit on the foot end, facing me. She dragged a chair from the pool area and sat alongside us.

"Thanks for coming, you guys."

"Thanks for the invite. How did your auditions go?" I asked.

"They went well. But that's always how I feel, so we'll see."

"Auditions?" Elliot asked.

She waved off his question. "It was nothing. I should check on my guests," Lacey said. "You two have fun." Her conspiratorial voice was back, and I knew she had planned this. Then she was gone, leaving me alone with Elliot.

TWENTY

Complete awkward silence followed Lacey's departure. I took several big bites of burger to try and justify it. After swallowing my mouthful, I panicked. Could I really not hold a normal conversation outside my friend group? The image of that lone fish swimming toward my foot crept into my mind, and I wasn't sure why. But then I realized I was feeling the same anxiousness now. Once I had let it happen, I was fine. Just give this a chance, I told myself.

Crickets literally chirped in a nearby bush and Elliot's eyes were drawn to the sound. Then he smiled. "And the crickets break the silence."

I immediately relaxed with a laugh. "Kind of ironic."

He nodded to where Lacey had retreated. "For an actress, she's not very subtle, is she?"

"I don't think she was trying to be. Subtle is not necessarily her thing."

"She got me over here alone with you, so I shouldn't be complaining."

My cheeks went pink, and his statement was followed by a long silence that I thought we had already conquered but was apparently back for round two. I tapped on the plastic arm of the lounge chair, then ate some watermelon. "What is your favorite thing to sculpt? What do you always go back to?"

"My favorite?" he asked. "I don't know that it's my favorite, but I sculpt a lot of trees. I think I'm trying to make the perfect one."

"Do you sculpt with clay or stone?"

"Clay."

"I've never painted a tree. Well, I mean, not as the sole subject. I've painted them as background or part of a scene. I should try a tree."

"What's your favorite thing to paint?" he asked.

"I don't really have a favorite. I painted a sunrise recently, and that was fun."

"I didn't see a sunrise in the living room."

"The living room just has some of my paintings. I have a back room full of my stuff."

"Why didn't you show me that?"

"Weren't you the one who talked about pretension?"

"There's a fine line between feeling like a show-off and wanting people to see your work, isn't there?"

"For sure," I said.

"Well, I want to see it."

I smiled.

"Abby!" I heard my name called from a distance. I looked over to see Cooper standing by an ice chest, holding up a can of Dr Pepper. The patio lights were on now, and white lights were strung around trees and posts and lit the otherwise dark backyard. When had it gotten so dark?

I nodded. Then he pointed at Elliot.

"Do you want a soda? Cooper wants to know."

Elliot cupped his hands around his mouth and yelled, "Coke!"

Cooper jogged around the pool and presented us with our two cans. "Coke might be a deal breaker for Abby. She hates Coke."

I rolled my eyes. "He's kidding."

"So you *don't* hate Coke?" Elliot said.

"No, I hate Coke. But not a deal breaker."

Cooper cuffed Elliot on the arm, then left. We both

watched him go. That was weird. He joined up with Iris again and she slid her arm around his waist.

"You two are really close," Elliot said, breaking my stare.

"Aren't most friends?"

"True."

We were quiet for a time, and I tried to think of more art things to talk about. I put my plate of half-eaten food on the ground beside our chair and he did the same.

He leaned to the side, which brought him a little closer to me, and looked up at the sky. "Do you know any constellations?"

"Just the basics. Do you?"

"Same."

"You smell good," I said. Like hair product or dryer sheets or something clean and fragrant.

"Thanks. You do too."

"It's vanilla lotion." I held up my arm, and he took it in his hand and brought it to his nose.

"Like cookies," he said.

Cooper wandered back over to us, holding Iris by the hand this time, and sat down on the lounge chair that Lacey had pulled over. Iris sat down in front of him.

"Abby, Iris asked how we met, and I was trying to remember the very first thing I said to you in science when you moved here."

"You said, 'You're new,'" I deadpanned. "I said, 'You're observant.'"

He laughed. "That's right. You were always sarcastic. But then I said something really funny back."

"Cooper thinks he's funnier than he is." I actually didn't remember exactly what he said when I walked into science class my first day at another new school. But I remembered he was the first person to talk to me and we'd been friends ever since.

He gasped in faux offense. "She's just jealous."

That word jolted something loose in my brain. Is that what was going on here? Why Cooper kept coming over and interrupting us? Was he jealous? That thought expanded in my chest until I felt like it would burst.

"I remember the first thing *I* heard you say," Iris said.

"Oh yeah, what?" he asked.

"You said if given the choice between seeing ghosts or zombies, you'd choose ghosts, because then they could tell you your future."

"Ghosts don't know the future," Elliot said.

I grabbed hold of his arm. "That's exactly what *I* said!"

"My ghosts would," Cooper reiterated.

"When we met Iris we were playing *would you rather*," I explained to Elliot. Well, when she met *Cooper.* She didn't remember me.

Lacey walked up right at that moment with a couple

of people in tow. "We're playing *would you rather*?"

"We weren't," Cooper said. "But we can."

Lacey sat on the end of our lounge chair, then gestured for Elliot to scoot closer to me. He did, and she settled into her spot more. The other two girls who had come with her sat on the grass at the foot of the chairs. "Do you all know Lydia and Kara?" The group greeted them.

"I have one if we're playing," Elliot said. "Would you rather have to jump in the pool right now or eat a live cricket?" He pointed to the bush, where I could no longer hear the insects, but I was sure they were still there.

"Pool!" almost everyone said at once.

Cooper and I looked at each other and both said, "Live cricket."

"What?" Lacey asked with a look of disgust.

"We've eaten the dried version before. A little salt and pepper and they're golden," Cooper said.

I raised my eyebrows. "Golden?"

He swatted his hand at me. "Don't start."

I held his sparkling eyes and laughed.

"I have one," Lacey said, tilting her head at me. "Unrequited love or not being able to love at all?"

I shot her wide eyes, but she just gave me innocent ones back.

"Is it better to have loved and lost than never to have loved at all?" Elliot asked. "Did you seriously just ask that question?"

"Is that a famous question?" Iris asked.

"Tennyson," I said. "Do you really not know that age-old quote?"

"It sounds familiar," she said. "And I think I'd rather not love at all. Unrequited love is so pathetic."

"Ouch," Lacey said. "I don't think it's pathetic. But very tragic. Artists use it to feed their muses. Muses are such ravenous things."

Now I couldn't help but laugh. I picked up a piece of watermelon from the plate I had abandoned on the ground next to me and threw it at her. She jumped off the end of the chair with a scream, which sent the chair teetering backward with its now uneven weight distribution. I rolled off onto the ground and Elliot landed on top of me.

"I'm so sorry," he said, pushing himself off, then helping me up. "Are you okay?"

"I'm fine."

Cooper was there too, obviously having jumped out of his chair when ours toppled. "You sure you're okay?" he asked, giving me a once-over.

"Whoever said chivalry was dead?" Lacey asked.

I held my hands up. "Boys, seriously, it was, like, a one-foot fall."

"I wasn't worried about the fall. Just the weight that landed on you," Cooper said, smacking Elliot on the back playfully.

I tilted my head at Cooper. He was definitely acting weird. "I'm fine."

We all settled back into our spots and spent the next hour playing the game. Finally, Lacey stretched and said, "I better go see a man about some fireworks." She stood up, this time making sure we'd repositioned our weight before taking hers completely off.

"Need any help?" I asked.

"Sure. We'll be back," she said to the rest of the group as I joined her. "The best view will be on the deck by the pool. You all might want to move there."

When we were out of hearing range of the group, I said, "Are you trying to give me away?"

She laughed a little. "It was harmless. I don't think he suspected anything. Besides, he's here with his girlfriend."

"She is *not* his girlfriend. They've only been on, like, two dates."

"Not too serious yet then."

"Did you notice Cooper acting different tonight?"

"I don't know him well enough to know his normal."

"Do you think it's possible that . . . could Cooper be . . . jealous of Elliot?" I said it out loud and I sort of wanted to take it back.

"Possibly." We walked around the side of the house toward the garage. "Have you thought about just telling Cooper how you feel?"

"I'm trying to get *over* Cooper."

"Even the Cooper that may or may not be showing signs of jealousy?"

I groaned. "He's my friend, and I'll go and ruin everything. I gave him a chance, and believe me when I say it wasn't well received."

She shrugged. "Things change."

I wasn't sure if they'd changed enough. Regardless of his weird behavior, he was here with Iris and I was here with Elliot. So tonight definitely wasn't a night for confessions.

The garage was big and housed four cars. One had a cover over it, only shiny black wheels showing. A man, I assumed Lacey's dad, stood looking in some boxes in the corner.

"Are the fireworks ready?"

He straightened up and turned around. "If we only shoot off a couple of the illegal ones, we should be fine, right?"

"Abby won't turn us in," Lacey said.

"I'd actually hand you both over pretty quickly with just the threat of torture."

"She's kidding," Lacey said, when he seemed worried by my statement. "Come on, we'll help you carry boxes." Between the three of us, it only took one trip to deliver the fireworks to the side of the pool. Then Lacey and I joined the others on the deck.

The fireworks weren't professional city-quality ones or anything, but they were cool. And as the illegal sky rockets lit up the sky with their loud bangs of color, I noticed Cooper looking at me. He averted his gaze. Maybe things *could* change.

TWENTY-ONE

When I walked in the house several hours later, Mom and Grandpa were sitting in the living room pretending to watch television.

"You're still awake?" I said, stopping in the entryway. "Isn't it past your bedtimes?"

Mom turned off the TV. "We wanted to see how your date went."

I sat down on the couch next to her. "It was fun. He sculpts."

"Sculpts?" Mom asked. "Is that a workout term?"

"No. He literally takes clay and molds it into cool

things. Or at least I think they're cool. I've never seen them before."

Her face lit up. "He's an artist."

"But don't get your hopes up, because I'm not sure if things will go any further." The fact that I ended the night hopeful that Cooper was jealous was not the right way to start a new relationship.

"Sometimes it takes a while to know if you like someone."

"I know."

"Well, I'm proud of you for trying. Maybe now that you saw how fun it can be, you can go out again. Or ask another boy out," Mom said.

That sounded like the worst idea in the world. "Yep. Sounds like a plan." When I realized they were waiting for something more, I said, "I'll just pick one of the boys lining up at the door waiting to court me."

"See, I knew she was being sarcastic," my mom said.

"Do you have anything to add to this interrogation, Grandpa?"

"I'll interview the line of boys to see who's after you for only your wealth and beauty."

I stood and kissed my mom on the cheek, then my grandpa. "I'm going to bed. I love you both. Good night."

★ ★ ★

The next day I woke up in the best possible way. With a Cooper text. It said:

My sister's goldfish died. We're having a ceremony. Get over here now.

I mean, I guess that wasn't *exactly* the best way. If the life of the goldfish could've been spared, it would've been much better. But it had happened, and he had texted *me*.

Roger. On my way.

I brushed my teeth, replaced my bed shorts for jean shorts, and headed for the door. "Going to Cooper's. I'll be back later."

"Okay, have fun," Mom said.

A thought occurred to me and I backtracked, grabbed my newest painting—the one of the fish—and left.

"Did you even brush your hair?" Cooper asked when he answered the door. "And you slept in that tank top, didn't you? For the love of Pete, this is a memorial service."

"Ha-ha."

He smiled and pulled me inside by the arm. He shut the door, then paused for a moment. The entryway was dim and I looked up, confused. His eyes met mine, holding them for three breath-stealing seconds. Then his smile brightened. "Let's go," he said.

His sister was already in the bathroom, holding the

fishbowl gravely. "I think I forgot to feed him," she whispered when she saw me.

"Sometimes fish just die," I said, putting my arm around her shoulder.

"Especially when they don't have food," Cooper said, and I elbowed him in the ribs. He grunted but then added, "It's okay, Amelia. I'll get you a new one."

"I don't want a new one."

"Well, let's at least give this one a proper end." Cooper gestured to the toilet. "I think it's time."

"We must have a memorial first," Amelia said. "Think of nice things to say."

"Okay." Cooper tapped his lips with his finger. "He was a quiet fish."

"It's a girl," Amelia said. "Lindsay."

"Your fish's name was Lindsay?"

"What's wrong with Lindsay?" I asked.

"That's a person name. You can't name animals people names."

"Says who?"

"I don't know. It's just a rule."

"I think the most common pet name is actually Max. Which makes it not a rule."

"Yes," Amelia agreed. "What Abby said. She likes the name Lindsay."

"I do."

"Abby likes everyone's name," Cooper said.

I barked out a laugh, then quickly covered my mouth. "So untrue."

"It seemed like the right thing to say."

"I thought we were saying things about my fish," Amelia said.

"Right. Your fish." Cooper thought for a moment. "She was quiet and kept to herself."

I sucked my lips in to keep from laughing again. I knew Amelia was upset, and I wanted to take this seriously for her. Cooper's smirk in my direction wasn't helping.

I added, "She was very bright. The prettiest shade of orange I've ever seen."

Cooper nodded. "And Abby is an artist, so she's seen a lot of orange."

Amelia smiled. "She was a pretty color." She looked into the bowl and her expression darkened. "Now she's kind of gray."

"What about you, Mil?" Cooper asked. "What nice things do you have to say about her?"

"When I left for school she would go to the top of the bowl like she was saying good-bye to me. I think she was smart."

"For sure," I said.

We stood there for several more moments, waiting for

Amelia to say more, but she didn't.

"Okay, it's time." Cooper walked to the toilet and placed his finger on the handle.

Amelia dumped her fish into the toilet bowl slowly and I tried not to cringe when it landed with a plop, splattering some water onto the lid.

"Bye, Lindsay," Amelia whispered.

Cooper flushed and we all watched until she was gone. Amelia gave me a long hug and I patted her back.

"Oh," I said. "I have something for you. Meet me in your room."

Cooper trailed after me as I made my way to the trunk of my car. "What do you have?"

"You'll see."

"By the way, I think we just watched a life go out of the world," he said. "For the list."

I stopped with a gasp, just short of opening the trunk. "You're right. We totally did. Nice." I was smiling and I stopped myself. "I mean, not nice. Not for your sister."

"It's okay, Abby. I think she'll be fine."

I opened the trunk of my car and pulled back the soft cloth from over the painting.

Before I could lift out the canvas, Cooper stopped my hands. "Did you paint this?"

"Yes. I'm going to give it to your sister."

"You can't *give* this to my sister."

"You don't think she'll like it?"

"I think she'll love it, but you have to show this to Mr. Wallace. It's amazing."

"It's good. But I can do better. This one is for Amelia." Mr. Wallace wanted more feelings, but this one felt like too much feeling and not enough technique.

"When did you do this?"

"The other day, after I went to that fish spa."

"This is what came of that? Now I wish I'd gone."

"It was pretty awesome." I picked up the painting.

"You really are just stalling, aren't you? You don't think this is good enough because you don't want to show Mr. Wallace until you think you've reached perfection."

"No, I don't think it's good enough because I didn't feel right when I was painting it."

"What does that mean?"

"You don't know what feelings are?" I asked with a smirk.

"Funny."

I held up the painting. "I still have sixteen days until he's making final decisions. And three more experiences to try. If two more paintings don't result, I'll use this one. Don't worry. I'm going to show him."

"Good. Because I want this for you."

"I know. Thank you."

Cooper nodded and took the painting from me, carrying it the rest of the way into his house.

Amelia loved it and made him hang it on the wall above her bed right that second. "Abby, you are the best. Thank you so much. This will remind me of Lindsay when I see it."

"Good. I'm glad you like it."

"She might have to borrow it back in a week to show the museum director for the showcase."

"Of course," Amelia said. "I'll keep it safe in the meantime."

The three of us stood back and stared at the painting like we were in our own art museum.

Cooper put his arm around my shoulder, still looking at the painting. "My little Abby is growing up."

I rolled my eyes and pinched his side. "You always know how ruin a moment."

"And here I thought I always knew how to make a moment even better."

I sighed, but conceded. "You do."

We left Amelia in her room with the painting and headed toward the kitchen. "Last night, you and Lacey seemed . . . ," Cooper started.

"Seemed what?" I asked when he raided the pantry without continuing. He came out with a bag of Cheetos Puffs. "Isn't it a bit early for that?"

He looked at the clock on the microwave. "It's eleven. That's nearly lunch." He opened the bag. "Chummy."

"Chummy? You mean cheesy?" I squinted to read the bright-blue print on the bag he held.

"No, you and Lacey seemed chummy."

"Oh. Right."

"When did that happen?"

"I don't know. I like her. We talk a little."

"I thought you said you weren't friends with her."

"Yeah, well, things change," I said, repeating her line from the night before. I studied his expression—tight around the eyes but trying to play it off as uninterested. I threw my head back with a groan.

"What?" he asked.

"You're jealous."

"Yeah, maybe I am. You're supposed to be *my* best friend."

I swiped the bag of Cheetos from him and headed for the front door.

"Where are you going?" he asked.

"To paint. You've given me all sorts of emotions to work with." Frustration being the main one. I had thought the night before that Cooper had been jealous of *Elliot*. But I was wrong. He was jealous of Lacey. That's why he'd been acting strange. That was definitely a check in the *absolutely nothing has changed* box.

My phone buzzed in my pocket as I walked out the door. I pulled it out to read the text I already knew was from Cooper. If I must, I will challenge Lacey to a duel.

I'll relay the message.

TWENTY-TWO

The next morning after waking up and getting dressed, I surveyed the pantry.

"Are you looking for your sugary cereal again?" Mom asked. "I think Grandpa ate it all."

"No. I'm looking for a sketch pad."

"In the pantry?"

"I already searched the rest of the house. It was my last hope." I hadn't sketched out my ideas in a long time, but when, despite my frustrations with Cooper, I was left staring at an empty canvas the day before, I knew I needed to try something different.

"I think I saw one. . . ." My mom stood up and went to a bin on the counter she put scrap paper and ads and coupons in. She dug through it and came up with a notebook.

"I know it's not a sketchbook," she said. "But will this work?"

"Beggars can't be choosers," I said, taking it from her.

"That's my line," Grandpa said. He'd just come in the sliding door from outside. He carried a watering can and a misshapen cucumber. "What are you begging for?"

I waved the notebook at him. "Nothing anymore. I'm going for a walk."

"I don't think . . . ," my mom started.

"No," I said, realizing she thought I was going to try to convince her to go with me. "Alone. I want to walk alone this time."

"Oh." My mom almost looked hurt. "Okay. Have fun."

I glanced at my grandpa, who seemed just as confused by the interaction as I was. "Did you want to come?" I asked.

She shook her head, and her normal smile was back. "Not at all."

"Tell Cooper we said hi," Grandpa said as I headed for the door.

"Cooper is not going with me. I really am going

alone!" I called back and let the door shut behind me. "I can be alone," I grumbled, walking down the steps.

I wasn't sure what I was looking for. I'd shoved a few charcoal pencils in the back pocket of my shorts and now pulled one out as I walked. I flipped to a clean page in the notebook, then waited to be inspired.

I had been walking for at least forty-five minutes, and all I'd doodled was a single bird that had been sitting on a fence. It wasn't even a very good doodle. I was about ready to give up and head back home when across the street I saw Tree Man, chain and all.

I looked both ways, waited for a car to pass, then walked across. I approached him with a wave. "Hi. You're still here."

He pointed to the bulldozer. "I'll be here until that isn't."

He looked younger than what I had thought he was. Definitely not my grandpa's age, but maybe close to thirty. It was hard to tell. His long, stringy hair was receding, leaving him a large expanse of forehead. His skin was tanned and looked slightly leathery, which made me assume that before becoming Tree Man he was definitely Beach Man or at the very least Long Walks Man.

"Can I sit up there or is that missing the point?" I

nodded toward a low-hanging branch.

"Be my guest. I used to sit up there all the time."

"Like when you first started your *save the tree* mission?" I asked, taking my pencils out of my back pocket and tucking them into my ponytail.

"No. Growing up. I have history with this tree."

"Did you grow up on this lot?" I set my notebook on the branch, then tried to swing up to join it. It was harder than it looked.

"Twenty acres. My parents owned it and sold it six months ago. They made a verbal agreement with the purchaser that he wouldn't tear this tree down. It's a hundred years old. But they didn't get it in writing. So . . ."

"That sucks."

"It does. Are you a reporter?" he asked, nodding to my notebook.

"Oh." I was surprised by the question. "No, I'm an . . ." I paused, then finished with determination. "Artist. I'm an artist."

"Cool," he said, like he meant it.

I'd finally managed to hoist myself onto the branch and sat against the trunk, my feet dangling. "Have you been getting lots of reporters?"

"Sadly, no. I was hoping for some buzz to get more support."

I stared up at the branches above me. They were heavy

with leaves dancing in the breeze. It made the tree look alive. I pulled a pencil out of my hair and grabbed my notebook. "It's a beautiful tree. When is it scheduled for death?"

"I'm sure they would've done the deed already if I weren't here."

"Isn't there a way the housing development can build around it?"

"I guess when they drew up the plans they realized the road would have to come right through here."

"And the tree is in the way."

"Yeah."

My conversation with Elliot came to mind, how we'd talked about what we loved enough to chain ourselves to. "You must have some great memories that involve this tree."

"I do. I have read no less than fifty books in the exact spot you are sitting."

"Really? I don't think I've ever read in a tree. It seems like the best place to read though."

"Now I just knit by the tree." There was a green reusable grocery bag by his feet that he kicked as he said this.

"You knit?"

"Yes."

"I've never knit. What are you knitting?"

He reached down, more easily than I thought he'd be

able to, being chained to a tree and all, and picked up the bag. He pulled out a multicolored hat that looked close to completion. "I'm making this."

"Is knitting hard?"

"At first, it can be. But with practice, it gets easier."

"Like most things."

"Exactly."

My phone rang in my pocket and I looked at the screen. Cooper. "Hold on a sec," I told Tree Man. I didn't know his name. Why had I not asked his name? I answered the phone and said to Cooper, "Wait." Then to the man chained to the tree I said, "What's your name? I've been calling you Tree Man in my head."

He laughed. "I'm Lance."

"Lance. I'm Abby. Okay, hold on." To Cooper I said, "Hey."

"Who's Lance?" he asked.

"The man chained to the tree."

"You're hanging out with Tree Man?"

"Yes. I am sitting on a branch that I climbed to."

"Wow."

"I know."

"So you're actually staying there?"

"Yes."

"For how long?"

"Don't know. Until after bulldozing hours."

"Bulldozing has hours?"

"I assume they work during the day. Gotta run. I'm sketching." I hung up before he had time to respond. Had I ever hung up on Cooper like that before? I thought about calling him back to make sure he wasn't mad about it, but didn't. I really did need to sketch. I'd call him later.

For the next thirty minutes I sat on a branch sketching, and Lance sat on the ground knitting. As my hand moved across the page, I realized it had been a while since I hadn't felt pressure across my shoulders while creating. The pressure of expectation. I was happy, relaxed. So I kept going. My first drawing had been of the leaves above me. Now I was focused on a one-inch section of bark and was drawing a close-up version of it.

My hand began to cramp and I stopped and stretched it. "What other stories do you have involving this tree?" I asked, filling the silence.

"My brother fell from that branch there and broke his arm." He pointed to one above my head.

"Bones should be stronger than they are, considering they're what holds us up."

"I agree. Sometimes it seems we're very fragile creatures."

On the trunk of the tree by my ear I had noticed some

carved initials. "What about this? One starts with an *L*. Is this you?"

He didn't look up from his knitting. "My first kiss."

"Right here? I'm sitting where momentous events happened in your life."

"That's what I'm telling you."

"Well, when I go home tonight, I will write a strongly worded letter to . . ." I paused. "The television station? The mayor?"

"You don't have to do that."

"It's not my cause, so I can't sit out here with you for the next month or whatever, but I am good at strongly worded letters."

"How many strongly worded letters have you written?"

"Okay, fine, it will be my first, but I wanted you to have confidence in me."

He smiled. "I have confidence in you."

I leaned my head back and looked at the tree towering above me again. "I can see what made you do this," I said. "Do you mind if I take a picture of us?"

"Sure."

I held up my camera and took a pic of the two of us—me on the branch, him right below me. I thought I'd include it in an email to my dad, but there was also someone else I wanted to send it to. Elliot.

Chaining myself to a tree for my art.

You're chained to that tree? He responded back almost immediately.

Not really, but I just learned the story of what made him want to and remembered your chain-worthy sculpture. I still want to see it.

You're welcome to see my art anytime.

When I got home, I flipped through the notebook of sketches I'd done. Then I combined some of each and painted a tree with its memories—a broken branch to represent the broken bone, two branches twisted into a heart shape to represent the kiss, words carved into the side for the books, and at the bottom I painted a chain. The chain represented Lance. I used one of my bigger canvases, and the tree's branches filled every corner. Now I knew why Elliot often made trees his subject. They were gorgeous.

But still, my painting was missing something, because no matter how gorgeous it was, I knew this wasn't a tree I'd chain myself to.

TWENTY-THREE

The next day I sat on my bed with my notebook trying to add something more personal to the sketches I'd done of the tree. I'd told Lance's story in my painting, but what about mine?

My computer, which was sitting next to me, dinged with an instant message.

Hey, kid.

I smiled, set the book down, and typed back. Dad! Can you video chat?

Calling now.

My computer rang and I moved the arrow to the video

icon. His face came up on the screen.

"Your hair is so short," I said.

He ran his hand over the buzz cut. "It's hot here. Had my buddy clip it yesterday."

"Should I go get Mom too?" I stretched up in my bed to look at the door, like she might be lurking there, waiting for the invite.

"I just got off with her. She's in her room."

I laughed. "I like how you know that and I don't."

"It's nice knowing more than you about home life every once in a while."

I smiled, and his smile slid off his face. "How is she?" he asked. "She was putting on a brave face, but I'm sure you know much more about that than I do."

"She's okay. She's been on a few walks lately. That's good. She promised me she's going to my art show."

"So you're in the art show now? Your heart list worked!"

"Well, no, not yet. I mean, I haven't shown him my new paintings yet. I will."

"I'm still not happy that Mr. Wallace said you have no heart. You have the biggest heart I know."

I blew air between my lips. "You have to say that because you're my dad. And because you hardly know me."

He narrowed his eyes, and I laughed.

"Just kidding. You sort of know me."

"I know you're more sarcastic than . . ."

"You went down that comparison road knowing you were going to crash and burn."

"Your grandpa!" he said, finally producing an end to his sentence.

"Yeah, nice try, but I think Grandpa might still have me beat. He is older and much more experienced."

"Speaking of your grandpa, how is he?"

"Still alive."

A door opened and closed behind Dad, and he looked over his shoulder. "I'm so sorry," he said back to me. "I have to go. Email me some pictures of your latest paintings. And Abby, don't let anyone tell you that you have no heart."

"Thanks, Dad."

"I wish I could be there for your art show."

I shrugged. "There might not be an art show. I mean, I might not be in it anyway, so it's fine. . . ."

"I love you," he said.

"Love you too."

He clicked the End button and a grainy image of him froze on my screen for a moment. I reached out and touched the smooth surface.

I was busy trying to change the bark sketch when a head appeared around my door.

"Hey," Cooper said.

"Who let you in?"

He smiled and came all the way into my room. "You're not happy to see me? Is that why you hung up on me?"

"I hung up on you because I was busy." I smiled.

"Are you still mad at me for wanting to duel Lacey?"

"No. I've learned long ago that you're a dork."

His eyes went to my hands. "What are you doing?"

"Drawing."

"Drawing? When's the last time you drew?" He sat down next to me and looked at the open book. "What is it?"

"Bark. Up close."

"Okay," he said skeptically.

He was right. It didn't look like bark anymore. It had at one point, but I'd drawn over it so many times, trying to make it cooler or better or more dynamic, that it now looked like a bunch of scribbling. "I know you're impressed."

"Why aren't you painting?"

"I was . . . sort of. I'm letting my mind brainstorm." I pushed his shoulder. "Now stop mocking me." I went over a line again on the page.

He took the book and pencil from me and placed them on my nightstand.

"Hey! Give them back."

"I'm saving you from yourself."

I sighed. "Fine. Let's do something on the list then." Maybe that would help.

Cooper let himself fall onto my bed, then glanced across the room at the list and gave a noncommittal shrug. His enthusiasm over the list had been declining steadily, much to my disappointment. But I still had a show to earn my way into. I couldn't quit while there was still time. Plus, the things I was experiencing had been fun. Yesterday, after talking to Lance, I'd marked "learn a stranger's story" off the list. I hadn't even set out to do that and I had.

"Let's do the 'Cooper faces a fear' one," I said.

"I still haven't thought of anything for that."

"Yeah, right. I'm convinced you know your biggest fear, you're just too afraid to tell me. Come on, I'm going to root it out of you." I stood and held out my hand.

"That sounds painful."

"I'm willing to make that sacrifice."

"I meant painful for me."

"I'm willing to make that sacrifice as well."

He smiled. "And why do we have to leave the house to do this?"

"It's part of the rooting."

He let me drag him to his feet and out the door.

★ ★ ★

Cooper and I had a spot by the ocean. One we liked to go to that wasn't overrun with tourists. Most days, there wasn't another soul there. Mainly because it lacked what most people went to the ocean for—a beach. This place didn't have yards of sand littered with shiny seashells dying to be collected. It didn't have a place to anchor an umbrella and build sand castles. Or even a rock-free zone to jump waves as they crashed onto shore. No, this place had to be hiked to. It was secluded and small and pitted with tide pools and obstacles. It smelled like fish and seaweed and salt. But this was where we came sometimes to escape everything else. I'd grabbed my notebook along with my beach bag as we had left the house, and I turned to a clean page and held my pencil ready now.

"I'm conducting an interview," I said, perched on a rock. One of the many purple wildflowers that grew along the cliff tickled the side of my foot.

"Of who?"

"You."

"Why?"

"It's part of the rooting process. I am going to discover your fear. If you don't know it and I don't know it, you must've hidden it somewhere deep in your subconscious."

"Okay, hit me." He leaned back on his palms.

"What is your earliest memory?"

"Easy. Four years old. Clinging onto my uncle as he drove me on a quad. When we got back, my mom told him off."

"You obviously have strong emotions attached to this or you wouldn't remember it. So was it fear?"

"Nope. Pure excitement."

"I could've guessed that."

He laughed.

I jotted a note in my book. "Okay, how about this. You find out tomorrow that you're going to die. What is the one thing you regret not doing?"

He seemed to consider this for a long moment but then said his answer like it was a throwaway one, like he'd really thought of something else but decided to keep it to himself. "Seeing the world, I guess. What does that have to do with fear, though?"

"I just thought that maybe fear was holding you back from doing something you really want to do."

"No, that's more about money and being underage."

I chewed on the pen cap. "Seeing the world, huh? I don't remember you ever talking about traveling."

"Like I said, it's not possible right now, so why dwell on it."

"Okay." I tried to decide what else to ask him. "Do you have any recurring nightmares?"

"Not that I remember." He tilted his head. "Do *you*?"

"Yes."

"Really? What happens?"

"I'm at school staring at the big brick wall by the amphitheater. You know which one I'm talking about?"

"Yes. The one that everyone always tags and the principal gives lectures about every year because apparently he wants it big and blank?"

"Yes, that one."

"Okay. Do you destroy it? Because that thing is begging to be destroyed."

"No. I paint it."

"Of course you do. How is that a nightmare? It sounds like perfection to me so far."

"Well, I paint it and then the principal tells me to try again. It immediately turns white. I paint the same thing. And again he tells me to try again. Over and over and over." I'd analyzed this dream, and I knew it all came down to me not feeling good enough. Not good enough for Cooper. Not good enough for his parents, not even good enough for my mom sometimes. And definitely not a good enough artist. It sounded overly dramatic, and that's why I wasn't going to admit to that out loud.

"Wow. That sounds awful."

I shrugged, committing to nonchalance. "It's not like I dream it every night."

"I was thinking you meant like monsters or demons, but when you put it that way, maybe I do have one."

"Yeah?"

"I'm standing in a windowless, door-free room, and I'm the only one there."

I wrote down his dream in my notebook. "Then what happens? Do you try to claw your way out or anything?"

"No. That's it. I wake up feeling bad."

"Scared?"

"Not really."

I sighed. "You're hopeless."

He stretched up to try to peer over my notebook. "Those are the only questions? You're done digging into my brain?"

"No. One more."

"Okay."

I looked him in the eyes. "What are you scared of?"

He laughed loud, throwing his head back. When he stopped, a smile still lingering, he said, "You thought this time I'd know?"

I smiled as well but then sighed. "No, but it was worth a try."

He toed my bag. "Did you bring any towels? Or treats?"

"Both."

He held up his hands and I threw him a towel, then

a granola bar. He lay back on the rock, wadding up the towel and putting it under his head. "You know, you're the only person I can sit still with."

"What do you mean?"

"I mean, I like to be in motion. I get antsy when I'm doing nothing. But you're so good at it that I don't mind it at all."

"So good at what? Doing *nothing*?"

"That came out wrong."

"Did it?"

"I just meant being laid-back. It was a compliment."

I kicked his foot. "You need to work on giving compliments."

He chuckled and unwrapped his granola bar. "I know."

I opened my notebook again and started sketching the flowers growing through cracks in the rock. "Why do you think that is?"

"Why aren't I good at giving compliments?"

"No. Why can't you sit still?"

"I can. Look at me. I'm a study in Zen." He took a large bite of granola bar and chewed it slowly.

"Are you afraid to be bored? Afraid of people thinking you're boring?" I pointed at him. "Ooh. I got it. You're afraid to be in your own head."

He pinched the bridge of his nose. "Ah. Here comes the painful rooting-around-in-my-skull part."

"So yes, then?" I wasn't sure why I was so intent on finding his fear. I claimed it was for the list and to pay him back for the terror-filled quad ride, but part of me felt like it was something beyond that.

"No," he said. "My head is the best place to be. There's a constant party up here all the time."

I continued drawing. This was a pointless exercise only reaffirming my belief that Cooper had no fears. It was time to change the subject. "How is your sister? Is she still upset about her goldfish?"

"No. She's trying to talk my mom into a pet bird now."

"She's moving up the food chain. Nice."

"Do you need her painting back so you can show Mr. Wallace?"

"Not yet."

"You still have one more to paint?"

"No, well, sort of. If I count her fish, then I finished the fifth one last night, but there's something not quite right about it."

He hummed. "You're stalling."

"I'm not. I have time."

We were silent for a couple of beats while Cooper finished his granola bar. Waves crashed against rocks in the distance, sending water filtering through the tide pools and closer to us. In a couple of hours the spot where we were sitting would be underwater with high tide.

"What happened with Elliot, Abby? We never talked about it."

"What do you mean, what happened? We hung out at a party. Were you expecting a wedding invitation?"

"You didn't like him?"

"Who said that?" My voice rose an octave, and even I could hear the defensiveness in my tone.

"I can tell. I thought you said your relationship goals were that you wanted to date an artist."

"How did you know he was an artist?"

"He told me."

"When?"

"I don't know."

I shut my notebook and sat forward, but Cooper didn't move from his reclined position. "I thought the first time you met him was at the restaurant."

"It was," he said.

"And the second time was at the party." I could feel frustration rising in my chest.

"Yeah, but maybe I asked around."

"Why?"

"I like to know who my friend is about to go out with."

I hit him with my towel. "Don't ask around, Cooper. Not for things like this."

"So why don't you like him?"

He's not you, I wanted to say. "I don't know. He's nice. We'll still be friends." At least I hoped we would be.

"You don't need another guy friend."

I crossed my arms. I wasn't used to Cooper being so serious. We sniped at each other occasionally, but where was this coming from? "Excuse me. What's that supposed to mean?"

"It's not supposed to mean anything but what I said."

"Maybe I don't need the *guy* friend I already have."

He scooped up a pile of sand from beside him and threw it in my direction halfheartedly.

"That was a toddler's response," I said, the tension dissolving a little.

He smiled. "It's just that you frustrate me sometimes."

"Ditto."

He pulled a piece of the towel over his eyes. "Fine. I'll drop it."

"I'm fine. I'm happy. I don't need a boyfriend. Maybe you always need a girl to make you feel special or whatever, but I don't. Okay?"

"Okay. I said I'd drop it."

"Good."

"Good." He took the towel off his face and sat up. "I don't always need a girl."

"Okay."

"I don't."

"I said okay . . . it's just, you seem to always have one."

"I don't."

"Maybe that's your fear."

"What?"

"You fear being alone. Stuck in a room with no door or windows and no way out. All by yourself."

"Why are you so hung up on my fears? Maybe you should analyze your own dream, Abby. Your own fears. Dig around in your brain for a while. Find out why you keep painting the same thing over and over. Find out what's holding *you* back."

I swallowed a surprised breath. Nothing was holding me back. "I'm pretty sure I'm transparent."

He scowled at me, then stood. "I should probably get home."

I stood as well. "Yep. Me too."

TWENTY-FOUR

I paced my room when I got home, back and forth, forming a thick line in the carpet. Cooper had no idea what he was talking about. I *was* trying to paint better. I was trying to grow. I was trying to change. Wasn't I?

The image of that brick wall and that same painting I kept painting for the principal flashed through my mind. I knew it was just a dream, but why had I painted the same thing over and over? Why did I never change it up?

I was scared of change.

The thought came to me like a revelation, and I knew it was true. I claimed I wanted to try to grow and change, but really everything I did lent itself to things staying exactly the same. When confronted with change, I dug my heels in. When Grandpa mentioned a therapist for Mom, I stopped it. When Lacey tried to be my friend, I kept her at arm's length. When Cooper showed the least bit of resistance to my feelings, I shut them off. I wanted to stay in my perfect bubble, where I knew that even if everything wasn't perfect, at least it was manageable.

This realization made me angry with myself. I marched to my art room. I tugged off the coverings on all my recent paintings: the sunrise, Cooper on the dunes, the stage, the tree. It was time to stop resisting change. To stop digging my heels in. Whether my paintings were ready or not, I needed to try.

I'd faced fear before. It was time to do it again, regardless of the outcome.

I stood at Cooper's front door and knocked. His sister answered.

"Hi, Amelia," I said.

"Hey. He's not here."

I hadn't talked to Cooper since our fight on the beach two days ago. We'd get past it, I was sure. But right now wasn't about Cooper and me. "That's okay. I actually came over to see if I could borrow my painting back."

"You're going to show it to the art guy after all?" she asked with a big smile.

"Yes, actually."

She clapped and bounced on the balls of her feet. "He's going to love it." She took me by the arm and pulled me through her house. Her parents were in the kitchen and I waved as I hurried past them.

The painting was on her wall, and she jumped onto her bed and helped me take it down.

"If it doesn't sell, I want it back when the show is over."

"Of course. I will bring it back that night or I'll paint you a new one."

She squeezed my hand. "Good luck, Abby."

"I'm gonna need it."

I hoped Mr. Wallace was otherwise occupied as I carried two of the five paintings into the building. My nerves were buzzing. Last time, I'd marched in here with my portfolio so sure that if he'd just look, he'd love them. Now, I didn't know. I wasn't even sure how *I* felt about them.

I wanted him to see all the paintings at once, so I snuck across the high-glossed tile of the museum. It felt like I was in some spy movie. I passed paintings hung on display and tried not to look at them. I was already intimidated. I didn't need to compare myself to the professionals at the moment. A couple of patrons looked at me curiously as I passed, but I had yet to see Mr. Wallace.

The painting in my left hand was longer than the one in my right and it gave me an awkward gait. I reached his door and tried the handle. It was unlocked. And when I swung the door open, it was dark. I sighed in relief and flipped on the light. It was still as messy as ever, and like I'd hoped, the stack of broken easels still lined the wall on the right.

I carefully leaned my paintings against the closest wall and went to inspect the easels. I found five that if propped just right—one against the desk, two against each other, two against the wall—would hold my paintings. Then I rushed out and retrieved the others.

Sweat beaded along my lip as I finished placing them each on an easel. The tree on its large canvas was the centerpiece. I stepped back to analyze. My heart pounded hard in my chest. For a moment I allowed myself to look at them objectively, not as their creator. And in that moment I thought they were good. Really good.

I wiped at my upper lip with the back of my hand, steeled myself, then went to find Mr. Wallace. He was talking to a woman in a pantsuit. They stood in front of an impressionist painting. Maybe now wasn't a good time. It would never be a good time. It had to be now. Now or never. He turned toward me.

I gave him a slight wave. The woman moved on to another painting and Mr. Wallace didn't follow her. He waited. So I took the thirty steps between us.

"Are you busy?" I asked.

He glanced at the woman. "No. I didn't think you worked today."

"I don't."

"I need you starting Wednesday to help with prep work for the show. It's coming fast."

"I know. I'll be here Wednesday."

"Okay, good." He started to walk away, like that was what I'd come to say.

"Wait," I called a little too loudly. "Wait," I said again, quieter. "I need to show you something."

"What is it?"

"Follow me." I led him toward his office.

"Did a mouse get into the storage room again?" he asked.

"No, no mouse."

The doorknob was slippery. I wiped my palms on my jeans and took hold of it again. Then I opened the door and stepped aside, gesturing for him to go first. He did. I stood there for two beats with my eyes closed, then followed after him.

He saw them right away. They were impossible to miss. He walked to each one, analyzing them, not saying a word. I had taken up post by the door, like a guard. Maybe it was so I could run at the first sign of rejection. Maybe it was to give him a moment to process alone.

I swallowed hard, then stepped forward.

"These are yours?" Mr. Wallace asked.

"Yes."

"They're interesting."

I wasn't sure if that was a good thing or a bad thing. "Yes, I've been working on emotion."

"I can see that."

"I want to be in the show. I want these pieces to be in the show."

"I already informed the winning applicants. We're full."

My heart dropped to my feet, and I was so tempted to flee like I had last time. I didn't. I stood my ground. "What? You said you weren't doing that for a couple more days."

"I did it early." He looked at my tree painting again. "But . . ."

"But?"

"Maybe," he continued, "we can analyze the layout and see if we can squeeze an extra artist onto the sales floor."

"Yes? Is that a yes?"

"What happens if you get no offers?"

"I'll be fine with that. I just want the opportunity."

"You have a lot of drive, Abby."

"Sometimes."

"Okay, I want you to draw up a chart of a new layout that can include everyone and bring it in for me to approve."

I clapped my hands together once. "So that's a real yes."

He smiled. "Yes."

I let out a short scream and threw my arms around him. "Thank you so much!"

"This is not professional, Abby." There was a smile in his voice.

I dropped my arms. "You're right." I gave him a handshake instead, pumping his hand way too enthusiastically. I couldn't control the adrenaline coursing through me. "Thank you." I started to rush the door before he changed his mind, but then I whirled back around, remembering my paintings.

"Just leave them here," he said. "So you don't have to haul them back in. Stack them against the wall. Did you bring some cloths?"

"I did."

I made quick work of the paintings, then left in a blur of happy emotions.

TWENTY-FIVE

I made it to the car without falling all over myself and climbed inside. I immediately texted Cooper: **He said yes! He said yesssssss!!!**

His response came seconds later: You asked someone to marry you?

I couldn't even conjure up a sarcastic response, I was so excited: **My paintings are in the show. He said yes. All five! I guess my heart has grown to epic proportions.**

It's about time he recognized your genius. I'm taking you out to celebrate. Your house in ten minutes?

Give me thirty. I need to pretend like I didn't share this with you first and tell my family.

"Mom! Grandpa!" I burst into the house.

My mom jumped to her feet, her book clattering to the floor. She stepped over it and rushed to me. "What is it? Did something happen? A car accident? An earthquake? Did you get fired?" She'd grabbed me by the shoulders and was examining me from head to toe.

My mouth opened, then shut. "Really? Those were your first guesses?"

"You've never come in the house like that before. It worried me."

"I'm fine. Better than fine. Where is Grandpa?"

"Outside."

I went to the kitchen and opened the back door. Mom followed. "Come inside, Gramps! I have an announcement that supersedes the health of your vegetables!"

Grandpa went straight to the kitchen sink when he walked in the door and began scrubbing his hands with soap and water. "Is everything all right?"

Okay, maybe I needed to work on my tone when making announcements. "Well, there wasn't an earthquake," I said.

"Am I supposed to get that reference? Is that a young-person phrase for something earthmoving? Has your earth moved, Abby?" He turned off the water and dried his hands on the towel hanging on the oven.

I laughed. "Yes. Actually, it kind of has. I got into the art show!"

"What? You did?" Mom clapped her hands and gave me a hug. "I knew you would!"

I hugged her back, then turned to my grandpa.

Pride shone in his eyes. "Well, of course you did," he said. "Am I supposed to be surprised?"

"You don't have to be surprised, but you do have to be happy for me."

"Done." He gave me a bear hug.

"I need to go email Dad," I said, rushing to my room.

I had just hit Send on my email when the doorbell rang. "Cooper is going to take me out to celebrate!" I yelled as I ran to answer the door. Cooper was there, fresh out of the shower. His hair was wet, his eyes bright with a smile. I threw my arms around his neck in a hug. He lifted me off my feet.

"Congrats!"

"Thanks. And thank you for doing the list with me." It had given me insight into myself that I hadn't expected.

He set me down and I started to go inside when he grabbed me by the wrist. I whirled back around to face him.

"I'm sorry for our stupid fight the other day."

"Me too."

"Can we both agree not to analyze each other's brains again?"

I nodded resolutely. "I'm fine with that arrangement." I pointed over my shoulder. "Let me grab my shoes and we can go."

"Okay. I'm going to say hi to your grandpa and mom."

"Sounds good." I went to my room and he went to the living room. I heard his greeting as I searched for my flip-flops in my closet.

"It's great news about Abby," he said.

"Yes, we're proud, and so is her father," Mom said.

My father? I'd just barely emailed him. Had Mom called him too? I pulled out one polka-dot flip-flop but couldn't find the other. I dug under a pile of clothes. I needed to clean my closet.

"Me too," Cooper said.

"Where are you taking her?" Grandpa asked.

"I don't know. Milk shakes, maybe? She likes milk shakes."

"Aha!" I said as I freed my second flip-flop. I slid them onto my feet and went to join the others.

"Have fun," Mom said when she saw me.

"Did you call Dad tonight?"

She looked at the clock on the wall. "No. It's too early there right now. I'll let him know."

"But you said he was proud."

She smiled. "Of course he's proud. He always talks about your art."

"Oh." She just meant in general. "Thanks, Mom."

"You ready?" Cooper asked.

"Yep. Let's go."

For a Sunday evening, the milk shake place was packed. We'd already been waiting in line for ten minutes when the bell on the door rang for the millionth time and a new group of people walked in.

"Cooper!"

Cooper's smile stretched wide. "Ris! Hi."

She joined us in line, leaving her other group behind. "I thought you said you were busy tonight."

"I am. Abby had some good news, so I had to take her to celebrate."

I tried not to smile with this statement, but I couldn't help it, and Iris noticed.

"What good news?" she asked.

"Oh, it's nothing big," I said.

"It's really big. She gets to have her paintings in an art show at the museum. She's the only minor in the show."

"Wow," Iris said. "That's great. Congratulations."

"Thank you."

"Can I join you guys?"

I should've said no. I wanted to say no. But how would that make me look? Like a petty best friend? "Um . . . yeah, that's fine," I said, hoping Cooper would turn her away.

He didn't. He put his arm around her and said, "Of course."

Maybe I was imagining it, but I could've sworn she was the one giving me a smug smile now. I turned my attention to the lit menu, even though I pretty much knew it by heart. Cooper and I had tried almost every shake combination they offered, plus some we'd made up. But looking at black words on a white board was better than watching Cooper nuzzle Iris's neck.

We finally made it to the front of the line and Cooper looked at me, then nodded to the menu. "Hey, remember the time we combined the—"

"We are not doing that again."

"It wasn't bad."

"It wasn't good either," I said.

He laughed. "Fine. Do you want the—"

"No, I want the banana pie shake."

"But you only like that if the bananas are the perfect amount of ripeness."

The guy behind the register raised his eyebrows when I looked at him.

"Are they?" I asked him.

"Are who what?"

"Are the bananas perfectly ripe?" Cooper asked. "That means zero brown spots but zero green as well."

"I'll find you a perfect one," he said.

Cooper nodded. "Then we'll take one of those and I'll have a brownie batter."

"That made you sick last time," I said.

"I've been conditioning my stomach." Cooper, whose arm was still around Iris, said to her, "What would you like?"

"Surprise me," she said.

Cooper hated that line. My smug smile was back.

"Nope. Your taste buds are your own," he said.

She let out a short sigh, then asked the worker, "What's your favorite?"

"I don't know. I like the cheesecake shake."

"Okay, I'll try that one."

He rang us up, and we went to look for a table. All the ones inside were taken, so we were forced outside to the circular metal ones while we waited for our shakes to be made.

Iris slid her chair as close as possible to Cooper, and he put his arm around her. Really? This was my celebration, but suddenly it felt more like I was the third wheel on one of their dates. I tried not to let it dampen my spirits. If Iris was going to be around more, I needed to make a better effort to get to know her.

"What do you like to do?" I asked.

"I like to bake."

"Bake? Like food?"

"No, like kittens," Cooper said, kicking my foot under the table. "Of course, food, Abby."

I scrunched my nose at him.

Iris put one hand to her chest. "My dream would be to own my own bakery one day."

"That's cool. Unlimited sugary treats is my dream, too."

She seemed to think I was mocking her or maybe not taking her seriously enough, because she said, "It's not all about the food. I'll need to figure out how to run a business too."

"Abby wants to see her paintings in museums around the world one day," Cooper said.

I said, "Speaking of museums, you can pick my mom up for the show on the twenty-first, right? I'll have the car, plus it will help get her out the door."

"Of course."

"But don't come right away. It will be too crowded. Maybe like eight?"

"Sounds good."

"Why does he have to pick your mom up?" Iris asked.

"Because she hates to drive," Cooper said without missing a beat.

And it was true, among many other things. She did hate to drive.

Our order number was called and Cooper left to collect our shakes. I smiled at Iris and started to ask her what her favorite thing to bake was when she stopped me with, "I like Cooper."

"I know," I said.

"And you need to stop trying to sabotage our relationship."

"What? I haven't been."

"It's obvious you wish I wasn't around. But it's you who needs to step back and let him have a girlfriend. You scare away anyone he wants to be with."

How would she even know that? Had she been talking to Cooper's past girlfriends? "And here I thought I was trying to be nice."

"We both know that's not true. It's obvious you're jealous."

I raised my eyebrows. "Wow. Okay. I'll tell you right now that getting on my bad side isn't a smart move."

She brought her smirk back out. "Ditto."

Cooper pushed the door open with his foot and came out carrying all three shakes. Iris's face transformed back to sweet innocence. Mine did not.

I collected my shake and stood. This was my celebration that she had butted her way into, not the other way around. "Cooper. Can we leave?" *Please, don't fail me now, Cooper.*

"What?" He had just sat down and taken a long drink. He looked between Iris and me.

She gave him a pouty lip. "Don't leave me here."

"Where are we going?" he asked. "Can Iris come?"

I'd never done this to Cooper before, but I needed this right now. "Can it be just the two of us this time?"

Cooper stood. "You came with friends, right?" he asked Iris. "They can take you home?"

She waved her hand through the air like it was no big deal. "Yes, of course. Have fun."

"I'll see you sometime this week?" he asked her. She nodded.

"Thanks," I said, hooked my arm in Cooper's, and led us back to his car, so relieved that he came with me that I almost broke down in tears. He came with me. He chose me over her.

"What was that about?" he asked.

"Your girlfriend hates me."

"Girlfriend? I've only been on a few dates with her. Don't tie me down yet."

They weren't girlfriend/boyfriend yet? Interesting. "Well, either way, she hates me."

"She does not. I think she's just intimidated by our friendship. She'll be better once Justin and Rachel are back."

"She told me to back off."

He laughed, like this was something to laugh about. "That's so cute."

"It didn't feel cute. It felt threatening. Like she was going to try to tear us apart."

"You probably misunderstood her."

"I didn't. But whatever. Let's not talk about it."

"Let's go make a sand castle on the beach."

"It's too dark."

"I have two flashlights in the car."

"Okay, let's go."

"How come your castle looks so professional and mine looks like a shoddy contractor built it?" Cooper asked as I used a small stick I'd found to carve windows.

"I can't help it that I'm awesome."

Cooper's foot shot out and collapsed the right tower of my castle.

I gasped. "You did not just do that." He was on his knees leaning over his castle, so I jumped up and landed right on top of it, the damp sand squishing between my toes. Cooper grabbed me around the legs, causing me to collapse onto his shoulder. He picked me up and spun me around. I pounded on his back but couldn't stop laughing.

"All the blood is going to my head. Let me down."

He did, but I was dizzy, so I fell to my hands and knees and then flung myself onto my back. I'd need a shower after this to get rid of all the sand that was now in my hair.

Cooper, who stood over me, poked my ribs with his foot. "I'm proud of you, Abby."

"For what? My amazing sand-castle-building skills?"

"You know what for. You worked hard. You put yourself out there. You deserve it." He held his hand out for me and I let him help me to my feet, where he pulled me into a hug.

We stood like that, staring out at the waves rolling in, for several long perfect moments. "Thank you," I said. And in that moment I knew I had to try. I had to put myself out there in another way too. Maybe it would change everything. Maybe, like I knew I'd feared all along, I'd lose him as a friend and nobody would speak to me again and I'd be alone. Or maybe, just maybe, things would change for the better.

That night, still high from my time with Cooper, I texted Lacey: You're right. Things do change. I'm ready to try with Cooper. Will you help me figure out a plan?

She texted back right away: Absolutely.

TWENTY-SIX

The next week passed by quickly in a flurry of gallery showrooms to lay out and invitations to send. I'd seen Cooper for a couple of hours here and there, but without the list directing our every move, we were back to our normal routine of lazy beach days and Friday night movies and milk shakes on the pier. Lacey had told me to hold off on any admissions while we concocted a brilliant plan.

Now, with only a week left until the showcase, I sat on the floor of Lacey's bedroom, scheming. She held a notepad in her hand. "This is like a play I once saw," she said.

I sat next to her, staring at the blank page, feeling like it represented exactly how I felt. I had no idea how I was going to win Cooper over. It wasn't like I was going into this with no history. Would he still react the same way? It didn't matter. *I* had changed. I wasn't going to run away from something because I was worried it would make things different any longer.

"A play you once saw?" I asked.

"Yes, it was about a girl and a clueless guy."

"And did it end well?"

"Let's not talk about the play. This is real life."

"So it *didn't* end well?" I asked, widening my eyes.

She waved her hand through the air. "Oh, you know, typical dramatic ending: death, destruction, heartbreak. But anyway, the point is that she had to show her clueless boy what he was missing."

I decided to ignore her horrible comparison and asked, "How do I do that?"

"First you have to make him miss it."

"Huh?"

"Today is Monday. The art show is Sunday. That is six days from now."

"Yes."

"You can't see Cooper until the art show."

"Why not?" I couldn't remember the last time I'd gone that many days without seeing Cooper.

"A boy has to miss that which he doesn't know he desires before he realizes he desires it."

"Sounds . . ."

"Completely logical."

"I was going to say, sounds like a lot of head games."

"Cooper needs a few head games, obviously. You tried the straightforward approach. Time to try something else."

"Okay, so no seeing him for six days." That was going to be hard. Cooper just showed up at my house all the time. How was I going to avoid him?

"Text him now. Tell him you'll be setting up at the museum all week."

"I *will* be setting up at the museum all week. Starting tomorrow."

"There you go. No head games involved then."

"He'll stop by the museum. He'll bring me cheesecake or something."

"Why will he do that?"

"Because he does that sometimes. We're friends."

She growled. "Then you'll have to keep a lookout for him and hide if you see him."

"This sounds complicated," I said. I didn't like complicated.

"Love is complicated."

"That should be on a T-shirt."

"It probably already is."

I smiled and looked back at her notepad. She hadn't written any of the plans we'd discussed. She'd just drawn two stick figures holding hands with a heart between them.

"Which one am I?" I asked.

"The shorter one, obviously." She added a dress onto the stick figure's body. "You need a new dress. A perfect dress. Something that will make him see you as a woman and not a girl."

I tried not to laugh, because I knew she was being serious. "*That* sounds like a line from a play."

"But it's a true line, nonetheless. Let's go shopping this week. When do you get off every day?"

"Probably around sevenish."

"Okay, we'll go tomorrow. That way I can be sure you're not sneaking to see your addiction."

"I'm not addicted."

"One time I tried to give up caffeine," she said, ignoring my statement. "I got a headache. I wonder if you're going to get a headache this week."

Lacey may have been new in my life, but now I knew she was teasing me. I took the notepad from her and added a few embellishments to the dress she'd sketched—some small flowers along the neckline, pleats below the waistline, and pockets. I loved a dress with pockets.

"When you can make a stick figure's dress look nicer than anything I own, you're a true artist."

I handed her back the notepad and she studied the dress.

"No flowers," she said. "We're ditching the girl and embracing the woman, remember? But I like the rest. And it needs to be red."

"Red? I was thinking black."

"Trust me on this one. You are wearing red."

"Okay, so he sees me at the art show in my new red dress that makes me look more woman than girl and then . . . what?"

"Then you tell him how you feel and you kiss him. You won't be able to joke your way out of that."

"You want me to kiss him right in the middle of the art show surrounded by people?"

"No, you don't want an audience when you kiss him for the first time. It needs to be a life-changing kiss. A kiss that turns stubborn hearts."

"But no pressure," I mumbled.

"Wait, this isn't your first kiss in general, is it?"

"No, I've kissed a few guys." Not any in the last year, but enough before a year ago that I wasn't worried about my ability.

"Good. So is there a close place you can pull him away to? A quiet, romantic place, preferably?"

"The broom closet?"

She was adding more details to her drawing. "Not a broom closet."

"I was kidding."

She looked up to see my expression. "Right. I always forget how sarcastic you are."

"It's a gift."

"You have a different place in mind then?"

I had a different place in mind. The sitting area overlooking the ocean. It was closed in by trees and shrubbery, and as long as it wasn't occupied by other guests, it would be an amazing spot for a first kiss. "I have the place."

"Then the rest should be easy."

I let out a single forced breath. "So easy. He'll be in love with me before the night is over."

"Plus, you'll have sold all five of your paintings that night. It will really just be the best night of your entire life."

"This is starting to sound more and more like a play."

"Exactly." She held up her finished drawing, like this summarized everything we'd talked about. And for some reason it felt like it did. I smiled, a surge of confidence jolting through me. Cooper and I were going to be together. It was fate.

TWENTY-SEVEN

I was tired. I'd spent the last four days at the museum with inventory and clearing and storing art and everything else we had to do to prepare for the show. And I'd spent every night with Lacey going over our game plan.

She'd taken me to pick the perfect dress—red, sleeveless, just above my knee, high waistline, with pleats and pockets—and we'd researched hairstyles. And most importantly, I hadn't seen Cooper since Lacey and I had come up with the plan. I had a headache, but I was pretty sure it was from worry and not from my detox.

It was Friday night. The show was in two days. We were in Lacey's room going over the final details of how Sunday would play out. I was sitting on her bed, which had more pillows than existed in my entire house.

She was surveying a shoe rack that took up one entire wall of her walk-in closet.

"What size shoe do you wear?"

"Eight."

She pursed her lips. "You think you can squeeze into a seven and a half for the night? Because these are perfect." She held up the shoes in her right hand. They were black peep-toe heels with red bottoms.

"I'll be on my feet for at least four hours."

"So that's a no?"

"That's a big no."

"Fine. But you need to pick out cute heels. None of your comfy flats."

"Okay, okay. I'll go tomorrow."

"Good. I wish I could go with you. I wish I could see this all play out. Maybe I should skip my latest LA audition."

"You're kidding, right? You should not skip the audition. You need to go and you need to get that part like I know you are capable of doing."

She gave me a salute. "Yes, ma'am."

I smiled.

"You're good at giving pep talks, not so good at taking them."

"Hey, I'm about to kiss Cooper my-best-friend-in-the-whole-world Wells on Sunday. Pretty sure I've taken an innocent pep talk to the extreme."

"Well, I wouldn't call my scheming an innocent pep talk, but I know what you're saying. And you will be great. I know you can do it, even if I can't be there."

"I can. I will." I put my fist halfheartedly in the air. "Ouch. My shoulder is sore."

"From what?"

"We've been moving a lot of paintings around at the museum."

She tapped her lips with her fingers. "I've been thinking. Is it too late to paint a special painting for Cooper? Something that would mean something to him that you could include in your display?"

"The show is in two days!"

"So that's a no?"

I laughed. "Do you normally say things and people just make them happen?"

She looked up in thought. "Not all the time. But enough to spoil me. We're good for each other, I think. You bring me down to earth and I make you dream big."

Maybe she was right. Because she did have me dreaming big. She had me thinking that in two nights, I could make Cooper mine. "I actually already have a painting for him. I revamped a painting of him on his quad. I haven't shown him the new version yet. I think he'll love it. I was going to gift it to him after the show if it didn't sell."

"Perfect. Look at that. I said something, and it happened."

I picked up one of her hundred pillows and threw it at her.

She caught it and twirled around like it was her new dance partner. Then she plopped it on the floor and sat on top of it. "So what are you going to do about his girlfriend? If she shows up to the museum with him, I mean."

My smile melted off my face. "They're not together," I said, repeating what he'd told me. "They've only been out a few times. I don't think he'll bring her."

"Okay, but if he does, you must steal him away from her to your secret location."

"That will be awkward."

"Remember, Cooper should've been yours a year ago. *She* is stealing him away from *you*. Think about the first time she met him. He was with you, and she didn't have any problem flirting with him."

"True."

"Say it like you believe it."

"True!"

A knock sounded at Lacey's closed door.

"Come in," she called.

Her dad poked his head in.

"Hello, Bill," Lacey said.

"Hey, your mother and I are going to run to the store. You brother and sister are watching television. Can you just keep an ear out for them?"

"Yes, I can."

"Thanks." He left, leaving the door open this time.

"You call him Bill. Is that an *I treat my dad like my peer* thing or is that a *my dad and I are distant and therefore I must call him by his first name* thing?"

"That's a *he's my stepdad* thing."

"Oh. That makes sense. Not sure why I didn't think of that one first."

She laughed.

"Is that why your brother and sister are so much younger than you?"

"Yep. Half siblings."

"Got it. And your not-stepdad?"

"You mean my actual dad?"

"Yes."

She threw the pillow back at me and I caught it. "He's around. Since I'm seventeen now, I kind of get to pick when I see him. It used to be they had fifty-fifty custody. But it's so hard to pack up my life for half a week. So now we mostly do meals together once a week, or I'll stay with him for three weeks here and there."

"Does he live close?"

"About an hour. And he's not super enthusiastic about my career choice."

"Acting? Why?"

"He thinks I'm too young. Wants me to grow up a little first."

"But your mom is fine with it?"

"Very. The consummate stage mom. And it's what I love to do, so I'm glad at least one of them has supported me. It's hard to be taken seriously as an artist. *You* know."

"I do. I'm lucky neither of my parents have given me grief about art."

"You are."

My phone buzzed in my pocket and I freed it. It was a text from Cooper.

I'm sick. Come take care of me.

I held up my phone for Lacey to see.

"Tell him no. You've lasted four days. He's going to

ruin our plans. No seeing him until Sunday."

I texted back: **I'm sure your mom is doing a perfect job of taking care of you.**

Parents are out of town.

Can't Iris take care of you?

I'm on death's door. Please.

"Gah!" I grunted in frustration. "He said he's on death's door."

"Abby," she said in a warning tone.

"I know, but what if he's really sick and all alone?"

"He has Iris, remember?"

"That will just further their relationship if she's there to take care of him while he's sick. The fact that he's texting me says a lot, right?"

"It does. It says our plan is going to work."

"So I'll just go check on him."

Lacey leveled me with a cold stare. "You're going to go no matter what I say, aren't you?"

"He's my friend."

"I know. Get out of here. Hopefully he's incoherent and our plan will still work."

I smiled. "Thanks for everything."

She hugged me. "Text me Sunday night with a detailed report."

"I will."

She swiped up the heels she'd dropped at the foot of

her bed. "Take these just in case you can't find any. Sacrifice is the start of any great relationship." She smiled. "Yes, you can put that on a T-shirt."

I took the shoes and ran out of the house. My heart was pounding. I'd let Cooper talk me into coming over so easily because *I* missed *him*.

TWENTY-EIGHT

Amelia let me in when I got to Cooper's house.

"Where is he?"

She pointed to the hall.

I dropped my bag by the front door and made my way to his room. I knocked softly on his door. "Hey, it's me."

He just groaned.

"You were well enough to text ten minutes ago. Have you deteriorated that much since then?" I walked into his room. The only light came from a small desk lamp, so it took my eyes a bit to adjust. He lay on his bed, his breathing labored. I put my hand on his forehead. It was burning up.

"Wait, you're really sick?" I had kind of thought he might be faking it a little or overplaying it to get me over. "You have a bad fever. Have you taken any medicine for this?"

"I don't know."

"What do you mean, you don't know?"

"Maybe." His lips were dry and cracked, and his words came out as a whisper.

"How long have you been like this? For longer than today?"

"What?"

"I'll be right back." I searched for his sister and found her eating ice cream in front of the television. "Has Cooper taken anything for his fever?"

"No. He got home about three hours ago and went straight to his room. I tried to wake him up to ask him if Mom left us any money for dinner, but he told me he was sleeping."

"So this just started today?"

"I think."

"Okay. I have money if you want to order a pizza or something."

"Thanks!" She ran to the phone and I went to the

medicine cupboard. I found a bottle of NyQuil. I also wet a rag. With my offerings in hand, I went back to his room.

"Hey, sickie, sit up for a sec. I need you to take some medicine."

"Abby?"

"Yes."

"What are you doing here?"

"You texted me. Now come on, sit up." I helped him sit up. He took the medicine and lay back down on his side. I placed the wet washrag on the back of his neck, where he felt the hottest. "How did this happen?"

"Dunno," he mumbled.

"If I make you some soup will you eat it?"

"Not hungry."

"What do you need?" I flipped the rag to the other side.

"Just stay with me."

"Okay. I can do that, but if you get me sick I won't be happy. I have a big show in two days."

He smiled a little and I crawled into bed next to him, sitting against the headboard instead of lying down.

His arm immediately went over my lap and his forehead found my hip. I could feel the heat radiating off him. I hoped the medicine helped soon, because I didn't like seeing him like this. I moved the rag from his neck to his temple and lightly ran it along his face.

"You've been gone this week," he said.

"Just busy."

"It's annoying."

I smiled and pushed his hair off his forehead.

"I'm cold," he said with a shiver.

"You're actually very hot."

"I know." One side of his mouth attempted a smile.

"Wow, even incoherent you can still pull out the jokes."

He let out what he probably thought was a small laugh but was really more of a moan.

The cloth was now warm and I moved stand up so I could rewet it, but his grip around me tightened.

"I just need to make this cold again, and get you some crushed ice to chew on, okay?"

"Don't leave."

"I won't leave. I'll be right back." I pried his arm off my waist.

Amelia was in the kitchen when I got there. "Did you order pizza?"

"Yes, a little while ago. They said thirty minutes or less."

I pulled a twenty out of my bag and handed it to her.

"I'm glad you're here," she said. "Is Cooper going to be okay?"

"Yes, he'll be fine. He just has a fever. I'm sure it will be gone by tomorrow."

"Okay. I'll wait for the pizza guy."

"Come get me when he comes, okay? Don't answer the door by yourself."

"I am fourteen, you know."

I gave her a hard stare.

"Okay, okay."

With ice and newly cooled rag, I went back to Cooper's room. He appeared to have gone back to sleep.

I laid the rag across his forehead and set the ice on his nightstand. I sat down next to him again. It was rare that I got to stare at Cooper for long uninterrupted moments like this. But as I sat next to him, his arm around me again, his eyes closed, I couldn't help it. He had long blond eyelashes that curled up. His nose had a knot in it from where he broke it falling off his quad when he was a kid. His lips, which were normally soft and full, were dried and cracked. Man, did I love this boy so much.

His head was still on fire, and I was worried. I picked up some ice and ran it along his lips. Tingles spread from the back of my neck all the way down my arms. No. What was wrong with me? I dropped the ice back in the cup, clenched my hands into fists, and forced them to my sides. I sat like that for a long time, listening to him breathe, willing his body to heal.

The doorbell rang and I slipped out of Cooper's hold and stepped out of his room. It was a good excuse for a break.

The pizza guy was in the open door by the time I got there, giving Amelia some change.

"I thought I told you to wait for me," I said to her.

"Oops," she said, taking the pizza and shutting the door. "Sorry."

I hip-checked her.

"You want some?"

"What kind?"

"Pepperoni and mushrooms."

"Sure."

She put the pizza on the table and pulled two plates from the cupboard. "I heard the fish painting is going to be in the show. I knew it would work."

"I'm happy it did."

"Do you think Cooper will let me come to the art show?"

"Yes. Of course. You're all invited. Your parents can come too. It's Sunday night."

"My parents are out of town."

"Oh, right. Well, tag along with Cooper. He's bringing my mom for me too." My plans for the night involved me taking Cooper outside anyway, away from everyone, to the overlook. Was I still going to be able to do that?

Was he going to be well enough?

She took a big bite of pizza. "He'll have to come get me at my friend's house. My mom arranged for me to spend Sunday over there."

"Where'd your parents go, anyway?" I asked, sitting down.

"My dad took my mom on some anniversary cruise trip for the weekend."

"Fun."

"She called. She's seasick."

"Oh. That's not so fun." I slid a slice of pizza out of the box and onto the plate that now sat in front of me. "And where was Cooper today?" I tried to ask casually, like I didn't care. It was weird not knowing what he'd been up to this week.

"I guess he took Ris to some fish spa?" She said it like she didn't know what that was.

"He did what?" I asked, mad that he wouldn't do that with me but had stolen the idea to do with her.

"I know. Weird, right?"

"Yeah . . . weird." I took a couple of deep breaths. I was not going to get mad. "Do you like her?" I asked.

Amelia shrugged. "She's okay. She bakes a lot."

"Yeah, she told me she liked to bake. That's cool."

Amelia leaned forward and lowered her voice, like Iris

was in the next room. "She needs a bit more practice."

A laugh burst out of me before I could stop it. Amelia's cheeks went pink.

We each ate two slices of pizza before I threw my napkin on my plate and pushed myself away from the table. "I better go check on your brother."

"He's a baby."

"Most of the time, yes."

"Did he call you to come over here?"

"He texted me."

"Huh," she said with a small nod.

"What?"

"Nothing . . . he's just a baby."

I could tell I wasn't going to get what she was really thinking out of her, so I left. Cooper's shoulder rose and fell in a steady rhythm as I stared at him from the door. I let myself inside and gently placed my hand to his forehead. His head felt a lot cooler and I took a breath of relief. Hopefully this was just some twenty-four-hour bug.

I walked slowly around his room, looking at the things on his walls. I'd been in his room a million times before, so I'd seen them all a million times before, but I hadn't really looked at them in a while. He had lots of pictures. For his birthday a couple of years ago, I'd bought him a Polaroid camera, the one that immediately spits out a low-quality picture. And there were tons of those, like a border, at eye level around his room. His eye level, not mine, so I had to stand on my tiptoes to look at them. So many were of him and me in various places over the years—beach, Taco Bell, dunes, school. There were some of the four of us too—Cooper, Justin, Rachel, and me. But they were mostly of just the two of us.

He'd carried that camera everywhere for a while, like it wasn't easier to just snap a picture with his cell phone. "These ones, I can hold in my hands instantly," he'd said when I told him as much. But gradually, he stopped bringing it places, and I hadn't seen it in several months. That's why the last string of pictures surprised me—him and Iris. Him and Iris on his quad, him and Iris at the beach. She made the wall. That was new too.

My hands started to sweat as I stared at those pictures. It was fine. It wasn't too late. My plan was going to work. He'd chosen me the other day. He'd chosen me tonight. He'd choose me again.

But what if he didn't? What if it *was* too late? I swung around and was almost to his door when Cooper said, "Abby?"

"Yes, what, huh?" I said, a little too loudly. I rushed to his bedside.

"I thought you left."

"I didn't leave. I'm here."

"Good. I like it when you're here."

"Me too."

"You're my favorite," he mumbled.

My shoulders relaxed. "I know. You're mine too."

TWENTY-NINE

I'd gotten to Cooper's house at eight. It was now almost midnight—my curfew. He'd been in and out of sleep. We had several incoherent (on his part) conversations. I'd wet and rewet his rag tons of times. But now that his fever was gone and he was sleeping comfortably beside me, I could leave. An hour before, Amelia had come in and said good night. Everything was going to be fine. I needed to leave.

I lifted Cooper's heavy arm from where it rested on my lap and got out of his bed. His phone sat on his nightstand. It was nearly dead—I'd heard it buzz its low-battery signal earlier. I plugged it into the charger so he'd have a way to text me if he woke up. Then I pulled out my phone and sent him a text.

Curfew. Had to go. Hope you feel better.

I lingered by the door. Why was I lingering? Why did I hope he'd wake up and beg me to stay? I needed to leave. So I left.

That night, I dreamed that I slept through the show. I woke the next morning in a panic before I remembered it was only Saturday. I still had a full day before I should've had a dream like that, but I was relieved it was only a nightmare.

I had two texts waiting for me on my phone. The first was from Lacey: You saw him last night. Avoid him like the plague today and tomorrow to counteract your weakness.

Yes, boss, I texted back.

The second was from Cooper: I heard I was a baby last night. Thanks for taking care of me.

So he didn't remember? Is that what he was saying? I answered: You were. Does this mean you're feeling better?

Much. Good enough for my quad and the dunes. You in?

Funny.

I thought you conquered that fear.

I faced it. Didn't conquer it.

The next text that came through was from Lacey

again: And don't text him all day either.

I laughed and did just as she directed. I didn't text him another word. He must've figured I was busy setting up for the show, because he didn't text me another word either. I didn't dwell on it (too much) because I *was* busy setting up for the show. I scrubbed so many baseboards and chair rails that day that my shoulders ached.

"Grandpa, I need a shoulder rub. But no deep tissue," I said when I got home that night. I plopped myself on the floor in front of his chair.

"How else am I supposed to get the knots out then?"

Mom turned the computer to face me and I saw my dad's smiling face on the screen. "Hey, kid! You made the show!"

"Yes! I did. You got my email?"

"I did. I answered back, but you've had a busy week, I hear."

"So busy. Sorry."

"It's okay," he said. "Good luck. I'm sad I can't make it."

"Can't make it, huh? Yeah, right. You're going to surprise me, like those soldier dads I see on the internet all the time jumping out of boxes at football games or cakes at birthday parties, aren't you?"

"They jump out of boxes at football games?" he asked.

"Yes, it's very dramatic and there are lots of tears."

Grandpa started rubbing my shoulder, and I sucked in a painful breath.

"No, kid, that's not happening. I wish," Dad said.

"That's what they all say. They try to play it off. But I'm onto you. Just don't jump out of any of my paintings or you'll have to pay for them. I will work on my good crying face though."

"Abby, I—"

"She's kidding, Paul," Mom said. "She knows you're not coming." She waved her hand at me behind the computer telling me to knock it off.

Grandpa, who was always quick to jump on board when he thought people were the most uncomfortable, said, "I hope you have a videographer set up for all this, Paul. Those kinds of videos get millions of views online."

My mom sighed and turned the computer back toward her with an apologetic look on her face. "You know how they are," she said. "They like to take things just beyond the funny point."

"What?" I said indignant. "I thought we were just under maximum level of humor on that one."

"Me too," Grandpa agreed while digging into the knot on my neck. "I had at least two more rounds in that volley."

"Nobody says *rounds in a volley*, Grandpa."

"I do, so that's not true."

"Ouch. I said not deep tissue."

He backed off a little. "Are you all ready for tomorrow?"

"Yes. I think so." I was ready to show my art. I wasn't sure if I was ready to kiss Cooper, but both were happening regardless of if I was ready or not. I just hoped *he* was.

THIRTY

I paced my station in Lacey's heels. I hadn't had time to shop for my own, and hers were definitely too small. They pinched my toes and rubbed at the side of my foot. But they did look good. What was it she had said about sacrifice?

She'd sent me a text earlier, and I smiled remembering it now.

Good luck. Remember: your lips will change hearts.

The doors hadn't been opened to the public yet, but they would be soon. I pulled out my phone to look at the time. Six forty-five. Fifteen minutes. I'd told Cooper to wait until eight though, so hopefully he remembered that. It would be better for my mom. I sent him off a quick text just to make sure. Because of my strict charge to avoid him, I hadn't gone over the schedule with him since a week ago at milk shakes, with Iris listening in.

A low-grade headache pressed at the back of my skull and up into my temples. I hoped it stayed mild.

The other stations around me each had three or four people arranging and rearranging paintings and placards. I twisted my hands around each other, then smoothed my dress again. My mom had helped me put my hair up in a loose twist with strategic pieces left down around my face.

My paintings hung on the wall behind me like a backdrop. I adjusted one of the placards: *The Tree of Life.* Which was obviously the tree painting. I'd named all my paintings that week. The one of Cooper on the dunes I'd named *Fearless.* The spotlight from the stage I called *New Perspective.* The fish-spa fish I'd decided to call *Distorted.* And finally, the sunrise. For some reason that painting represented all the new things I had tried over the past several weeks with Cooper. A coming to life. That painting was my favorite, mostly because that morning had been my favorite, sitting there and taking it in. So I named the sunrise *The Heart List.*

I was excited for people to see the paintings. I was especially excited for my mom to see the theater one. It was like a premonition of tonight. She'd finally get to see me in the spotlight.

Mr. Wallace was making the final rounds. He was visiting each artist, asking them if there was anything else they needed. I knew the drill. I just hadn't been on this side of the drill before. When he reached me, he squeezed my hand. He looked a little more put together tonight. He had on a dark suit that wasn't quite as big as usual. His gray hair had been cut recently, giving him a more polished look.

"How are you feeling?" he asked.

"Excited."

His eyes flitted over my paintings. "Good luck," he said.

"Thanks."

"You should put your phone away. Try to be as professional as possible."

"Yes, I was planning on it. Thanks." I tucked it back into my purse and set my purse on the chair behind a screen I'd set up for my mom. I'd found the pretty painted screen in the back room and thought it would be a perfect place to escape if she needed a breather.

The doors opened seconds later, and then there were people. There were people walking around the museum looking at paintings. Looking at *my* paintings. I hoped I could keep my excited feet on the ground.

A familiar face came into my view.

"Elliot!" I said. I hadn't seen him since the party and hadn't texted him since talking to Tree Man.

"I didn't realize you were an artist featured here tonight," he said.

"I wasn't sure if it was actually happening either."

"You look great."

"Thanks." I stepped aside, because he was trying to peer around me to look at my paintings.

"These are amazing, Abby."

"Thank you." I followed him as he stepped in front of each one. "Have you ever entered your sculptures in a show like this?"

"No. I haven't. I should." He stood in front of the sunrise now. "I like what you did with color here. Cold to warm."

It was nice talking to someone my age who understood the nuances in art.

"Have you had a lot of people come by?" he asked.

"I've had a few that seemed interested. Lots of lookers."

Speaking of lookers, a well-dressed older couple came alongside Elliot to look at the sunrise piece. Some patrons were the silent type, and it was nerve-racking not hearing what they thought of my art—good or bad.

"It's amazing, right?" Elliot asked the man who was closest to him.

"Is it abstract or realism?" the man asked.

"It's abstract meets realism."

The man grunted a little, like he wasn't into twists on classic forms. Then they moved on.

"He's stupid," Elliot whispered.

"It's fine. Art is subjective, that's what makes it great," I said. "We each get to love or hate something on our own terms."

"Well said."

I turned away from my paintings to face the room again. My feet were killing me. "You haven't seen my family or Cooper around, have you?"

"Around here?"

I smiled. "No, at the McDonald's up the street. Of course around here."

"I haven't. You want me to go make a loop and see if I can find them?" He pointed to the second level, where the other half of the displays were set up.

"No. That's okay." They'd come find me once they were here.

"I'm going to finish my round then. Check out the other artists."

"Of course. Go. Tell me your favorite when you're done so I can look at it later."

"But art is subjective, Abby. You'll have to pick your own favorite." He winked at me.

I gave him a shove to help him on his way, and he smiled at me over his shoulder. Then I went back to waiting. After three more groups of people came by my display, I couldn't help myself, I snuck out my phone and slipped behind the screen.

My phone said it was already eight thirty. Only an hour and a half left of the show. There were three missed calls, all from our home number. None from Cooper. I texted him again: Where are you?! My mom and grandpa are waiting!

I pulled up the Find Your Friend app and tried to locate him, but it said *inaccessible*. It only said that when his phone was powered off or out of battery.

I quickly dialed the home number. Grandpa picked up after the second ring.

"Where is Cooper?" he asked.

"I don't know. I was calling you to find out."

"He hasn't been here," Grandpa said.

"How is Mom?"

"She's okay, but she does much better when things go like she meticulously rehearsed them in her head."

"I know. Cooper was sick Friday night. Yesterday

morning he said he was feeling better, but I haven't talked to him since then. I wonder if he took a turn for the worse."

I felt a presence to my left and looked up to see Mr. Wallace. I let out a short yelp of surprise. "I have to go," I said to Grandpa. "Can you try to call Cooper?"

"I'll try."

"Come even if he doesn't."

"Without Cooper we have no car. You have it."

I had forgotten that minor detail. "A cab?"

Grandpa gave an ironic laugh. "You think your mother would get in a cab?"

"No."

"Either way, Abby, have fun tonight. Don't pin all your success on your mom."

I hung up because Mr. Wallace was still there, still staring.

"I'm sorry," I said quickly. "My mom was supposed to come, and my friend, and I was getting worried. . . ." I trailed off when I realized he didn't care about my excuses. "I'm sorry."

"Please try not to show your age tonight, Abby. This isn't a show about parents seeing their kids' artwork."

Ouch. I nodded and stepped out from behind the screen. There was nobody at my station, but I went to stand by my paintings anyway.

Another half hour went by. At least that was my guess. I couldn't be certain without my phone. My excitement from before was melting to disappointment, and my head started to ache even more. I saw Elliot across the way, and I waved him over.

"What's up?" he asked.

"What time is it?"

He looked at a smart watch on his wrist. "Five after nine."

"There's less than an hour left. Cooper was supposed to get my mom. I have the car. Will you do me a favor?"

"Sure."

"Text Cooper for me." I had a feeling his phone wasn't on, but maybe it was just the Find Your Friend app that wasn't working. Or my phone was being weird. Or . . . something.

"What's his number?"

I recited it to him.

"What do you want me to say?"

"Say, Abby is looking for you. Where are you? She said that if you're not sick, she's going to break into the nearest science facility, steal their deadliest virus, and release it in your bedroom."

Elliot raised his eyebrows at me. I watched him type—Abby wants to know where you are—into his phone.

"That works too," I said.

We both stared at his phone, waiting for a reply. When nothing happened, I sighed.

"Excuse me," a voice from behind us said. "Are these your paintings?" I turned to see the woman looking at Elliot.

"No," he said at the same time as I said, "No, they're mine. Here, let me show them to you." As I walked her to the nearest one, out of the corner of my eye I caught Mr. Wallace staring in my direction. Had he seen that whole exchange? My grandpa was right, I needed to stop thinking about it and let tonight be about my paintings and not about a breakthrough for my mom . . . or Cooper and me. As I let both of those ideas slip to the floor, my heart followed suit.

THIRTY-ONE

As soon as the woman moved on to another artist, Mr. Wallace was at my side again. Elliot must've moved on as well, because he was nowhere to be seen.

"Abby, I'm disappointed," Mr. Wallace said. "Your father assured me you would be mature."

"My father? You know my father?"

"He emailed me. Didn't he tell you? I thought that's why you brought your paintings by last week."

"He . . . emailed you? That's why you picked me?"

"He said one of the paintings you were displaying was already sold, so it would be financially smart of the museum to allow an opportunity for the others to be seen. I meant to tell you earlier that you should put a Sold sticker next to the placard of the one that is sold."

My dad had lied to get me into the show tonight? My paintings hadn't earned their own way in?

"You have a patron." Mr. Wallace nodded behind me, then left me standing there with that new information swirling around in my head and trying to drain out my eyes. I sniffed back the tears and joined the older gentleman looking at the painting of Cooper on the sand dunes. The painting looked so juvenile now. Nobody else at the show tonight had a quad on their canvases.

"My grandson would love this," the man said.

I nodded numbly. "It's my friend. He rides."

"So does my grandson. How much?"

He was the first person to ask me my prices and I became tongue-tied. This man was buying this for a kid. My eyes slid to the fish painting next to it. My paintings—loved only by children. Maybe they *were* immature. I suddenly felt embarrassed. Like I was selling stuffed animals while everyone else was selling live exotic ones. Like I was the only amateur in a room full of professionals. Maybe Mr. Wallace really had been protecting me by telling me no. I wasn't ready. My paintings weren't ready.

"Young lady?" the man asked, sympathy in his voice. "Are you okay?"

"Um. Yes. I . . . uh . . . I'm not sure how much I should sell that for." I had researched and priced my paintings before the show, but now those prices seemed too high.

"Should I make you an offer?"

I turned to face him fully. I could do this. He wanted this painting, I was going to sell it to him. Just as I opened my mouth to speak, my eyes collided with a pin on the lapel of his suit coat—a US flag alongside an army one.

He knew my dad. My dad had sent him here. If my dad had been willing to lie to Mr. Wallace to get me in the show, I had no doubt he talked some of his friends into coming to support me. He probably even told them he'd buy a painting for them. Anger coursed through me.

"No. That one isn't for sale, actually." I'd planned to give it to Cooper, and if this was just someone my dad had told to come in, I wasn't about to let it go. Where was Cooper? I was worried about him. His parents were still out of town, and his sister had gone to a friend's today. Was he at home burning up with a fever?

"Oh. Okay. Someone beat me to it I guess," the man said. He handed me his card. "If you ever paint another one featuring a quad, give me a call."

"Okay. Thanks."

He left and I paced, regardless of the blisters I now had on both feet. I paced and looked at the door. Before, I'd been begging time to slow down, and now I just wanted tonight to be over. My phone was buzzing. It rattled my bag on the chair behind the screen. At this point, I didn't care what Mr. Wallace said. I pulled it out. Elliot's name flashed across the screen and I furrowed my brow in confusion.

"Hello?"

"Hey." It was Grandpa, and now I really was confused. "Thanks for sending Elliot, but she can't do it. Take lots of pictures for us."

"Elliot's there?" I whispered back.

"Yes."

"You can't talk Mom into coming?"

"I've tried and it's not working."

"Then *you* come."

"Abby, I can't leave your mom like this. She's a mess now."

"What?" I asked in disbelief. "She doesn't want *you* to come either?"

"It's not that she doesn't want me to come—"

"Is she telling you to come?"

"I don't think I should leave her like this."

"Okay," I snapped and hung up the phone, angry tears stinging my eyes.

I didn't take pictures. They could see all the paintings when I got home. They would all still be mine.

Cooper, are you okay? I tried one last time.

My phone said five minutes left. Five minutes. I counted to one hundred, then one hundred again and again, until Mr. Wallace stood by the door, saying good-bye to the last guest. Then as quickly as possible, I cleaned up my station, making several trips out to the car to store my paintings.

"Abby," Mr. Wallace called as I passed him with my last armload.

"I can't talk right now!" I answered over my shoulder. "I have to go. Emergency." I didn't look to see his face. I knew it would register disappointment.

At the car I took off my heels and threw them behind the driver's seat. My paintings were tucked away in the back. I started the car, my hands shaking. I made it to Cooper's in record time. His house was dark. I parked across the street.

First I rang the doorbell. I didn't wait long before I was at his window though. "Cooper! Are you okay?"

I pried it open like I had before and climbed in. His room was pitch-black. I clicked on his desk lamp to see his bed was empty. I tore through the rest of his house, even checking his parents' room. There was nobody there. The worry that had driven me to his house melted first into relief and then into anger. If he wasn't here, where was he?

I could wait. I sat on his bed. It smelled like him, so I moved to the floor by the window. Ten thirty came and went. Then eleven. My phone buzzed.

The text was from Grandpa: Are you still at the museum?

No. Out. I'll be home late.

Avoiding them right now felt like the best way to punish them. I knew I shouldn't have been mad at my mom. She had an illness. One I realized now that she obviously needed help for. But my brain and my emotions weren't playing well together. Because I *was* mad. I was mad at everyone really. Cooper, obviously. Grandpa, for not being able to talk Mom into coming and then not coming himself when he couldn't. Dad, for forcing it to happen at all when I hadn't earned it. I leaned my head back, letting it hit the wall. That sent a painful jolt through my already aching head. I rubbed my temples and thought about getting some aspirin from the medicine cabinet in Cooper's bathroom but couldn't find the energy to stand.

I hadn't shut the window all the way, and a slight breeze played with my hair. I wondered if I should call the police. Had Cooper gotten in an accident? My mind wanted him to have a really good excuse for tonight. He would have a really good excuse.

My mind was also conjuring up something I had tried my hardest not to think about. But all that hurt I had pushed deep down inside me was rising to the surface as this new hurt filled me up.

Last year. The fateful night on the beach. Cooper and I had been hanging out after celebrating his one millionth win. Justin and Rachel hadn't been able to make it to the after-party for one reason or another. But it didn't matter. Cooper was high on life and his smile felt like the center of mine. I had realized, quite suddenly in that moment, that I lived for his smile. That every time I saw it, my own smile couldn't help but appear. And I knew then and there that I'd do anything to see it. Happiness bubbled in my chest all fizzy and intoxicating. "We're good together," I'd said.

He'd met my stare, and his smile slowly fell away. I thought it had been because he was recognizing the seriousness of the moment, of what I was about to say, so I'd barreled forward. "I think I love you."

His expression went darker, and then I knew. He didn't feel the same way.

He'd punched my shoulder playfully and said, "You too, you're a great friend."

I hoped the dark night hid my red cheeks. I managed to keep the sting in my eyes from turning into tears and I forced myself to laugh. "You should see your face right now. Did you think I meant as more than a friend?"

His face went from horror to levity faster than I'd finished the sentence. He laughed too and let it go as easy as that.

I was pulled out of last year's memory by a car door shutting out front, followed by laughter. It was crystal clear through the open window.

"I had fun today," Cooper said. "Thanks for the surprise."

"Of course." That was Iris. "Thanks for coming so last-minute. I'm sorry about your phone."

"It's okay. I'll try the rice thing."

Cooper must've started walking away because Iris said, "Hey! Don't I get a hug or anything?" There was a pause and then a squeal. Obviously Cooper had picked her up in a hug. I forced myself not to cry. I was too mad. I couldn't let hurt take over.

When her car drove away, I stood up and tugged down the bottom of my dress. Why was I still here? I could just climb back out the window and confront him the next day, when my emotions were more reined in. I didn't.

Cooper walked into his room and flipped on the overhead light. Then he let out a startled yell followed by a laugh. "You scared me."

I didn't respond.

"Did you miss me?" He took in my dress. "Wow. You

look hot. Did you have a date tonight?"

Was he really asking that? He *forgot*? "No. I had that whole art show thing. Nothing big."

His smile slid off his face and his brows went down. "No, that's tomorrow."

"Really? Huh. I guess nobody told all the artists and guests who showed up tonight." My voice was like ice.

"You said it was on the twenty-first."

"Today *is* the twenty-first, Cooper."

"No, it's the twentieth, right? Saturday?"

I snorted out an insincere laugh. I wanted to rip down all the pictures from his wall and shred them to pieces because the anger throbbing in my chest was so intense.

He shook his head. "Is it really Sunday? I'm a total jerk. My phone fell into a tide pool today. It's completely busted. You haven't been texting me at all this week. I'm not used to zero reminders about things."

He was blaming this on *me*? Something washed over me. It started at my scalp and poured down my body in a numbing wave. It wasn't exactly peace, but it was acceptance. Resolution, maybe. "I'm done," I said, and I found that I truly meant it.

"I must've lost a day when I was sick," he continued, without acknowledging what I'd said. "It's summer. The days all blend together. Plus, I think Iris said it was

Saturday this morning. She must've been confused too."

"Oh, I'm sure she was *so* confused."

"Why was that dripping sarcasm?"

I held up my hands in surrender. "No reason, Cooper. I'm done."

"What does that mean? Why do you keep saying that?"

"This one-sided thing isn't working. I can't do it anymore. Have a good life." I either had to climb out the window and look like a major buffoon with my short dress riding up to my waist or walk by him out the door he was still blocking and maintain my resolve.

I sensed it deep in my chest. I could walk by him.

He didn't move when I reached the door. I looked up at him. His eyes were pained. It cracked my heart a little more.

"I'm sorry, Abby. Please don't walk away like this. Let me make it up to you." This was the Cooper that could normally get me to do anything. His pleading eyes, his charming smile, his persuasive voice. It didn't work this time.

"Cooper. Move."

"Abby, please don't leave like this. How was the show? Does your mom hate me for not picking her up?"

"She didn't come."

He pushed his fingers against his closed eyes. "Oh no. I'm so sorry. I'm a huge jerk. The biggest one in existence."

"Move," I growled.

He reached out for my hand and I yanked it away violently. He wasn't used to that from me, I could see it in his surprised expression. I didn't ask him to move again. I pushed him aside and fled.

I made it to my car and drove down the block before I let the tears come. And they came.

THIRTY-TWO

Mom and Grandpa were waiting up for me when I got home. Mom was a mess. Her eyes were puffy, her makeup washed away. I didn't want to hear another round of apologies. It didn't seem to matter what I wanted tonight, because apologies were what I got.

She collapsed on me, her hands around my shoulders, her face in my neck. "I'm so sorry."

"I don't want to talk about this tonight." I pushed her off. I never pushed her away, and now anger *and* guilt pressed against my chest so hard that I couldn't breathe.

Mom let out a sob.

"You need help," I spit out.

She nodded. "I know."

"I need to go to bed." I knew I wouldn't be sleeping anytime soon. I really just needed to get out of this room before I said more things that I could never take back. I whirled around and stormed down the hall.

Grandpa, who hadn't said a word, followed after me.

"What?" I snapped.

"Do you need to talk about it?" His voice was calm, like that would make this all okay.

"I need to be left alone."

"You're mad."

"Yes, I'm mad!"

"You should be. I would be."

"Good. Because I am."

"I'm sorry she couldn't make it."

"I'm mad at *you*, Grandpa! You!"

"I couldn't leave her."

"Really? *Really?* That's the excuse you're going with? You. The one who's always trying to push her to do more. This time it was too much?"

"I'd never seen her quite this bad, Abby."

"Then maybe you could've asked Elliot to stay with her. Maybe you could've left her for just thirty minutes and come and shown me some support! This was an important night, and it's like you didn't even care about me."

"I care about you. You know that."

"Well, you certainly didn't show it! Now please get out of my room." I knew half of this tirade was for Cooper, but at least half of it was for my grandpa too, so I didn't call him back when he lowered his head and left.

Somehow yelling at him didn't make me feel any better. My head was pounding, and my eyes felt like they were on fire.

I should've waited until I had calmed down to send an email to my dad. But he deserved some of this anger too. The email was short, but true to how I felt.

> Dad, never ever lie or bully someone into including your daughter in anything again. Let her earn her own achievements.

I hit Send and closed my laptop. Then I went to my bathroom, downed two aspirin, and crawled into bed.

My phone woke me the next morning with lots of buzzing. I sat up. I'd slept in my clothes and makeup. My eyelashes felt clumpy. I looked at my phone. There were exactly thirty-two texts from Cooper. Guess he'd fixed his phone somehow. Most of them were just the words *I'm sorry* over and over and over again. I had a text from Lacey as well: You didn't send me a report. That must mean it went exceptionally well.

I groaned and got out of bed. I took a long and very hot shower. My skin was red and splotchy when I climbed out. In the twenty minutes I'd been in the bathroom Cooper had sent five more texts. I ignored those as well.

There was no reply to the email I'd written my dad. It wasn't like he had time to just sit around checking his email. I knew it might take a few days. I hoped I didn't regret sending it by then.

I steeled myself and went out to the kitchen. Grandpa sat at the table. I looked around but didn't see my mom anywhere.

"She's still sleeping. She had an emotional night."

"Didn't we all," I mumbled.

"Can we talk about it?"

"Not yet, Grandpa, please not yet." I felt dizzy and leaned against the counter.

"Can you at least tell me if Cooper is okay? I was worried last night when he didn't show up."

"I never want to talk about Cooper again."

He raised his eyebrows.

"No. Really. I'm done with Cooper. Forever." I knew this was my emotions speaking. If it had been Rachel or Justin, I would've been mad at them for a few days and moved on. But it wasn't Rachel or Justin. It was Cooper. The guy I loved. And that love was now making forgiveness feel impossible.

"That's . . . um . . . forever?" Grandpa asked.

My headache was back and my head throbbed. Grandpa narrowed his eyes at me, then reached forward and felt my head.

"You're burning up."

"Cooper," I growled.

"I don't think heartbreak causes fevers," Grandpa said.

"No. He was sick." On top of everything he gave me his bug. Grandpa dug some medicine out of the cupboard, and I took it and went back to bed.

Cooper called and texted all day long. I had to turn off my phone at one point.

Mom hovered in my doorway later that day. "How are you feeling?" She stared at me with a pained expression that I knew had nothing to do with my illness and everything to do with her guilt.

"Not great."

"Can you give me a play-by-play of the night?" she asked.

"No. I can't. I feel like I've enabled you for a long time," I said. This was something I'd been thinking about since the night before too. "And I'm not up for talking right now."

"Grandpa told me about Cooper."

"Of course he did."

She pretended not to hear me. "You have a big heart,

Abby. I know you'll get through this."

I felt like I had no heart at the moment. Like a certain someone had ripped it out and eaten it. Okay, maybe he hadn't eaten it, but he fed it to some rabid dogs or something. Last night, I had been prepared to hand him my heart. I was going to put myself out there again. And this time, he didn't even show up at all, not even as a friend. He was supposed to be my best friend, but a best friend wouldn't have dropped the ball on such an important night for me. I wasn't sure what hurt more—realizing I really lost the guy I loved or realizing I lost my best friend. Probably the second.

Mom left me alone, and I stared at the walls of my room. My phone lay on the nightstand next to me, full of unanswered texts from Cooper. I needed a distraction. I texted Lacey: **Worst night ever.**

My phone rang and I thought I was going to have to avoid another Cooper call, but it was Lacey. I picked it up. "When do you get back?" was how I answered.

"In two days."

"I hope I last until then."

"Tell me everything."

And I did.

The next day and fifty-four more unanswered texts from Cooper, I was sitting on the floor in my room wielding a pair of unruly knitting needles I had bought, when Grandpa knocked on my open door.

"Come in."

The door opened wider with a squeak. "Hey, you feeling better?"

"Physically? Yes." I could tell my fever was gone and the headache I'd had for the last couple of days was gone with it. But anger still glowed in my chest like an evil that needed to be exorcised.

"What are you doing?" he asked.

"I'm working on the last four items on my list." I held up the yarn and needles. Lance had made this look so easy, but it wasn't. "Well, three, technically, since the reciprocated-love thing isn't happening anytime soon."

"The heart list? I thought that was only for the art show."

"No. It was to improve my painting, and that hasn't happened yet."

"Of course it did. You got into the show."

"Dad wrote Mr. Wallace. It's why he let me display my paintings."

He cringed. "Sorry, kid."

If I never heard the word *sorry* again it would be too soon.

Grandpa moved to where my list hung on my wall. "Is there something on the list about lopsided knitting?"

My phone buzzed from the ground next to me. I looked at the screen.

Abby, please. Talk to me.

I growled and flipped it over.

"Did you need anything else?" I asked Grandpa curtly.

"Nope." And with that, he left my room.

Yes, I definitely needed a good exorcism.

THIRTY-THREE

It was Saturday and officially the longest I'd ever gone without seeing Cooper in over a year. Six days. That number bounced around in my head as I ate breakfast. As I brushed my teeth. As I powered on my computer. Other numbers were in my head too. Like ten. That was how many voice mails Cooper had left me in six days. I'd listened to the first two, but when I realized they were just repeats of the night in his room—*I'm sorry I mixed up my days, I'm a jerk, please forgive me*—I started deleting them right when I saw them. Two hundred and eleven . . . and counting. That was the number of texts he'd sent. Three. The number of times he'd shown up at my door and my grandpa sent him away. Twenty-three. The number of days it had been since I'd painted anything. And I still didn't feel like picking up a brush or going into the museum. Four. The number of times I'd called in sick this week to work. I didn't want to face Mr. Wallace. What was I going to tell him about my horrible behavior that night?

I checked my email. Still no message from my dad. Had he even gotten the email I'd sent? Between not talking to my grandpa, my mom, my dad, or Cooper, I'd never felt more alone.

I picked up my phone and called one of the only people I wasn't mad at.

"Hello?" Lacey answered.

"I need to get out of my house."

"Well, you're in luck. We were just on our way to an adventure. I'll text you the address. Meet me there."

I didn't even ask her to give me more details. I got up, got ready for the first time in six days, and left.

There were three other cars in the parking lot of the abandoned church on R Street when I pulled in. I parked next to the BMW, which I knew was Lacey's. I still wasn't sure why this was where she said to meet, but at this point, I was up for anything. I was trying to replace bad habits with good ones. Going anywhere without Cooper was a good habit. Six days. Six days.

I jumped out of my car and hopped my way up the weedy stone pathway to the front doors. Stained glass windows that were missing several panes of glass surrounded the doors, which were nailed shut with several long boards, and created a colorful mosaic in the dirt. I knocked, not sure if I expected someone to answer but not sure how to get in.

Nobody came, so I walked around the building. On the backside I found another door, a missing board providing a space just big enough to crawl through. I took a deep breath and dived in. I pulled my phone out to light the area.

"Hello?" I called, in more of a whisper than a shout. Nobody answered. The whole place smelled like stale dirt. I stepped over and around broken bits of colored glass until I found a large room in the center of the building.

"Lacey?" I asked, seeing shadows of people in the middle. The scene made my heart pick up speed and I was seconds away from turning and hightailing it out of there.

"Abby?" her voice sounded loud in the otherwise quiet room.

"Yes."

"Come over."

I did. "What are you guys doing here?"

"We just got here. Give me a sec." She clicked a button, and a lantern glowed to life.

"Am I the sacrificial lamb in some weird hazing ritual you all have?"

"No, nothing like that. It was that thing I was telling you about. Perspective outings. We like to look up weird places to visit near us. It helps stretch our creative brains. Gives us new experiences. All that."

Ah. Right. She had told me she did this. Like their own version of the heart list. "Got it." I lowered myself to the ground next to Lacey, disturbing some dust that immediately made me sneeze.

Lacey patted my back, like that was the correct response to a sneeze, then said, "Abby, have you met Lydia, Kara, Nick, and Colby?"

It was hard to see their faces in the shadows. "I met you two at the party."

Kara's teeth glowed with a smile.

"So what do you do once you're here?" I asked.

"Tell stories. Improv a bit," one of the guys said. Nick? Colby? I wasn't sure which was which.

"What's improv?" I asked.

"It's a theater term that basically means to make things up as we go along."

"Are you in drama?" Nick/Colby asked.

"No. Art."

"Art. This is a good place for an artist to get inspired too," Kara said.

I looked around. Kara was right, this was a place that could inspire someone. Everything from the dusty pews to the statue of Mary up front glowed a soft yellow in the lantern's light. Muted evening sunlight tried to permeate the dirt-stained glass windows that bordered the room. An old piano sat up front, half of its white keys missing, creating the appearance of a gap-toothed smile. For the first time in a while my fingers itched for a paintbrush. Remembering the art show, and my poor outcome there, quickly took that feeling away. I shrugged. "Yeah, it's cool."

"Update," Lacey said, squeezing my arm, like she knew I was ready to be out of the spotlight. "I got a callback."

One of the girls shrieked and it echoed off the walls and sent dust showering on our heads.

Colby/Nick (the one who hadn't spoken yet) threw his arms over his head. "Lydia, come on. You want us to get caught?"

She covered her mouth with her hand. "Sorry. That's just so exciting. When do you go in? What part are you reading for?"

"Next week. And I'm reading for the lead girl."

Now they were all a clamor of voices and excitement.

I leaned over. "I'm sorry I didn't ask you. I've been too caught up in my own problems."

"It's okay, I understand."

"Congrats," I said. "That's really exciting."

"Thanks." She smiled, then put her hands up, and everyone went silent. "Okay. Let's get started. Everyone pick one object in this room, and you're going to tell its origin story."

I was going to be horrible at this game. Game? Is that what they called it? Exercise? Whatever its official title, it was not my strength. I picked the piano, since I'd already given it human character traits in my head, and told the story of a girl who got turned into a piano by an evil queen. They had tons of follow-up questions, like I had actually thought this through at all. Once I was done with my part, I was happy to listen to their much more creative stories about women frozen in time and benches made of gold and keys that unlocked portals. They were fully realized stories, with details and twists.

"Did you make that up just now?" I asked Lydia when she was done.

"Yes."

"How?"

"Practice, I guess."

It was more than the stories themselves that impressed me. It was the confident way they told them. Like they didn't care what anyone thought.

I wasn't sure how long we were there, but the shadows became more pronounced and the stained glass no longer shone at all when we stood and I dusted off my jeans. Lacey linked arms with me on the way out.

"Thanks for letting me come," I said.

"Anytime."

I was the fourth one to climb through the hole to the outside, and it took me a moment to realize that the three who had climbed out before me were staring at something in the distance. I thought maybe we'd been caught. That the cops had shown up and we were going to get hauled away for breaking and entering. Even though technically there was no breaking. Only entering. But it was worse than cops.

It was Cooper.

He held something I couldn't make out in his hand. A box with a handle of sorts.

My not-quite-weaned heart did a flip.

How had he known I was here? It took my brain two seconds to remember the stupid app on our phones—Find Your Friend. My phone had tattled on me. I needed to delete that app immediately.

Lacey had climbed out of the hole behind me, and

she saw Cooper too. "Do you want me to tell him to go away? I'll go tell him right now."

"No, I'll talk to him."

She gave me a disbelieving look.

"No, really, I'm in no danger. I'm dead inside now."

Her disbelief turned into sympathy. "Come to my house when you're done, okay? We'll eat chocolate and watch a movie about killing boys. Is there a movie like that? We'll find one." She squeezed my arm. "Be strong."

I smiled, then watched as all my new friends got into their cars and drove away. My gaze went back to Cooper. Six days strong. I'd have to start the count over after this. I walked slowly until I stood ten feet away from him. There I stopped. I may have been stronger, but I didn't need to smell him too.

I could feel the grime on my hands and face from the building we'd just emerged from. I wondered if I was covered in dirt. Then I remembered I shouldn't care.

Cooper looked at the building behind me, and I knew he wanted to ask me what we had been doing in there. I could see it in his familiar questioning brow. He didn't ask. He held up the box in his hand—four glass bottles in a carrier.

"Chocolate milk," he said. "Chocolate milk makes everything better."

I nodded and swallowed. "It does."

"Permission to approach enemy lines," he said, holding out the box.

I sensed my old habit taking over—the one that wanted everything to go back to how it was. The one that wanted to patch things up and pretend everything was fine. I resisted. "Cooper. I can't do this."

"When?"

"I don't know. I need time. You're not giving me time."

"I gave you six days. That's a long time. I feel terrible. Do you think I wanted to miss your show? I didn't. I wanted to see it. You're my best friend in the world."

"I know you think you wanted to see it. But the thing is, Cooper, when you truly want to do something, you do it. It's that simple."

"I got the days mixed up."

"Exactly."

"You're not going to forgive me." He said it as a statement.

"I don't know. Maybe. I need time."

"Time for what?"

"To stop loving you, Cooper," I blurted out. "To get over you. To change."

His eyebrows dipped down, but so did his chin.

My breathing was shallow, my cheeks red, but he

didn't say anything. "You remember that night on the beach a year ago?"

"I remember."

"The night I told you I loved you and then played it off as a joke." I realized, as I stared at him, holding those chocolate milk bottles and looking at the sidewalk, that he knew it hadn't been a joke all along.

"I wish you would've told me that you knew a year ago. Then maybe all of this would be resolved by now. I put myself out there and you let me take it back so easily."

I hadn't been angry that day, or even in the year since, at how that all played out. I had been more embarrassed and hurt. Now I was angry. For the last year he knew, and he hadn't even given me the courtesy to talk it through with me, to let me explain or tell him why we should be together or why I loved him. He basically blew it off. Dismissed my feelings.

Tears drained down my face now as I stared at him. I felt all the hate and resentment draining out with them.

"I . . . I don't know what to say," he said. "I can tell you I was a jerk again. I can tell you I handled that all wrong."

I don't know what I hoped would happen once the truth was finally out there. In the very corner of my brain, I hoped that this was when he realized he actually *did* love me. That the horror I'd seen on his face that night at the beach was because it was surprising, not because it wasn't reciprocated. That his feelings had grown over this year. That being without me this week was so hard for him that he realized he must love me. But that wasn't going to happen.

"Cooper. I'm letting go. I have to let you go, regardless of how much that scares me."

I watched his Adam's apple bob with a hard swallow. He gave a single nod, then set the box of chocolate milk on the ground in front of him and took a wobbly step back.

I held my ground. I held it while he walked away backward, not breaking eye contact with me the whole time. I held it when he climbed into his car and the engine roared to life. I even stayed perfectly still while he backed out of his parking spot and drove away. When his car disappeared around the corner, I sank to the ground.

THIRTY-FOUR

I showed up on Lacey's doorstep. I hated to bring her down after the good news that she'd delivered earlier, so I tried my best to plaster a smile on my face.

"Oh, please," she said. "I saw you try out for a play. You're not a very good actress."

I hiccuped out a laugh and she pulled me inside.

"You have chocolate milk," she said. "Wait, is that what Cooper was holding? *Four quarts* of chocolate milk?"

I nodded. "Chocolate milk makes everything better."

She swiped the carrier from me and took it to the sink.

I thought she was going to pull out some glasses right then, but instead she uncapped a bottle and began pouring it down the drain.

I gasped. "Lacey, that's like liquid gold."

"It's like liquid poison. We are purging ourselves of Cooper." The empty bottle clanked on the counter, and she got the next one and began pouring.

"Can we at least deliver it to needy children?"

"Do you hear that?" she asked. We went quiet and the *glug glug* sound of large amounts of liquid making its way through a small opening rang out.

"All I hear is you pouring chocolate milk down the drain."

"Exactly. That's the sound you need to remember. The sound of freedom."

I shook my head and couldn't help but laugh. "*That's* the sound of freedom?"

"Those words sounded better in my head."

I stopped her from uncapping the next bottle. "Let's save some for your family. I bet your little sister and brother would love to drink this liquid poison."

"True." She opened the fridge and put the remaining two bottles inside. "I found the perfect movie for us."

"What?"

"It's called *Body Count.* You'll like it. Lots of death and revenge. Then later we should have a bonfire. Do you have any Cooper things you need to burn?"

I hugged her. "Thank you for this."

She hugged me back. "I'm sorry he hurt you."

I shook my head, feeling the tears threaten again. I pulled away and changed the subject. "I like your friends."

She led me to the living room. "They liked you too. So, welcome to the world of having more than one friend group. It's a great place to be for the inevitable moments like this."

"Moments like what?"

"When you want to murder one of them, of course."

"Of course." I looked at my hands, which still felt grimy. "Can I use your bathroom?"

"Yes, down the hall, second door on the right."

The bathroom mirror proved I was in worse shape than I thought. Dirt streaked my cheeks, turned more mud-like from the tears I'd added to it earlier. I pulled the handle on the faucet and scrubbed my hands and face with water. Then I patted dry with a hand towel. I leaned against the counter and took several deep breaths. A single drop of water clung to the end of the faucet, and I watched it drop. Then I reached for the handle on the sink and twisted. Water poured out and down the drain with a glug.

"The sound of freedom," I whispered.

Lacey was settled on the couch when I rejoined her.

"How are you feeling?" she asked.

"Okay. I'll be fine." And I would be. Eventually.

She pushed Play. The first scene proved the title of the movie was an appropriate one. "Maybe *that* should be the real sound of freedom," Lacey said, imitating gunfire.

"It's much less pathetic, but maybe that's why it's not as fitting."

Lacey gave a small laugh. "You got this. And I'm here for you. You'll be on to your next victim in no time."

The next day I stood in the center of my room taking in everything I chose to surround myself with. Most of the clippings and pictures were years old. I began taking things off my walls one by one, sorting them into piles. One pile was "definitely throw away," one was to file in my desk drawer, and the other pile would be to hang back up on my wall in a new order so my space wouldn't feel so stale.

Like Cooper, I had Polaroid pictures of us on my walls too. Ones I had either stolen from his wall or he'd given me after he snapped them. I put them in the "file away" pile for now.

My phone rang. It was an out-of-area number. I knew what that meant.

I answered. "Dad?"

"It's me," he said. His voice always sounded far away when he called. Which was appropriate, because he was. Very far. "You still mad at me?"

I considered his question. The anger that had brewed all week was mostly gone, but that didn't mean I wasn't upset at what he had done. "You thought if you gave me some time, I wouldn't be?"

"I called you as soon as I could. We had drills this week. So that's a yes? You are still mad."

"I'm not happy that you reached out to Mr. Wallace without my permission."

"If I see my baby girl in need of my intervention, I'm not going to just sit back and not take action," he said.

I had been willing to forgive him, but he was being unapologetic. That made it harder. "Dad, I'm telling you I don't want you to do that. Especially without talking to me. If I had asked you to, it would've been one thing. But I didn't."

"Well, I did it."

"I know! And you may have ruined a relationship for me with the person who I need to write a recommendation letter."

"He better still write that letter."

I growled and hung up the phone. Why were the men in my life so pigheaded? I'd never hung up on my dad before, and I felt guilty immediately. It wasn't like my dad got unlimited phone time.

My Cooper wound felt fresh again. I ripped the heart list off the wall and threw it into the "throw away" pile. That list had been pointless.

A few minutes later my door squeaked open.

"Honey." It was my mom.

I turned to face her.

"Your father has something to say to you." She held up her phone.

I took it from her. "Yes?"

"I'm sorry," he said.

I sighed. My mom was good for him. I wished he were home more, because they really did balance each other out.

"Thank you," I said. "That's all I wanted to hear."

"I know. Sometimes I just want to protect you, and it's hard for me to remember you're not a child anymore."

"I know. I'm glad I have a dad who wants to protect me, but let's wait for me to call for help first, okay?"

"So I don't need to beat up Cooper when I get home?"

He knew what happened with Cooper too. I looked at my mom with narrow eyes, and she acted innocent.

"No. I took care of that on my own."

"You beat him up?" he asked.

I laughed, but then stopped. "Yes, Dad. I think maybe I did."

"I found something for you out here."

"You did?"

"I was going to wait until I got home to show you, but when we hang up, I'll email you a picture."

"Okay."

"Love you, kid."

"Love you too."

We hung up, and I waited two minutes to log onto my email. My dad was true to his word—he'd sent an email. The only thing it contained was an attached picture. I clicked on the image. A small gray stone resting on the palm of his hand filled the screen. It formed a lopsided heart. He'd found a heart rock, after all. I swallowed hard and smiled.

After throwing away, filing away, and rehanging my piles, I knew I could no longer avoid work and Mr. Wallace if I wanted to keep my job.

He was in his office when I arrived at the museum. He had done some cleaning of his own and the room looked bare.

"Hi," I said, trying to be as humble as possible.

"Abby, are you feeling better?"

"Yes, for a while now, actually. I've been avoiding you."

He shook his head, but a smile took over his face.

"You're always very honest."

"I'm sorry for how I behaved last Sunday night. And I'm sorry my dad bullied you into letting me be in the show."

He sighed and stood. "Come in. Have a seat."

I did as he asked.

"He didn't bully me into it. I was already on the verge. And your paintings showed amazing growth."

"You think?"

"You still have things to learn, but yes. I hope you haven't decided to leave us. I really value your work here."

"I don't want to leave. I love being surrounded by art."

"Good. I have you on the schedule for tomorrow. Are you going to be able to make it?"

"Yes. Absolutely. And do you think . . ."

"Yes?"

"I want to go to a winter art program. Do you think you can write me a letter of recommendation?"

"I'd love to."

"Thank you."

THIRTY-FIVE

There were four weeks left of summer, and those weeks stretched before me like an undeserved prison sentence. With Rachel and Justin still gone, I was worried I'd have nothing but time to think about this. To think about Cooper and the failed art show and my still-strained relationship with my mom and grandpa. I wondered if Cooper had told Rachel or Justin what had happened. I wondered if we'd have to split up our friend group when school started or if I'd be able to get through these feelings of hurt and anger. My life was a mess.

But at least Lacey kept true to her word. She said she'd

be there for me, and she was. She invited me to parties and perspective-shifting outings and late-night food runs. Plus, Mr. Wallace put me back on the schedule, and I worked well past my scheduled hours.

Two weeks had passed and the gaping hole in my life wasn't getting any smaller, but it was easier to walk around it these days. I wondered if Cooper had a hole in his life too. He hadn't texted or called me once since the night outside the abandoned church building. He was giving me time. Just like I'd asked.

I tried not to think about if it was the right decision. I tried to be in the moment. And in this moment, I was riding in the passenger seat in Lacey's car. We were heading to Elliot's house. I'd asked her to go with me to check out his art. It was hot. Sweat was forming behind my knees and beading along my upper lip.

"Is there a reason the AC is not on?" I asked as humid air blowing in from the cracked windows did nothing to cool me.

"Yes, it's good to experience discomfort sometimes. It helps me channel that emotion better when performing."

"So all your life is a stage?"

"Pretty much."

I smiled and turned my focus back to the window just in time to see we were passing Cooper's neighborhood. I squinted my eyes, like I had gained the ability to see through houses. I had to literally clench my jaw to keep myself from asking Lacey if we could drive by his house.

We passed successfully only to come upon the now-empty field where the big hundred-year-old tree used to stand. They'd torn it down. The sight hit me in the gut. I placed my hand on the window. Poor Lance.

Lacey was asking me something, I realized. I needed to not let my mind wander so much. I looked at her, focused on the words she was saying.

". . . stopped seeing her?"

"What?" I asked, knowing I missed way too much of that question to try to fake an answer.

"I was talking to Kendra, who was talking to Delaney, who apparently knows Iris's older sister, and she said that Cooper broke it off with Iris. Is that true?"

My mouth opened and closed once before I said, "I don't know."

"Really? So no social media updates from him?"

"I haven't looked."

"Wow. I'm impressed."

She shouldn't have been. When I wasn't forcing myself to go out with her, I was working or sleeping. "Yes, I'm the queen of self-control."

"So are you happy about the Iris/Cooper breakup news?"

"Should I be?" It just made things worse, actually,

because now I knew he had nobody. At least I had Lacey. Who had Cooper been hanging out with? Justin and Rachel would be home soon, but they weren't home now.

"I wondered if I should tell you or not. I thought maybe I shouldn't, but then I thought, if I were you, I'd want to know."

"I'm glad to know, but it doesn't change anything."

"No, it doesn't." She nodded like she was the one that needed to be convinced, not me.

Elliot lived beachfront. I should've known this, after all his talk about hiring private teachers and worrying about sounding pretentious, but I was still surprised. His house was stunning. Ivy climbed redbrick walls and bright flowers filled boxes beneath windows, all with the backdrop of the ocean.

"Wow," Lacey said. "Does Elliot seem a little more attractive all of a sudden?"

I smacked her arm.

"What?" she asked, laughing.

We exited the car and walked the stone stepway up to the house, where a gnome statue sat in a flowerpot to greet us. Its expression seemed to warn us away. I wondered if Elliot had sculpted it.

Lacey didn't care about the gnome's warning. She rang the doorbell.

Elliot had a much friendlier expression when he

answered the door. "Hi. Welcome, ladies. Come in."

He stepped aside. His house was just as charming inside as it was out. Someone with an artist's eye had decorated. There were benches tucked in nooks with eclectic mismatched pillows and paintings on every wall and shelves filled with colorful glass shapes and twisted metal and foreign masks. There was something to look at everywhere, and yet it didn't feel cluttered.

"My mom loves to collect things," he said, noticing my gaze.

"She has great taste," I said. "Are any of these your pieces?"

"No. There's a room devoted to me. The Elliot shrine, I call it." He said it in a joking manner, but I could tell it was to hide some embarrassment.

He led us farther into the house, and every room we encountered was more beautifully decorated than the one before. The kitchen was my favorite. The cabinets were a pale yellow and the countertops a brighter shade. The walls were stamped tin. It seemed like it shouldn't work together, but it did. Especially with the pops of colorful dishes on open shelves.

"I wouldn't leave my house if I were you," I said. "I could paint in here all day."

"Could you? You're welcome to come over and paint anytime."

Maybe I would. I still hadn't picked up a brush. It had been over a month now. I needed something to jolt me out of this slump, and maybe this house would help me.

"Can we see your shrine?" I asked.

He ducked his head, his cheeks reddening. "I guess that's what you're here for."

He had described the room right. His pieces were set on shelves on every wall, spotlights shining down on them from the ceiling. But I could see why his parents were proud. They were amazing. I slowly walked around the room, studying each carefully made piece. There were trees and faces and intricately carved shapes and vases, and on and on.

"Is the chain-yourself-to-your-art piece in here somewhere?" I asked.

"You've chained yourself to your art?" Lacey asked.

"No," he said. "I haven't. We were discussing if we had ever made any pieces that we would defend with our lives."

"Well, with our bodies," I said. "We never said anything about lives."

He smiled at me. "True. And no, that piece is not my mom's favorite, actually, so she didn't know of its importance. Which I was happy about, because that means I get to keep it in my room."

"Let's see it then," Lacey said.

His room was barer than I had expected it to be. I just assumed it would be like mine, with art and inspiration all over the walls. But it wasn't. The furniture had clean modern lines, simple. And in the corner was his heart. I could tell by the way he looked at it. It was two shapes, twisted together, like bodies wrapped around each other. I wasn't sure why I thought they were bodies. They had no distinct human form. But the long, elegant shapes seemed drawn to one another.

"That's beautiful," I said.

"I liked the big tree in the shrine room better," Lacey said.

He shrugged. "We all have our own views."

She fiddled with one of the bracelets around her wrist. "Do you mind if I raid your fridge for a soda or something?"

"Oh, yes, of course. Go for it. Do you want anything?" he asked me.

"I'm good."

He and Lacey headed for the door. I spent one more moment with his sculpture. I ran my hand along the smooth surface. It felt surprisingly cold.

"He texted me," Elliot said, and I jumped. I hadn't realized he was still there.

I turned around. Lacey was gone and just Elliot stood in the doorway facing me.

"What?" I asked. "Who?"

"Cooper. He asked if I'd seen you. Wanted to make sure you were okay."

The words made me want to cry all over again. "What did you say?"

"I haven't answered yet. I won't, if you don't want me to."

"Tell him I'm . . ." What? Fine? Miserable? I didn't want him to know that. Still in love with him? What was wrong with me? "Nothing. Tell him nothing."

He waited, as if he thought I'd change my mind, then held up his phone as if Cooper were inside it. "I shouldn't even try with you, should I? He still has a hold on you."

I took a deep breath. "Maybe now is not the best time to try, because yes, he does."

"I understand."

"We can be friends though, right? I could use a friend right now."

"Of course."

I nodded toward his statue. "It's really good."

"Thanks, that means a lot coming from you."

"From me? The amateur?"

"You were in a professional art exhibit."

"I found out I didn't earn my way in."

"That only matters if you don't believe you deserved it."

That's exactly what I believed. He seemed to read my

expression, because he said, "Nobody else's opinions about your art are going to matter to you until yours does."

"When did you get so smart?"

"I always have been, really." His eyes sparkled with his joke.

"Thanks for trying to get my mom that night, by the way."

"I knew you wanted her there. Sorry it didn't work out."

"It's okay." I knew I needed to explain to him about my mom and why she didn't come and how it wasn't him, but I wasn't ready to talk to him about it just yet. "She's working on it," is what I said instead. "Our household is a big work in progress right now."

"Isn't everybody's? Come on, I'm sure Lacey has prepared us a feast by now."

In the kitchen, I grabbed hold of Lacey's hand and squeezed. "Thanks, both of you," I said to her and Elliot. "I didn't realize I needed more friends in my life, but I really do. It's been nice."

Lacey squeezed my hand back.

THIRTY-SIX

Nobody else's opinion about my art would matter until mine did. Elliot was right. I had been so concerned about what everyone else thought about my work. It was always about my parents or Cooper, my grandpa. Everyone else. So what was my opinion about my art? I walked around my small studio back at my house. I studied each piece. I had been quick to adopt Mr. Wallace's opinions about my paintings when he'd mentioned them—immature, one-dimensional. And maybe I still thought that way about my early paintings. But my newer ones held emotion, depth. My newer ones were good, maybe even great. I could see the growth clearly, and I could see there was room for more growth. But wouldn't there always be room for more growth? Wouldn't I learn and grow as long as I was willing to try? As long as I was always willing to let things around me change?

I wandered back through the quiet halls of my house. My mom sat on the couch reading. At first I thought it was the medical book—it reminded me of one she'd read before—but then I realized it was a novel.

She met my eyes and shrugged. "A little progress."

"Good job, Mom."

"I have my first appointment this week with a therapist," she said.

"Really? That's great." I smiled.

"I'm glad you're happy about it."

"Does it make *you* happy?"

"No. It terrifies me, but I'm going to do it."

"Good. Sometimes we have to do the things that scare us, right?"

"Is that what *you're* doing?" she asked. "With Cooper?"

"Maybe . . . yes. I'm just trying to free myself."

"Hang in there," she said.

"You too."

"Are we going to be okay, me and you?" she asked.

"Yes, Mom. Love is about caring for someone even when they have weaknesses, right? I mean, you love me despite my sarcasm and laziness."

She smirked. "I love you *because* of those."

"I can see that." I leaned down and hugged her. She didn't let me go for several long breaths.

"Where is Grandpa?" I asked. It was time to talk to him as well. I had been the hardest on him. Maybe because he'd never let me down before, and I expected the most from him.

She pointed to the back door, and I let myself outside. Grandpa was in the far corner of the yard on his hands and knees picking weeds from between vegetables.

"You're not going to break a bone, are you?" I asked, sitting on the retaining wall that boxed in his garden.

He took off one of his gloves and threw it my way. "Let's see if your hands can accomplish as much damage as your mouth."

I took a deep breath, knowing I deserved that, and put on the glove. I could see why Grandpa liked to garden. There was something about plucking offenders out of the warm, soft soil that was very satisfying. I wouldn't let him know that though or he'd put me on weekly weed duty.

I looked over at Grandpa through a curtain of my own hair that hung down, blocking part of my view. "I'm sorry for what I said."

"I'm sorry I couldn't get your mom there the night of your show."

"It's not your fault, Grandpa."

"But I'm *more* sorry I didn't come. I should've. I was only thinking of her and her needs and not you. I hope you'll forgive me. I do care about you, and it makes me sad you doubted that."

Tears dripped off my face and into the dirt. "I know. I've always known. I shouldn't have said that."

Grandpa stood, with some effort, brushed off his knees, then took off his glove. He sat on the retaining wall and patted the place next to him. I sat next to him and played with the fingers of the glove that I left on my hand.

"It's hard for me," he said. "I feel like no matter what I try, she struggles. I try to push her, she pushes back. I try to be understanding, she sinks deeper. I want to take this burden from her." He got a little choked up and I looked over at him, surprised.

I slipped my glove-free hand into his. "You can't. She has to make that choice herself."

"But I'm her father."

"You feel like it's your fault somehow."

"Who else's?"

"Grandpa. She's her own person."

"Your grandmother would've known how to handle this better. But obviously that's wishful thinking."

"I've learned a few things this summer."

"From your list?"

"From everything."

"What have you learned?" he asked.

"That we can only control ourselves. No matter how much we wish we could twist and bend someone's will to ours, they have to want it too."

"You're a smart kid."

I laid my head on his shoulder and squeezed his hand in mine. "You know, I could've turned out really screwed up."

"What?" he asked, seeming surprised by my statement.

"I have a mom who is great but who rarely leaves the house and a dad who is gone all the time."

"Yes, you could've let that turn you rebellious or jaded."

"But I had you, Grandpa. I always had you. You made me feel safe. You gave me my strength."

"And you, child, restored my heart."

My art room was bright that afternoon. It was like a representation of what I'd realized after talking to my grandpa. I had finally figured out what my tree painting was missing. My heart. Lance had chained himself to his tree because of his memories, but his memories weren't mine. I now knew what to add. What had helped define me. I hefted the large canvas up onto my easel, and for the first time in weeks, I slid open the drawer on my hutch and retrieved some colors. Then in the bark, on the strong, steady, trunk of the tree, and only noticeable if studied just right, I painted a face. My grandpa's.

By the time I was done, paint coated my fingers. It had even worked its way under a few fingernails. I smiled and tried to wipe as much as possible on my shirt. I left the painting on the easel to dry.

I was going to apply to the winter art program with or without a sale. It was what I wanted to do. And standing there staring at my grandpa's eyes in my painting, I believed I'd get in.

THIRTY-SEVEN

I sat on my bed in my room the next day gripping my phone. My finger hovered over the button that would instantly connect me to all of Cooper's online world.

I knew what I'd told my grandpa in the garden was true. We could only control ourselves. No matter how much I loved Cooper, I couldn't love him enough for the both of us. I had to let go.

And yet, I let my finger fall. Cooper's profile pic came up—a selfie of him and me making the goofiest face for the camera. My breath caught. The last time I'd looked at his profile, it had been a pic of him and Iris. So did that mean that they really had broken up? I scrolled through the screens, but that was the only update there was. The statuses were from weeks ago. Like my accounts, his were eerily silent.

I put my phone to sleep and tossed it onto my nightstand. A small piece of paper fluttered to the ground with the action. I squinted and retrieved it off the ground. It was a business card. Mr. Wade Barrett. My brain took a couple of seconds to recall why I had this card and who this man was. He was the guy from the art show who'd made an offer on my quad piece—*Fearless*.

My quad piece. The one I had planned on giving to Cooper. I retrieved my phone and dialed the number.

The voice that answered was loud and boisterous. "This is Wade."

"Hi, Wade. I mean, Mr. Barrett. This is Abigail Turner. I met you at the art museum. You liked my piece with the quad. You said your grandson liked to ride."

"Ah. Yes! Hello."

"Can I ask you a weird question?"

"Uh . . . sure."

"Do you know my dad?"

"What's your dad's name?"

"Paul Turner."

He hummed as if thinking. "Can't say that I do."

"Are you still interested in the piece?"

"Did you paint one similar?"

"No, but I've decided to sell the one you saw to you after all, if you're still interested."

"I am."

We talked numbers and settled on a price. I hung up the phone.

I had just made money from my art. It was the first time I'd ever sold any of my work, and a thrill went through me.

"Mail," Mom called.

"You got the mail, Mom?" I asked, emerging from my room.

"I know it's not a big deal. . . ." She trailed off.

"It is a big deal." As little as Mom went out, she went out even less by herself. I was proud of her, but I didn't want her to push past her breaking point. "You know I love you no matter what, right?"

"I know that, and that would be good enough for me if all of your life could happen in this house. But it can't. One day you're going to graduate from college, get married, or have a baby. I'd like to be there."

"I can only pick one of those?"

"What?"

"You said *or*."

She rolled her eyes. "You know what I meant."

"I do." I kissed her cheek. "Thanks for doing hard things."

"I'm surrounded by excellent examples." She paused, then said, "I saw your painting."

"You'll have to narrow that down. I have a lot of paintings."

"You know which one. I want to be that person for you, the one who can cheer you on."

"Me too, Mom."

I squeezed her hand, then turned to leave as she began flipping through the mail. I stopped in my tracks and turned back around, seeing something. "Underground gardens. I've been wanting to try this out." I pulled it out of the stack and held it up. "It even has a coupon. Two for the price of one."

"You should take a date." She winked at me.

I walked to the front door and opened it. "Suitors?" I called out the door. "Where are all my suitors?"

"Is Elliot out there?" she asked.

"Funny." I shut the door. "I told you, I have no feelings for Elliot. Not yet, anyway. We're just friends right now."

"Is there a law against going to an underground garden with your friend?"

"Well, in my brain, the underground gardens are the most romantic place in the world, so, you're right, I should totally take a friend."

I had been kidding, but I pinned that flyer and coupon to my wall, one of the few things left, and every day for the following three days, I walked by it. On the fourth day, I called Elliot. As a fellow artist, he was sure to appreciate the experience.

"This is beautiful," I said as we walked down two levels of wooden stairs. Vines dripped from the ceiling like stalactites and the air was thick with the sweet aroma of flowers.

"Isn't it?" Elliot said. He'd been to the gardens before, but when I called, he had said he would love to see them again.

Sunlight poured through sections of the ceiling that were open to the sky. The temperature was slightly cooler but also more humid, like we were in our own tropical forest. And the plants that lived there, I guessed, were tropical plants—big colorful flowers and broad-leafed shrubbery. Drip lines ran along the wall, bringing even more moisture to the area. I felt like I had been transported to an island somewhere.

"I love this," I said. The garden was divided into dug-out rooms and we walked slowly through each one.

We weren't the only ones there. Two little kids kept darting past us, their footsteps echoing off the walls as their feet slapped the ground. Their parents tried to keep up with them. A couple was there as well, holding hands and stopping at each display. They looked at each other more than they did the flowers. I remembered telling Cooper this would be a perfect date. I gave Elliot a sideways glance. It didn't feel like a date now. It felt more like a research mission with Elliot. It kind of was. We were both soaking in the inspiration.

"Are you ready for school to start?" he asked.

"Not really." This year would be different. I wouldn't have Cooper. Would I have Rachel? Justin? I hadn't talked to them in a while. I'd sent a few texts to Justin but hadn't wanted to explain anything until they were back. Which they would be in exactly three days. I was both excited to see them and nervous to tell them about the destruction of our friend group. I'd understand if they chose Cooper. I was the one who'd set off the bomb. "You ready?" I asked, trying not to think about it too much.

"It's senior year . . . so no."

We continued down the wide corridor toward the next dug-out room. "There are carvings on the walls," I said, tempted to run my hand along the patterns that manifested between plants and vines.

"I know. They probably took hundreds of hours to complete."

I heard running water somewhere and I left Elliot behind, examining one of the more intricate patterns, to follow the sound to a water feature that took up the corner of one of the rooms. The couple I had seen holding hands was in the room as well. I skirted around them and to the corner. Water poured over stacked rocks and followed a path carved into the floor ending in a pond. Several large koi fish swam in the pond. Images of that day in Cooper's bathroom while we had a memorial service for Amelia's fish came into my brain unbidden. I pushed the side of my fist to my forehead and turned around.

Cooper stood at the roughly carved entrance of the room. At first I thought it was my brain putting his face on someone else's body, since I had just been thinking about him. But then he spoke.

"Abby, don't be mad."

I shook my head. I wasn't mad. Well, I was kind of mad at my body that no matter how many weeks it had been separated from him, it still reacted to the sight of him. It was like feeling rain after spending days in the desert. He was, like my grandpa might say, a sight for sore eyes. His blond hair fell across his forehead just above his intensely blue eyes. I'd almost forgotten how tall and broad he was as well, his frame seeming to fill the entire doorway.

"I sent that flyer to your house."

"What? Why?"

"To get you here. You said this was your dream location. And I've been watching my phone every day since then, and now finally you've come."

"I knew I should've taken that app off my phone."

"I'm glad you didn't."

"Well, here I am."

He walked closer.

I looked around to see that the couple who had been in there before was gone. I crossed my arms over my chest, hoping they would protect me from whatever was about to come out of his mouth. Another speech about how we made the best friends? We *did* make amazing friends.

"I miss you," he said. His voice was rough, laced with emotion. Now that he was closer I could see the dark circles under his eyes, like he hadn't gotten good sleep in a while.

"I miss you too, Cooper, but . . ."

He held up his hand, and I stopped.

"Please don't say any buts until I finish. Please."

I nodded.

"It's been weeks since I've seen you, and in that time I figured out my fear."

"Being alone?" I asked.

He laughed a little. "No. Although that wasn't fun."

He still had the same amazing smile. The one that lit up his whole face. Why couldn't that have changed in the last few weeks? I found myself wishing he were missing a tooth or something. What was I going to say at the end of this if he asked to be friends again? I couldn't do this. My insides were already twisting back up again.

"My fear is being *with* you."

"What?"

"All this time, Abby, that's what I've feared. On the beach that night a year ago, you told me you loved me and I was scared. Terrified actually. I knew how much I cared about you as a friend. But I knew that if I let myself fall in love with you, that it would be like handing you my heart to hold. I'd be so exposed. So I held on to it tight. Kept it to myself. And I thought I'd succeeded. I thought that I didn't feel the same way about you as you did about me. But that's just because I didn't realize until now what love really felt like. I thought love was that first-meeting emotion. You know, the one that always fades over time. I kept trying to find my happiness there in that emotion. I'd date girls and think, yes, this is what love feels like. But I was never happy. It always felt empty. It wasn't until you left, until you took what my happiness really was away, that I realized love was this." His put his hand on his chest. "This deep, intense caring about someone's well-being. About wanting that person to be okay no matter what happens to yourself. The realization that you, Abby, are already holding my heart and I'm perfectly okay with that. I love you."

I knew Cooper really well. We'd been best friends for nearly four years. So I looked for the signs that he might be lying—avoiding my gaze, fidgeting, biting his lip. But they weren't there. His gaze was steady, as was his stance. "I think you're confusing love with missing me," I said.

His head started shaking back and forth before I'd even finished my sentence. "I knew you'd think that. I knew you'd think I was saying all this because I miss you. Or because I just want you back in my life any way I can have you."

"Yes. That's what I think." My arms were still crossed over my chest and my heart was crashing into them, asking me why I was making him question his declaration.

"I *do* miss you, Abby. Ugh. I miss you with everything in me." He grabbed hold of the front of his shirt in his fist. "And I *do* want you back in my life, but I do love you, with my entire soul, and I'm sorry it's taken me so long to realize that."

I swallowed hard. My whole face felt tingly and numb.

And then I heard Elliot's voice before I saw him. "Abby, did you see the huge tree growing up through the roof in the . . ." He trailed off when he turned the corner and saw Cooper. "Oh. Hey, Cooper." Then Elliot's eyes met mine and seemed to ask if I was okay.

I wasn't sure what I was, but it was definitely not okay. Cooper had just told me he loved me and my heart was racing and my mind was racing and I didn't know how to respond. I didn't know if I should grab hold of him and never let go or run the other way because he might change his mind and destroy me for good.

Cooper's smile fell as he looked between Elliot and me. "I'm too late?" he asked. "I'm too late." His face was painted with pain. "What can I do? A duel?" He met my eyes with a sad smirk, sharing our inside joke.

"No, Cooper," I said.

"I have to walk away, don't I? Let *you* go this time?"

I didn't speak, and I wasn't sure why. Maybe I wanted him to feel the torture of that thought for just a moment. Cooper took the three remaining steps between us and crushed me into a hug that eradicated the rest of my anger. "I'll wait as long as it takes," he whispered. Then he left.

"He finally figured it out?" Elliot asked.

I nodded. "I'm sorry. I need to go."

"I know."

I ran.

I ran through the maze of the underground garden and up the stairs. The sun blinded me for a moment when I made it outside, breathless. When my vision cleared, I saw Cooper's car in the parking lot. I ran to it, but he wasn't inside. I turned a full circle, but he wasn't anywhere, not up the street walking it off, not at the small gift shop where the admission tickets were sold. Nowhere.

I turned and practically slid back down the stairs underground again. When I reached the bottom, Cooper came stumbling out of one of the side rooms. I skidded to a halt.

"This place is like a maze. It doesn't let a guy trying to save a little dignity just leave." Tears were in his eyes, and my heart couldn't handle the sight of that.

I pointed over my shoulder up the stairs. "I made it all the way to the parking lot, but you weren't there. Just your car."

"It needs to be washed."

I laughed a little. "Your car?"

"Yeah, I was thinking about that earlier today. How it needed to be washed."

"Are we really talking about your car?"

"I'm trying to hold it together here, Abby."

I nodded toward where I'd left Elliot. "I'm not. We're not."

"What?" he asked, using his palm to wipe at his eyes.

My eyes stung in sympathy. "I don't think I've ever

seen you cry. Well, there was that one time you accidentally ate that really hot pepper."

He choked out a laugh. "Accidentally? You *put* it in my burger."

"I know. It was funny."

"For you," he said.

"I love you too. I've never stopped," I finally spit out.

"What?"

"I love you, Cooper. I never stopped."

He wiped at his eyes again. "You're not just saying that because you feel bad for me, right?"

I laughed. "You do look pretty pathetic."

He nodded to the side. "Come here, I want to show you something."

He walked ahead of me, back the way we'd come from, and reached back for my hand. I placed mine in his like I had so many times before and, like I'd thought so many times before, it felt perfect there.

"I found it while I was trying to flee," he said.

He led me to a portion of the garden I hadn't seen yet. The room was darker than the others. Small holes had been drilled into the ceiling, letting in pinpricks of light like a blanket of stars. When my gaze left the ceiling I found Cooper staring at me.

"I've always thought you were amazing," he said. Our hands were still linked and he tugged, pulling me closer to him. His eyes still shone with emotion. "And smart and funny and beautiful."

My heart jumped to my throat. After months of anticipation, now I was the one who was terrified. His free hand ran a path down my jaw. He kissed my cheek, lingering there. He smelled like Cooper—cherry ChapStick and mint gum and oranges and vanilla. His arm slowly wrapped around my waist, like he thought I might break. Then he hugged me close. His heart beat against my chest, fast and hard. "Is it weird yet?" he asked.

I smiled. "The only weird thing is that I don't know what you like. I thought about putting my fingers in your hair, but then I wondered if that would bother you."

"I feel the same. I wasn't sure if you'd like my arm here."

"I like your arm there."

"It's weird not knowing everything about each other."

"Are we stalling the actual kiss?" I asked.

He chuckled. "You've been anticipating this for months, and I'm worried it will disappoint."

"I know. What if we suck at this? Also, let me borrow your ChapStick."

He dropped his arm, laughing. "Best friends can't kiss. Even if they do love each other."

I laughed too. "Give me your ChapStick and then you're going to kiss me." I reached into the pocket of his cargo shorts where I knew he kept it and pulled it out myself. "We should make our first kiss purposely bad so that it can only get better from there," I said while applying the lip balm.

"What do you mean?"

"I don't know, pucker our lips really tight or move our heads a lot. Or slobber a lot."

He couldn't control his laughter, and it took him a while before he could say, "I missed you so much. And you are not making this easy."

"No, I'm serious. Come here." I pulled him toward me by the pockets of his shorts and puckered my lips as tight as possible, then nodded for him to do the same.

"You are the biggest goofball," he said.

When I didn't stop he sighed and said, "Fine. I guess our first kiss is going to be awful."

I had to purse my lips even harder to control my smile. I put my hands on his shoulders and stretched up on my tiptoes. He rolled his eyes and pressed his tightly puckered lips to mine. It was just as bad as I knew it would be. I smiled and pulled away.

"See, it can only get—"

He slid his hand to the back of my neck and pulled me to him. His lips were soft this time as they found mine. He kissed me once, then twice, then ran his lips along mine. "Better," he whispered, finishing my sentence.

I started to nod but we were kissing again, and I didn't have to think about where to put my hands this time, they just dug into his hair. His hands went to my hips, his thumbs applying the perfect amount of pressure there to hold me up. He deepened the kiss, his tongue finding mine. He tasted even better than he smelled, like mint and sugar. He backed me up to the closest wall and leaned into me. I couldn't get enough air, but I didn't want to stop. Cooper was pressed against me, breathing my breath and setting my skin on fire. He was warm and familiar and amazing. When it felt like I would burst, I finally pushed him away and gulped down several mouthfuls of air.

"We don't suck at that," he said.

I shook my head, still catching my breath.

"I love you so much."

I smiled and tipped my head back, looking at the starred ceiling. "I'm so happy."

"Me too."

I closed my eyes and he brushed a soft kiss to my lips again.

"Now," he said, "you have to tell me everything that's happened in the last several weeks. Starting with what you were doing in that abandoned church building."

THIRTY-EIGHT

"Do you think they'll want cheesecake before or after they kill us?" I asked as we sat in the Cheesecake Factory waiting for Justin and Rachel to arrive. They had both gotten into town in the past two days. Justin first, the night before last, and Rachel last night. Cooper and I had decided we'd tell them about our relationship in person, not over text or phone. So here we waited. I'd already told Lacey the night it had happened. She had been happy for me, but this was different. Lacey knew about my feelings. Justin and Rachel didn't.

"The real question is, should *we* get cheesecake now

or have faith that they won't kill us?"

"Probably now."

"That's what I was thinking."

I smiled.

He squeezed my knee under the table. "Do you know one of my favorite memories of you from this summer?"

"No, what?" I asked.

"Quad riding."

"Of course you'd like the thing that terrified me."

"No, I like the thing that made you cling to me with everything you had. We should do that again."

"I can do that without the quad if you'd like."

Cooper smirked.

My phone buzzed and I pulled it out, thinking it was a text from Justin or Rachel about their arrival time, but it was an email notification. My cheeks went numb. "The winter program," I said aloud.

"What?" Cooper asked.

"It's from Wishstar."

"Did you apply?"

"I forgot to tell you. I did."

"Wow. Congratulations."

"Don't congratulate me yet. I don't know if I got in."

"I was congratulating you for applying. It's about time."

I nudged his shoulder with mine. "Funny."

"Well? Are you going to open it?"

I nodded but took my time. This was the last moment to savor not knowing. After this I'd either be happy or devastated. And I'd handle either. I clicked on the email.

"Congratulations," I read out loud. "You have been accepted to our winter course at the Wishstar Institute of Visual and Performing Art."

"That's amazing," Cooper said, kissing me. "I knew you could do it."

"Thanks."

"Am I late?" Rachel's voice had me flying out of my seat. Had she seen our kiss? She didn't act like it as she continued talking. "How come you two are both already here? And how come you haven't ordered cheesecake?" She picked up a piece of bread from the basket on the table, which we hadn't touched, and ripped off a bite. "I'm starving. I've been sleeping for eighteen hours straight. I'm never going to sleep tonight. Jet lag." She flung her arms around me in a hug. "Hi!"

"Hi!" I said with a laugh. "Welcome home."

Cooper stood and hugged her as well.

"It felt like I was gone for years, but I'm back and everything is exactly the same. It's this weird time-warp thing. Where is Justin?"

Cooper looked over Rachel's shoulder. "Right there."

Justin headed toward our table with a big smile on.

"My friends," he said. We all took turns hugging him. "Next summer, we do a trip together. This was way too much time away."

"That's what I was telling Abby last month," Rachel said. "Was that last month? That we need to take on Europe together after we graduate."

"How come there's no cheesecake on this table?" Justin asked, looking around for a waiter.

"We weren't sure if you'd want cheesecake before or after you killed us," Cooper said, then laughed when I gave him wide eyes. That wasn't exactly how we'd practiced doing this. When we practiced, we'd eased into it, talked about how we'd been friends forever and how that had developed over the summer to something more. This wasn't that.

"Why would we kill you?" Rachel asked, sitting down in the seat next to mine. Justin sat as well, noticed the bread, and picked up a piece.

"Did you guys eat at all this summer?" I asked.

"I ate too much," Rachel said. "In every city, any new thing I saw. It was amazing. But now my body expects to be fed every two hours."

"I haven't had American food in a long time. Well, I guess last night, but . . . you know what I mean," Justin said through his mouthful.

"Abby has great news," Cooper said. "She got into the

art program she's been drooling over."

"What! That's amazing!" Justin said.

"So amazing. Congrats! Is that why we're going to kill you? Why would we kill you over that?" Rachel asked.

"We've all been friends for a long time," I started, back on track with how we'd planned.

The waiter appeared at our table. "I see your whole party is here now. What can I get you?"

"I love Abby," Cooper said matter-of-factly. "It wasn't until this summer that I realized what an idiot I've been for not making her mine." Then he looked at the waiter. "I'll take an Oreo cheesecake and some fries."

"Wait. What?" Rachel asked a piece of bread halfway to her mouth.

"Should I come back?" the waiter asked.

"No!" Justin said. "I want lemon cheesecake. This news doesn't change that fact. Also," he said to Cooper, "it's about time."

"What?" Rachel asked again, this time looking at Justin. "You knew this? Am I the only one who didn't know this?"

"You didn't tell Rachel about last summer?" Cooper asked. "I thought she would be the only one *not* surprised."

"I didn't tell anyone."

"Exactly," Rachel said. "In this friend group we all get

the same things or no things. You were right. I *am* going to kill you."

I should've told her about my feelings for Cooper a long time ago. I could tell she was hurt. "I'm sorry," I said softly, just to her.

"I'm going to come back," the waiter said.

"Wait," Cooper said. "Rachel. Order. Then we'll talk about your strange rules."

"Fine," she huffed. "I want chocolate. Your most chocolate cheesecake."

The waiter wrote down her order, then turned to me. Right, I still hadn't ordered. "White chocolate raspberry," I said.

"At least some things haven't changed," Rachel said with an eye roll.

The waiter left quickly and silence took over.

"How did this happen?" Rachel finally asked.

"What do you mean, how did this happen?" Justin threw a crust of bread at her. "They like each other. We left them alone for the summer, and they finally realized it."

She turned to us. "And you both thought this was a good idea? To put a ticking time bomb on our friend group? Soon we will implode and end up scattered into pieces, and then how will you feel?"

"Ouch, Rach," Cooper said. "I'm glad you have faith in us."

"Can we just call dibs now on who gets custody of who in the breakup?" Rachel said, a smirk finally coming onto her face. Oh, good. She would forgive me, eventually, at least.

"I call Abby," both she and Justin said at the same time.

I laughed.

"What?" Cooper said. "Why Abby?"

"She's funnier," Justin said. "And more chill."

"I guess that's reason number five thousand why I'm not letting her go."

"Oh, wow," Rachel said. "They say cheesy things about each other now. This is going to take some getting used to."

"For me too," I said.

"What do you mean, for you too?" Cooper asked, wrapping his arms around me and pulling me against his side. "Maybe I should say *more* cheesy things so you'll get used to it faster. All of you."

I pushed him away with a laugh.

"Justin, don't get any ideas," Rachel said. "We will always be just friends."

"Absolutely no ideas happening over here," he assured her.

The waiter came back with our cheesecake and a basket of fries for Cooper. Rachel reached across and snatched one of his fries. He smacked her hand.

"You still don't share?"

"The world didn't change while you were gone."

"Are you sure about that?"

Cooper smiled at me. *My* world had changed. I smiled back, then picked up my fork and took a bite of cheesecake.

"So does this mean no four-amigo trip next summer? Because it was going to be epic."

"Why would this mean that?" I asked. "We will definitely do that trip next summer. We will crush that trip."

Rachel pushed my shoulder. "I'm pissed at you for not telling me, but I'll be happy soon. Really."

"Enough about us," Cooper said. "We need to celebrate Abby's awesome news and then hear everything about your summers."

We stayed at our table long after our food was gone and probably long after the waiter wished we would leave. Rachel and Justin shared their adventures, and even though things were different, everything felt right.

As we left the restaurant, Cooper tugged on my hand, allowing Justin and Rachel to walk ahead.

"Are we good?" he asked. "Did that work out how you hoped?"

"Yes. It went great."

"You just seem quiet."

"I do?" He held open the door for me, and we stepped outside. Rachel had climbed up on the fountain out front and was walking around the rim with her arms out.

"You're not having doubts, are you?" His face had taken on a worried expression.

"What? No." I reached my arms up around his neck. "I love you," I said quietly, then threw my head back and screamed, "I love Cooper Wells!"

"Get in line!" Justin called out.

I laughed and Cooper's shiny smile was back.

"Good," he said. "Because unrequited love is the worst. If I had a choice between unrequited love and never being able to love at all, I'd definitely choose no love."

I smacked his chest. "So you *did* know what Lacey was talking about at that party. And here she thought you were clueless."

"Lacey. Is she going to be coming around more?"

"I think so. We're friends now."

"Better friends than us?"

"You're my best friend, Cooper. Irreplaceable."

"I love you." He kissed me, stealing my breath away.

Okay, maybe this wouldn't be too hard to get used to. "Thank you, heart list," I said under my breath.

"You're giving credit to that list for *us*?"

"I'm giving credit wherever I can. I won Cooper Wells's heart and I'm caging it up and never letting it out."

He chuckled. "Be gentle with me."

I went serious. "I will."

"And, Abby," he said. "It may have taken me a while to figure it out, but I'm the one who won."

ACKNOWLEDGMENTS

To all of you out there who have a dream that you feel is just out of your reach, keep reaching!

Thank you to my readers!! I love you all so much! I appreciate your support and encouragement, your kind words, your tweets, your Goodreads questions, your Instagram comments. I see them and they mean the world to me. Thanks for reading my books! Thanks for reading in general! I love readers. I'm a reader first, and I really feel like I've found my people.

To my agent, Michelle Wolfson, thanks for being my support always and my therapist sometimes (maybe more than sometimes). You are the best. I'm so happy I get to work with you. You make my job easier and a lot more fun!

To my editor, Catherine Wallace, who believes in me and helps make my stories better: thank you! And thanks to Jon Howard, Michelle Taormina, Alison Klapthor, Stephanie Hoover, Bess Brasswell, Sabrina Abballe, Meghan Pettit, Jen Klonsky, and the entire HarperTeen team. You took a chance on me in the very beginning, and I will be forever grateful for that.

As always, thanks to my husband, Jared West. Seriously, this guy is the best. He supports me in all I do, even when I have to go into hermit mode. I have some pretty fabulous kids that get me too: Hannah, Autumn, Abby, and Donavan. These are my favorite people ever. I love just hanging out with them. We laugh more than we should in this house, and I'm grateful for that. I love to laugh. Laughing is my favorite (every time I say that I think of the movie *Elf*).

I have some amazing writer friends who are not only fun to be with but are awesomely talented too. So much love to: Candice Kennington, Jenn Johansson, Renee Collins, Natalie Whipple, Bree Despain, Michelle Argyle, Sara Raasch, Shannon Messenger, and Jessi Kirby.

And to my nonwriter friends who I love and who make me happy: Stephanie Ryan, Rachel Whiting, Elizabeth Minnick, Claudia Wadsworth, Amy Burbidge, Misti Hamel, Brittney Swift, Mandy Hillman, Emily Freeman, Megan Grant, and Jamie Lawrence.

Last but not least, my amazing extended family, who

have all been so supportive of me: thank you, Chris DeWoody, Heather Garza, Jared DeWoody, Spencer DeWoody, Stephanie Ryan, Dave Garza, Rachel DeWoody, Zita Konik, Kevin Ryan, Vance West, Karen West, Eric West, Michelle West, Sharlynn West, Rachel Braithwaite, Brian Braithwaite, Angie Stettler, Jim Stettler, Emily Hill, Rick Hill, and the twenty-five children (plus some of the children's children) who exist among all these people.

Stephanie Ryan Photography

KASIE WEST

lives with her family in central California, where the heat tries to kill her with its 115-degree stretches. She graduated from Fresno State University with a BA degree that has nothing to do with writing.